SOMETIMES IVORY, SOMETIMES SAND

Mahek Jangda can often be found looking at the stars in the night sky and wondering about the universe. She spends the rest of her time conjuring up stories, writing poetry and dancing to her heart's content. Her poetry has been featured by *The Hindu Business Line* (*BLink*), Hyderabad Literary Festival, UnErase, Kommune, Habitat Studios, Filtercopy and the Poetry Club (Mumbai). She has a bachelor's degree in business administration from NMIMS, Mumbai, a diploma in Persian from Mumbai University and is currently pursuing a postgraduate diploma in the liberal arts from Ashoka University under the Young India Fellowship programme. This is her first novel.

SOMETIMES IVORY, SOMETIMES SAND

MAHEK JANGDA

hachette INDIA

First published in 2020 by Hachette India
(Registered name: Hachette Book Publishing India Pvt. Ltd)
An Hachette UK company
www.hachetteindia.com

SRD

ISBN 978-93-89253-12-2

Hachette Book Publishing India Pvt. Ltd
4th/5th Floors, Corporate Centre,
Plot No. 94, Sector 44, Gurugram 122003, India

Typeset in DanteMT Std 10.5/14
by InoSoft Systems, Noida

Printed and bound in India by
Manipal Technologies Limited, Manipal

MIX
Paper from responsible sources
FSC™ C043100

For Raunaq, who never fails to show me my own strength.
Urja, this book is as much yours as it is mine.

It's been weeks
That I've been trying to figure you out…
But you've kept me on the surface
Sometimes ivory,
Sometimes sand

– Akhil Katyal, 'Udaipur (early morning)'

ḳhudī ko kar buland itnā ki har taqdīr se pahle
ḳhudā bande se ḳhud pūchhe batā terī razā kyā hai

– Allama Iqbal

one

Jasmine

All the pieces are cream in colour, with hand-painted gold and pastel-green peacocks on the edges, and red roses in the centre. The last time Jasmine saw her mother use this crockery was six years ago. That was a time when they still lived in opulence. Her father had told her that this set was made with clay and the bone ash of a cow. Jasmine has never seen a cow. She has only seen pictures of the animal in one of her father's books. At times she wonders if she misses her father more or his books.

While Jasmine prepares the food, her mother lays a white crochet cloth on the low table placed between the two well-cushioned grey sofas in the living room. It is going to be a feast. There are deep-fried potato cheese balls and minced meat samosas for starters. The main course includes a decadent red chicken curry and spiced rice. The feast is to end with a rich cinnamon cake. Jasmine has cooked the whole meal by herself with little help from her mother. A showcase of her talent to make up for the lack of a father.

An entire month's savings have been used for this one meal. Her mother, Nina, said it was all worth it though – the expenditure and the effort are both necessary. If all goes well, Nina will never have to spend on Jasmine's hunger again. Imagine how much money that will save them. The dowry could have been a problem, but Kaiza, Jasmine's father, had arranged for that before he left. Fifty thousand rehats in all. That is enough to buy even a small car. Surely, it will suffice.

Jasmine admires her mother's commitment to giving her what she believes is a good life. Not once has her mother touched the 50,000 rehats. Not when Jasmine's older brother, Sabaar, was looking for work, not when they could only afford to eat once a day, not when the roof gave way, not even when they had to give their cat, Mr Jones, away. Jasmine knows that perhaps those times were more difficult for her mother than they were for her, to live without the man she loved. Jasmine also knows that the love between her parents was strained. She's almost sure that her parents were so used to each other's company that they could not let go of one another, even though most parts of them wanted to. Or maybe they had kept it together for her and Sabaar.

Many a times, a frightening thought crosses Jasmine's mind: What if Kaiza's argument for leaving had been a ruse? What if he had wanted to break free from Nina, to not have her around to pull him back? Or worse. What if he had also wanted to break free from Sabaar and Jasmine? What if they had been suffocating him, just as much as Nina had?

It is difficult for Nina not to stifle anyone. She constantly needs someone to leech on to, to suck love out of. It can be blamed on the lack of affection in her early years. Both of Nina's parents had passed away when she was only six. She lived with her father's brother for a couple of years, and then in an orphanage till she was married away at the age of fourteen. Fortunately for Nina, her suitor wasn't much older than her. He was only nineteen. The one coming to see Jasmine today is twenty-six. Jasmine is seventeen now, and only one more year of good proposals remains. And probably none better than this one. That explains all the expensive crockery and exquisite dishes. A good husband deserves a good deception.

Jasmine does not mind getting married. A married girl is not to be made meat of in society.

They arrive in a light-blue car. The car is small and not very well maintained. Even if the car were well kept, it wouldn't show. As it does with all things exposed, the sand in Mahlah has given the box on four wheels a diligent coat of ochre.

Ochre. Yellow. Brown. The only colours a child born in Mahlah is truly familiar with.

Mahlah is a desert and one of the more underdeveloped districts of the nation, along with Attara. The nation itself is made of five districts, with Rahat, the most advanced and prosperous district, being the capital. Rahat is bordered by the ocean on one side and shares borders with the other four districts – Samin, Baugh, Attara and Mahlah.

Like Jasmine's single-storey house, almost every house in Mahlah is made of sandstone. Jasmine is sure that her suitor's house has at least three storeys. They have a car after all. A man generally marries into a family a few ranks below his. No one with a three-storeyed house would give their girl away to someone who did not own a car and at least two two-storeyed houses.

Jasmine would not have been considered, but concessions are made when the girl is good-looking. Jasmine is olive-skinned, with a round face and razor-sharp features. She is neither very tall, nor too short. Years of malnutrition have thinned her body, but fortunately it does not show on her face. Her hair is long, straight and black, a preferred combination. Her eyes are as dark as her hair and, once upon a time, they used to always have a spark in them.

Nina is standing at the door to welcome the guests. Unlike Jasmine, Nina is not considered very good-looking. She has muddy hair and a nose that is as triangular as a samosa. Both her children, though, have inherited their father's looks. There's a bit of Kaiza everywhere in this house.

A tall, well-built man steps out of the car. A chirpy woman and an older man follow him. Jasmine peers out of the kitchen window to catch a glimpse of her future family. The Morans. They are all olive-skinned, much like everyone else in the city. The boy and his father have broad shoulders and wide bone structures, while the mother defines the words petite and plump both. There is a look of arrogance on the mother's face, while the father is grim and the boy looks like he is unsure of what he is supposed to do. They all shine though; they glow like only the wealthy can, like only the ones without daughters can. It is in moments like these that Jasmine misses her father the most. Kaiza would stand up to the visitors, not in arrogance, but with a sense of pride that no one could take away from him. He would make it clear, from the very first second, that his family was not to be taken for granted, not to be messed around with. But Nina is different; she is submissive, and in Kaiza's absence she has constantly tried to teach Jasmine that she is expected to be submissive too.

Jasmine walks out of the airy kitchen into the now modest but once well-done living room with a tray in her hand, bearing samosas, cheese balls and a pot of chai. She sees that the guests have already taken their seats. Jasmine's suitor is seated on the sofa alongside Sabaar. Mr and Mrs Moran are seated on the sofa opposite, while Nina is seated on a low chair beside them. Nina has covered up the torn plaster on the dull green walls with paintings that she had made years ago. After a long time, the living room does not look shabby.

Everyone is wearing fine clothes today. Sabaar has his pearl-white kaftan out, while Nina is wearing a maroon gown. But no one compares to Jasmine, who possesses a timeless elegance that she definitely did not inherit from her mother. She must be from another world, this one, single-handedly fighting every bit of Mahlah's ruggedness.

She is dressed in a beautiful deep-blue silk robe with matching pants – fashioned from one of Nina's old dresses they haven't sold yet. She has paired it with an embroidered turquoise scarf, draped around her head, as proof of her modesty. Counterfeit sapphires adorn her neck and ears. Jasmine looks like a princess. Jasmine likes looking like a princess. She likes the elaborate meal she's prepared for today, and she likes the air of festivity that surrounds her house.

The hustle and bustle and the action, in some way, help her fill the void that her father has left behind.

'Come, Jasmine, sit here.'

Nina is pointing towards a low chair placed beside hers.

'Mr Moran, Mrs Moran, this is my lovely daughter, Jasmine.'

Jasmine wonders what their names are, especially her suitor's. Now that she can see him up close, she realizes that she finds him very good-looking. He has clear blue eyes that perfectly complement his olive skin. The stubble on his face makes him look mysterious. His brown hair is a bit long. He is wearing a white shirt and khaki pants. His body looks well built. He must have worked for the army once, like most men from Mahlah do.

As Jasmine puts into use her often-practised shy smile, the Morans look pleased. At such meetings, there is never any talk of the compatibility of the future couple. Approval of the girl's manners, the dowry amount and the final confirmation, that is what these meetings are for. Oh, and for the soon-to-be-groom's mother, a chance to gloat about how her son has the ability to eat camels' faeces and shit out diamonds. In this case, almost literally.

'Oh, Jasmine, you are even more beautiful than we had imagined,' Mrs Moran exclaims. She is wearing a knee-length pink gown and matching pants. Her gown is encrusted with jewels. 'Let me tell you, Sabaar...' Sabaar is the only male from Jasmine's family present, and so Mrs Moran assumes that, by default, he is the decision maker, 'my son is indeed very lucky. But so is your sister. Amer is one of –'

Amer, Jasmine tells herself, *so his name is Amer. Such a nice name.*

'– the sharpest minds in all of Mahlah. He has doubled our jewellery trade in the last two years. People often say that he is the gem of the gemstone business of Mahlah. We even sold pearl pieces to the Jagirs recently. You must have heard of the Jagirs? Ahmed Jagir, the famous councilman from Rahat? The deal was completely arranged by Amer. He is truly a diamond in a coal mine.' Mrs Moran turns her attention towards Jasmine and smirks, 'Maybe you will get to wear *real* sapphires once you marry my son.'

Jasmine has no urge to retort, although she wishes she did. Years of staying with Nina and Sabaar have taught her to be patient. She knows how to take an insult and not say anything. She even knows how to take a beating and not say anything. But Sabaar has not hit her for a month now. He knows that bruises show and no one wants an already bruised bride.

Sabaar and Mr Moran have now taken to loudly discussing their family histories. Amer looks disinterested in the conversation that is happening, and Jasmine feels surprisingly disheartened by his disinterest. Their eyes meet, but for only a second as Jasmine hastily averts her gaze to the floor. Her heart flutters and she can feel a faint smile form on her lips. She can sense Amer's gaze on her now. It is difficult to hide the flush of red that is rushing to her cheeks. She notices that Amer's cheeks are red too.

Once the chicken curry and rice are devoured, and the last crumbs of the cinnamon cake disappear, the hide-and-seek between the eyes of the to-be-weds is interrupted by Mr Moran's gravelly voice.

'Sabaar, we have already taken a liking to your lovely sister. If Amer approves of the match, we will need some more cake here...'

All eyes, barring the most curious ones of Jasmine, turn to Amer. It is not considered decent if the girl looks her suitor in the eye. Jasmine has no say in this arrangement. Once the male heads of both families and the male suitor accept the proposal, the girl cannot reject it. But Jasmine wants Amer to say yes. Despite the obnoxious mother-in-law, Jasmine wants Amer to marry her.

Like a bolt of lightning bursting through the darkness, his voice fills the room. 'I accept this proposal. I will marry Jasmine Mir, daughter of Kaiza Mir.'

two

Jasmine

Once the rattling whirr of the old blue car is vanquished by the distance, Jasmine lets her tears fall. There was no reason for this one to be different. Although Pardad, the matchmaker, had assured them that this family would not run once they knew the truth, Jasmine should have held her doubts close to her heart. So should have Nina. And Sabaar. Oh, all this preparation, all this money, all of it down the drain. But Jasmine is not shedding her tears for the five hours it took her to cook the meal, or for the week they did not eat bread to save up for this day. Jasmine is crying because she thought that she and Amer had a connection. She wanted him to marry her.

Mr Moran was only being logical.

'We will fix a date once we have the final nod from her father. We have been wondering why he is not present here. But we understand that Kaiza sahib must be a busy man, so we will set an appointment as per his convenience. We only need his word now.'

There was a moment of silence around the table as Nina and Sabaar glanced at each other, while Jasmine continued looking down at the floor. Her eyes were struggling to contain the teardrops that were making her vision hazy.

Jasmine remembers the night her father sat them down and narrated his plans. Nina already knew. Nina had known for a long time. The power board had stopped the supply of electricity for a few days and so they were sitting on the bed, under the orange light of a small wick lamp. When Jasmine first caught a hint of his purpose for calling the household meeting, she let out a loud shriek. That was a time when Jasmine used to allow her body to express emotion. There was a lot of crying, mostly from Jasmine. Sabaar did not let more than a few tears escape his eyes. But Jasmine knows that Kaiza's absence pinches him too. She knows because she is a victim of his pain.

That night, helplessness coursed through Jasmine's body. And fear. A pang of panic clawed inside a portion of her chest that is now hollow, a pain that as a little girl she could not fully understand – the pain of separation.

She hugged Kaiza to sleep that night, clenching every bit of his strong arms tight, hoping that her hands were powerful enough to force him to stay, hoping that they could act as the authority that she could never be.

At the crack of dawn, Jasmine woke from her dreamless sleep to stretch her hands onto the mattress and found only the warmth that her father had left behind. She ran out of the room, past the grey sofas and the wooden front door to see the silhouette of a thin man on a camel fade into the distance. Before he disappeared at the turn, the tall man turned to witness his twelve-year-old daughter helplessly shout after him, and then feebly wave goodbye. It was only after a long time into the journey that he let his dark eyes water.

Kaiza had said that it was not a big deal. He would come to see them once every two months. Business was declining, and he had an excellent work opportunity in the capital – something to do with managing the income and expenditure of a recently set up but large company. It would provide for the family, and in a few years, they were to all shift to Rahat. It was for a better future, Kaiza had promised.

It has been five years since that dreadful dawn, and there has been not one visit, not one letter. Not even any news of his whereabouts. As days turned into nights, wait turned into worry, worry turned into rage, rage into resentment, and now there is only an unspoken pain so seamlessly etched into their lives that they would be incomplete without it. Kaiza's absence defines each of them and why should it not? After all, like today, their lives have been constantly shaped by his one decision.

Like all the others before them, the Morans apologized and left. Jasmine almost expected Amer to reason with his parents. But why should he reason for her, a girl whom he has not so much as had a word with? If speaking with their eyes doesn't count, that is. And so, Amer said nothing. He followed his parents straight out of the door, lingering just long enough to glance at the dark-eyed girl one more time, but incidentally not the last.

three

Jasmine

Hanz has decided to take the shorter route today. He usually avoids it past sunset because it is quite deserted. But his current situation demands incautious action. If he doesn't hurry up, this will be the third day in a row that he will be late for their family dinner at eight. He does not want to be beaten again. His father's strong black whip, with a carved wooden handle, is his arch-nemesis. He has successfully avoided it for two months now, but the scars from their previous encounter still haunt his pale chest. Hanz is almost nine years old and does not understand why he still has to take instructions from his parents. Surely, he is old enough to decide at what time he is to return home from his evening games. But his father doesn't seem to understand. Any effort at reasoning with him is always torn apart in a second with the threat of the whip. So, instead, Hanz has to hurry home. Running against the wind with minute particles of sand hitting his face, Hanz can almost imagine the whip striking his body. He can hear the sound of its crack.

A second cracking sound of the whip makes him stop in his tracks. A loud shriek follows. Surely, this is not his imagination. Startled and curious, Hanz follows the sound to a window around the corner. The window belongs to what looks like a bedroom in an old single-storey house that isn't very different from the other houses in the lane. Light from an incandescent bulb reveals a poorly kept bed with a man standing beside it. A woman cowers in front of him. The man, with a whip in his hand, is staring at his prey. Despite himself, Hanz crouches behind an old dumpster near the window and watches the dimly lit room erupt in violence.

The girl is beautiful, with her dark eyes and her olive face. There is something fierce about her even as she crouches in front of the beast of a man. She is wearing a blue dress and is adorned with jewels; she looks like a princess out of a dream. Hanz cannot help but feel a wave of terror pass through his body as he watches the man drop the whip and slap her face.

Despite the rush of blood to her face, the girl's expression is blank, as if the act is routine and she knows that it will eventually be over. The man pulls her hair and slaps her one more time. Then another. Then another. A savage set free, unleashing his rage upon an innocent solely because he can.

It lasts for almost twenty minutes, the carnage. When the beast has had his fill, he leaves his bedraggled prey and walks away. Slowly, the girl struggles to her feet and walks towards the window. Hanz feels like her piercing black eyes are looking directly into his tiny grey ones. But he knows that it is impossible for her to spot him. He is safe behind the dumpster, while she is not safe in her own house.

His father's wrath long forgotten, Hanz sits in his spot, frozen. As the girl shuts the blinds, Hanz finds he cannot move, afraid that with any movement, with any noise, the beast will appear right in front of him. Minutes pass, if not hours, before a voice shakes him out of his stony trance.

'What are you doing here at this time of the night, boy? It's not safe to be out alone.'

As Hanz looks up, he rubs his eyes to make sure he's not dreaming. It is the princess, standing right before him.

'Are you okay?'

Her sweet voice masks the events of the evening, but the fresh bruises on her face give her away. She is dressed in an off-white kaftan and olive-green pants. A colourful scarf draped over her shoulders carefully covers her head. She is carrying a large square bag on her shoulder.

'I don't want to go home because my father will hit me for being late. That is why I am hiding here.'

The princess sits down beside Hanz. Tears fill his eyes, and he tries his best not to cry.

She smiles at him kindly and asks, 'What's your name?'

'Hanz.'

'Hanz, I'm sure your father worries about you, and that is why he wants you back home. Where do you live?'

'Right here, in the next lane.'

'Come, I'll walk you to your house. Will that be better?'

Hanz doesn't respond. But when the princess holds out her hand, he gives her his. He doesn't know her, but he feels safe in her company.

It is a short ten-minute walk. They stop at the entrance of his lane.

'I can go home from here by myself,' Hanz says.

'Promise me you will go straight to your house?'

'I promise,' Hanz replies. The princess smiles at him once more, and then places her hand over his head.

'Goodbye, Hanz.'

'Goodbye.' Just before turning to walk home, Hanz asks her what her name is.

'Jasmine,' she replies.

four

Laila

Thick brown tea is poured into the ornate silver teacup. Laila lifts the teacup off the plate in protest. She does not like tea and thinks of this Friday evening ritual as obsolete, for it was put in place for the members of the household to engage in non-political chatter; but talking to each other casually is not something they do any more. During these sessions, there was a time when Laila would run into her father, Ahmed's, arms and sit on his lap. But time has made her body too big for his lap and her behaviour too reckless for eye contact.

It is just teatime, but as always, a feast has been laid out on the table. There are vanilla and chocolate cakes, cashew biscuits, buns with maska on them, some slices of toast and three different kinds of jam to go with them. The embroidered ivory cloth covering the round mahogany table is hardly visible underneath the plates of food. There is no need for such a grand spread, but it is an indispensable part of playing the role of being wealthy and powerful. Not one of the four diners has a large appetite any more. The food will either be consumed by the servants or be thrown into the garbage, to later be dug out and devoured by the homeless.

Laila has heard stories of Ahmed's once-large appetite. 'Your father could eat an entire basket of lamb kebabs on his own. He had the appetite of a rakshasa,' a friend of Ahmed's had told her once. But since her mother's death, a servant had to be hired just to make sure that Ahmed did not skip any meals. She's been named after her mother; one Laila to make up for the loss of another. The doctors told her father that her mother would not survive, regardless of whether she chose to have Laila or not.

'The doctor placed you in my arms. A bleeding, crying baby. But you were the only thing that could make the pain go away, Laila.

The most beautiful thing in my life,' her father used to tell her often. He brought her home, a daughter without a mother, born into a man's world. Many had told him to burn her, his own father, Thakur, being one of them. Twenty-two years ago, it was common practice. But he was a rebel, a thorn in the hard, rubber skin of society. He took on the role of being both mother and father and brought up his daughter like he would have a son. Growing up, she sometimes wondered what life would have been like had her mother still been with them, but with Ahmed around, Laila did not feel the absence of a second parent.

It was an ironic society back then, and not much has changed today. Having a daughter was akin to a curse, but a house without any woman was labelled bare and inauspicious. So, slowly, Thakur came to accept his granddaughter.

'Congratulations, you're in the papers again, Laila,' Ahmed Jagir raises his eyebrows over his thin rectangular reading glasses and hands over the *Street Daily* to his daughter across the table. Those bastards have done it again, morphed her protest into an action against morality.

Ahmed waits for the day his daughter will start to behave, though it's perhaps too late now. Laila is twenty-two, and the probability of her getting a suitor now is low. She was poised to acquire a great husband. After all, she was born with a silver spoon and blessed with unconventional good looks. Laila has a warm olive face that is highlighted by her large striking eyes and a petite frame. She is of average height, but her long legs make her look tall and authoritative. There was a time when the media used to sing songs about her big hazel eyes and long, wavy cinnamon-coloured tresses; but all that's talked about now is that the daughter of one of the richest and most powerful men in the nation has lost her manners and is sitting in a golden train that's gone off track. The tabloids tut, a girl without her mother will inevitably stray.

This time, though, Ahmed is making much ado about nothing. Laila is mentioned on the fifth page in a small hundred-word article, without her picture. She had interrupted the wedding of a ten-year-old girl to a fifty-year-old man. It had been a no-dowry wedding, and in fact, the man was paying the girl's family 100,000 rehats. He had even agreed to sponsor the ceremony, paying for a hundred people to eat kofta, naan and meetha. There had been a little ceremonial stage with white and mango-yellow drapes, jasmine and marigold flowers adorning the rest of the space. Disturbingly, there had also been a stack of dolls stashed away in the corner to pacify the child in case she started crying. Without a single thought, a little girl had become a business deal.

Laila had gathered a few like-minded people and gone to the venue to peacefully put an end to the proceedings. Neither of the families was of much importance, so the news hadn't made the front page, but it had still ended up in print – a testimony of the press's loyalty to the conservative.

The first person to throw herself at Laila had been the bride's mother. It was always the woman. Years of indoctrination made the woman believe that she was doing what was necessary. She probably thought it was the only way to ensure her daughter's happiness. That is always what scares Laila the most: how firmly people believe that they are doing the right thing.

The freshly formed folds around Thakur's flat nose warn Laila of her grandfather's impending wrath. The news in the paper has not gone down well with him. While Ahmed understands the futility of his words, Thakur still tries to curb the menace that has taken the form of his granddaughter.

Laila still remembers the first time she was harshly reprimanded. Her grandfather had caught her playing with one of the cook's children when she was eight. It had just been a simple game of hide-and-seek.

'Don't touch him,' Thakur had shouted; a quick parade of insults had followed. He had raced across the lawn, with his eyes firmly on Laila and his fingers tightly clenched around his brown shawl that seemed determined to fly away with the wind. He had clasped her arm tightly and taken her away into the house. The cook was never allowed to enter the house again. Laila had often felt guilty, until she realized that the cook had lost his job not because of her behaviour but because of her grandfather's sense of superiority.

Ahmed used to support her back then. 'She's a kid, Father. All she wanted was to play with another kid. Don't let class get in the way of innocence,' he had told Thakur upon finding out what had transpired that afternoon.

But things have been different since Ahmed became a councilman ten years ago. Her actions affect his political position and so rebellion is now deemed reckless.

Ahmed has been a hard-working council member. He is also considered to be handsome, giving the press something to write about when controversy runs dry. Ahmed has a pale rectangular face like his father's, and the same dark-brown eyes. His features are sharp though, unlike his father's or his brother's, and his well-defined jawline makes all the female writers in Rahat mention him in their magazines. Like most men in the family, Ahmed is tall with straight, dark hair. The Jagir men always keep their hair short and their faces clean-shaven; they are always disciplined.

Thakur used to be a councilman too. He was only twenty when he first campaigned and, at twenty-one had become the youngest-ever council member. Five members make up the national council, one from each district of the nation. Their word is only second to the head of state, making their position one of great power.

Ahmed's first campaign runs fresh in Laila's mind as if it had happened just yesterday. The phone would ring all day, and Laila had been warned not to answer it.

Reporters would stand outside, under the hot sun. They would want just one glimpse of her father. Something to write about, something to make a story out of. Anything to make a story out of. The Jagir servants would give them water, to compensate for all the drops of sweat trickling down their foreheads. Then there were the supporters, the ones waving white flags with yellow circles on them – her father's campaign symbol, and printed below the circles, his primary promise.

A complete life

He had promised to provide basic food, water and living necessities to the people of Rahat. In his ten years as a council member, Ahmed has changed the lives of many for the better. But this term is his last. He will be passing on the baton to his younger brother, Gulzar.

But Laila knows that her uncle doesn't want it. He does not enjoy large crowds, and pleasing the masses is not his forte. He instead wants to put on canvas all that he sees around him, and let colours do the talking. But the only thing his conditioning allows him to do is carry the weight of his father's and his brother's achievements on his shoulders and let himself to be crushed under the large boulder of their expectations. Sons of powerful families do not indulge themselves in the arts for a profession. They do not tear the fine tapestry of legacy for the sake of personal dreams.

five

Laila

Leftover crumbs of the lamb kebabs and butter naan are emptied into the dustbin. The silver utensils are dutifully washed until they're sparkling clean and are then wiped dry and put back in place. Once the soft chatter of the servants fades, Laila carefully climbs down the marble staircase. She is wearing comfortable blue cotton shorts and a white T-shirt. Rahat is warm throughout the year but not unbearably hot like some of the other districts. Laila has never visited any of the other districts. In fact, she hasn't even seen most of Rahat. Ahmed does not realize how suffocating his protection can be.

It's dark and Laila is careful not to tip over the metal vase at the bottom of the staircase. Once, her Aunt Helena, visiting them from her home district of Baugh, had knocked over the vase, and its clatter had been loud enough to wake the dead. Despite the repeated requests from Laila, Ahmed and Gulzar, Thakur had refused to let the vase be moved to another location in the house. The vase had been gifted to Thakur by the head of state when Thakur had returned from serving in the army and he wanted it where it was most visible. Every inch of their mansion has history attached to it.

Laila makes her way to the kitchen. Cold milk and cocoa-flavoured cereal await her. Only in the middle of the night can Laila find some quiet in this house. A slight tinkle of the crystal chandeliers can be heard, almost like a lullaby hushing the house into slumber. During the day, the ground floor is always bustling with visitors, either guests with a political interest or reporters for official statements and interviews. But the sweet lull of the night helps her think and clears her head. Once she's done with her midnight snack, she cleans her bowl and puts it back in place. The comfort and warmth of solitude give her a sense of liberation and make the din from headlines and opinions seem far away.

She stops in her tracks as Shadow lets out a soft woof. Her little black terrier has been trailing her. Just as she picks him up in her arms to give him some attention and stop him from barking, she hears the front door open. Quickly hiding behind a pillar, easily concealed by the darkness, she peeps round it and realizes that there's no need to worry. It's just Ahmed arriving late from one of his meetings.

Instead of heading straight to his bedroom though, Ahmed takes off his black leather shoes and enters the boardroom. Decorated in cream-and-gold upholstery, and laden with pictures of ancestors, this room is only used by the Jagirs to discuss matters amongst themselves. Not even servants are allowed inside, barring one ageing man, who has been responsible for the upkeep of the room for the last thirty years.

Laila was six the first time she entered the room. The exam results had been declared in school and she had scored the highest marks in her class. She couldn't wait to tell her father, but Ahmed was inside the room, having a conversation with Thakur. So, she knocked on the door and called out to Ahmed. Immediately, Ahmed opened the door to let her in. But Laila remembers Thakur shouting at Ahmed from the back of the room, 'You want to let that little brat in here as well? Just having her in our house is an insult to our family. Ahmed, don't slay our legacy, Ahmed, listen to me, Ahmed –' This is not the welcome all women receive. Laila has seen many photos of her mother inside that room. Thinking about Thakur's words often makes room for a chilling thought to enter Laila's mind that she sternly pushes away.

Laila hears footsteps come down the stairs and shifts behind the pillar. Thakur and Gulzar appear and make their way towards the boardroom. *A family meeting without her; they must have a lot of those.* Once everyone is inside, Laila tiptoes to the large dark wooden door that quite literally guards the family's secrets. It's not good at its job though, because if Laila crouches and places her ear at a particular spot, she can hear the conversation inside. It also helps that the Jagirs are a particularly loud bunch of people. Apart from Gulzar – he's the only one she can't hear, but he's usually silent, so it doesn't really matter.

'Is it true?' Thakur asks with a strange tension in his voice that usually appears either before election results are announced or after drinking tea that has a spoon or two of sugar missing.

Nobody responds, but Laila assumes that Ahmed is either nodding or shaking his head. After a moment or two she hears a feeble, 'Yes.'

'But why? Councilman James is retiring. He should not be allowed to dictate how the council is shaped in the future.' Thakur sounds furious now. Laila can sense the famous tiny wrinkles forming around his nose.

Laila presses her ear closer to the door. 'It is just a bill, Father. You know we need a clear majority to pass it. Three out of the five council members must vote for it.'

'And are you going to vote for it, Ahmed?'

Laila's heart stops for a second as she hears Ahmed's reply. Surely, she must be dreaming. A sense of euphoria engulfs her.

'Yes, Father. I think it's high time that women are allowed to be elected to the national council. After all, they make up more than 40 per cent of our population.'

six

Jasmine

It is noon and everyone around her in the train compartment is complaining about the harsh sun outside. The heat doesn't bother her much. She has seen only extreme temperatures in Mahlah, and this, to her, is somewhat pleasant. Jasmine focuses on holding the metal bar attached to the roof. Everyone around her, including the tiny red-haired woman standing beside her, seems determined to conquer her spot.

The electric trains that connect almost all parts of Rahat are different creatures. The trains do not make any noise as they start moving. There is no familiar clacking of wheels or snort of the engine. Everyone must always be prepared for the sudden jolt that indicates their departure. Kaiza had once told her that the company which makes these trains had offered him a job. It was good money, but Kaiza did not want to leave Mahlah and so he rejected the offer. How irony finds its way into people's lives is rather amusing.

The red-haired woman is wearing a blue skirt that ends a little above her knees. Jasmine glances at her legs and moves her own arms closer to her body, as if to cover herself, even though she herself is dressed in long pants, a full-sleeved shirt, and has covered her head with a scarf in such a way that all that is visible of her are her eyes. The old man standing at the other end, wearing a crisply ironed shirt and carrying a leather briefcase, is ogling the red-haired woman. So is the young lad dressed in hand-me-downs that are two sizes too big for him.

A woman must please a man to lead a happy and comfortable life. Do you understand, laado? Her mother's words ring in Jasmine's ears. Perhaps, this is another way to please a man. But something about the men's stares is making Jasmine uncomfortable.

The intermingling of class and gender in this moving box of metal is all but an illusion created for the sake of convenience. In her last few days here, Jasmine has realized that the rest of Rahat is like that too.

It's a beautiful city, Rahat, but a city where contraries can cohabit. A couple of six-lane-wide roads cut through the entire length of the city, but the interiors are filled with thin by-lanes that citizens treat as their waste ground. At local libraries, people who own multiple cars sit beside those who don't own even a bike. Class here isn't measured by the number of floors a person's house has; Jasmine has seen beautiful mansions that are only two storeys tall. Large cinema halls play movies that are made in Rahat itself. There are places that print books; there are people who write them – all in Rahat. Even women are allowed to write in magazines, she'd heard on the train. As she digs into her pocket and removes a black-and-white photo of a young Kaiza, she pushes away the thought nudging at her – what if Kaiza fell in love with the culture, the freedom, the madness of Rahat? What if this life was too good for him to compromise by taking on the burden of a family? What if he hadn't returned because he simply chose not to? The thought of how perfectly Kaiza fits into Rahat fills her with dread. Mahlah, where people's minds only want to stick to their narrow world view, was akin to a prison for someone like her father. Rahat is a never-ending open field where it is acceptable to explore, to be lost and to question.

No, Kaiza loved them too much, she tells herself as she shrugs away her fears. She is not here to look for a man who doesn't want to return; she is here to look for a man who couldn't.

Jasmine had arrived in Rahat a few days ago. The journey from Mahlah had been unexpectedly smooth. She told the bus conductor that she was travelling to live with her brother who had gone to Rahat to find a job, and fortunately he hadn't questioned her further. There have been incidents of girls running away from their families, and every man in Mahlah assumes that it is their responsibility to take a girl back to where she belongs. Even if everyone minded their own business, safety is often a concern for solo female travellers.

Jasmine has been sleeping in waiting rooms of different train stations since she arrived. Stations are the safest places to lodge in. People are always in a hurry and even at three in the morning, there are people getting on and off trains. There are also officers on duty throughout the night. As long as Jasmine doesn't attract attention, she should be all right. Sleeping in stations is also convenient. It's easier to follow leads or even to aimlessly set off in a direction with nothing but the hope that she will see the reflection of Kaiza on a window of a train.

Kaiza had said that he was going to work for a company called Fern Tree, but Jasmine has found no trace of it yet. She visited the company registrar. Two fat files and five cups of tea later, there was still no result, making Jasmine wonder if the company really existed or if her father had already set his mind to being a no-show long before he left home.

But it's not just her father she misses.

When they were younger, Sabaar and Jasmine would often play carom in the summer heat and Nina would bring them some icy rose sherbet as refreshment. In the evenings, when Kaiza would return home from work, they would all sit together and play a game of cards, which Jasmine would win most of the time. Each time she would win, Kaiza would give her 5 rehats. She was saving up to buy an encyclopaedia. She'd heard that it was a book containing information about everything – animals, birds and even inventions. There was a time she could read very well, but it has been years since she has read anything.

As night fell, Nina would bring in the dinner, and together they would relish every bite. Nina used to enjoy cooking back then; she would try new dishes every week. Now she merely puts the lentils in the pot and blankly stares into space as they cook themselves. Jasmine would wait for the day when biryani was cooked. It was her and Kaiza's favourite dish; made only on special occasions, Nina would layer the finest long-grain rice and perfectly spiced lamb meat in a clay pot and cook the biryani in dum style. Their neighbours would sometimes gather to taste Nina's special biryani. Some said that the royal aroma of the meat and the rice being cooked would spread through all of Mahlah.

Kaiza used to often ask Nina to start catering for small functions in their neighbours' or relatives' houses. 'It's your turn to do something with your life, Nina; take your passion forward,' Kaiza would say.

Nina would blush at Kaiza's suggestion, as if the thought was too outlandish, too dishonourable to let it enter her mind. 'Na, *jaan*. The household duties take up most of my time, and who will take care of the children? Anyway, I am satisfied with just cooking for my family.'

Kaiza's suggestions to split the household duties were always met with rage. How a man could offer to perform domestic chores was beyond Nina. 'It is not a man's job,' she would say.

The last time the aroma of Nina's biryani spread through Mahlah was two months after Kaiza had left. He was supposed to visit them that evening, stay for a few days and discuss future plans. The three of them had behaved like children all day, their hearts beating faster with every grunt from a passing camel, with every breath of the wind that teasingly rattled their door.

Every inch of the house was wiped clean. The children were dressed in new clothes, and Nina herself had worn one of her fancier dresses. When morning turned into night, Nina tucked a crying daughter and a furious son into bed. She went to the kitchen and emptied the entire pot of biryani into the dustbin, making sure to break the pot in the process. No one had eaten. They had all wanted to sit with Kaiza and take their first bite.

Since that night, hunger has been a predominant pang in the little house at the corner of the street.

seven

Laila

Dressed in denim overalls, with a matching blue scarf tied around her face, more to protect her identity than her modesty, Laila walks to the corner of the street and takes a cab. The sun is right on the top of her head, and she can easily be spotted by her father or one of his many servants.

There is a thin stack of carefully bound papers in her hand. Ten sheets with graphs and information that will hopefully aid in convincing Councilman Hooser to vote for the entry of women into the national council.

This is the first time such a bill has been proposed. Seventy-two years after the districts were united and the nation was formed, the nation has found a chance to redeem itself.

The council needs three out of five members to vote in favour of the bill for it to pass. As her father has decided to vote for it and as Councilman James, the proposer of the bill, cannot cast a negative vote, just one more positive vote is needed. Council members Briggs and Tony are young and will want to run for the council again, so they are more likely to play it safe. Councilman Hooser is Laila's best bet. Councilman Hooser is an old man in his mid-sixties and this is his last term. He has always been very respectful towards Laila. He agreed to meet with her at once. It was slightly more difficult to convince him to keep their conversation private. Hooser is a good friend of her father and grandfather.

As Laila enters Hooser's mansion, he gets up from his chair to greet her. He is dressed in a white kurta and matching crisp white pajamas. His clothes perfectly match his hair, or at least whatever is left of it. His pointy nose has a slight bend, which makes him look like he is always leaning forward. His pale face is complemented by his grey eyes. He is a man who didn't start out with big ambitions, but fate had handed him a golden opportunity and he used it.

Hooser is not known to be a sharp man. He is perhaps the most naive of all the council members. He takes life as it comes and doesn't like to get involved in playing the political game. He hails from Attara, the most underdeveloped of the nation's five districts.

As Laila sits facing Hooser, explaining all the advantages of having a woman in the council, Hooser's eyes and brain wander off into the distance. He probably hasn't even been listening. Despite presenting her long report, she knows that facts aren't going to get her his vote; her persuasion is. She politely clears her throat and asks him if he has made his decision.

Hooser brings his eyes back from the distance and answers, 'One woman is fine. But what if one day, all the council members are women? How will the nation run then? On emotions and mutton kulcha?'

What do they feed some men when they are born? Morsels full of a sense of superiority? Laila hides her distaste under a thickly plastered wide smile and replies, 'With all due respect, sir, around 70 per cent, even 100 per cent of voters in some districts are men. Do you think men will let there be a council full of women? I'm sure that your side of the gender is capable of making logical, apt decisions. Giving women the right to be in the council doesn't guarantee their presence, but it makes them feel like they have something more, which means that they will ask for less. Less whining from your wife; wouldn't you like that, sir?'

'You do make a good point, Ms Jagir...'

What do they say – lose a battle, win the war?

He waits for her outside Councilman Hooser's house in anticipation. It had startled him when he saw her.

Having made the biggest sale of the year, he was walking out of Councilman Hooser's mansion a content man. But as soon as her cinnamon tresses came into sight, a wave of uneasiness shook his entire body. He wonders why she is visiting the councilman.

Half an hour later, she finally steps out of the mansion and calls for a taxi. Why she must take a cab when her family owns a fleet of cars, eleven in total, is beyond him. But then, there are many things about her that he does not understand. A person can learn only so much by watching from a distance.

The crystal-clear memory of their last and only meeting plays in his head, as it often does. He had made sure to take note of every detail. She had been dressed in a white silk blouse and matching pants. Her father had been sitting beside her while she decided on what to buy. She jumped with excitement as she tried on every piece and looked at herself in the mirror, as if she herself was surprised by how marvellous she could look.

He sits in a cab and does not need to ask the driver to follow her taxi. He knows where she is headed. He knows the directions to her house.

It is not a mere house though. The Jagirs live in a mansion. Painted white, complete with a driveway and gardens of its own, the mansion is two storeys tall. Marble balconies protrude outwards from the structure, and Laila often likes sitting in a balcony on the first floor. It is perhaps a part of her room, he muses. No one can get into the Jagirs' mansion without an appointment. There is a security guard stationed every hundred metres.

Every time he sees her, he has to stop himself from making contact. But he can't stop himself from wondering if she would recognize him, even just as the man who once sold her some jewellery. That's all that he is for her.

From the window of his taxi, he watches as Laila gets down from the cab. Her lips take the form of a triumphant smile, which instantly lights up his face, and when she ties her long hair in a bun, he knows she means business.

Once Laila is inside the mansion, he asks the driver to take him back to his hotel. His eyes well up. He has grown used to the tears now and wipes them off like they are routine. He will spend the next couple of days swimming in sweet agony. His heart longs to talk to her, for he is aware that they share so much more than that singular meeting.

Laila is careful to not let the rich chocolate cake spill onto her denim overalls. Ahmed had got them for her during one of his many travels. She has waited for more than a couple of years to fit into them. Her father's sense of size is all wrong. This frenzied feeding of cake is worrying Laila. Her Aunt Helena from Baugh is here and so is her Aunt Rahia, who lives on the next street. Their husbands have joined the party too.

When she returned post her meeting with Councilman Hooser earlier this afternoon, they were all waiting for her. For a few moments she even feared that they had found out about her visit to the councilman, but soon she found out that it was not the case.

Aunt Helena's two-year-old has wet his pants and is about to start crying any minute. But no one is paying any attention to the little baby; all they are focused on is pushing the rather toothsome cake into Laila's mouth. Laila is sure that Amjad Uncle has made the cake. She can detect the hint of his special dark chocolate anywhere. Amjad Uncle has been the head chef of their in-house bakery for a little over two decades now. He doesn't prepare cakes by himself any more, unless a special occasion demands his expertise.

Thakur is watching this festivity from a distance, with an uncanny grin on his lips. The sparkle in her grandfather's eyes accompanying the grin has always served as a fair warning to Laila. He had it when she was taken out of school to be tutored at home. He had it when he had almost convinced Ahmed to send Shadow to an adoption centre; only a large, handsome and strong dog could be a Jagir, he'd said. And he has it today.

Laila tries to catch Ahmed's eyes. Even after years of arguments and miscommunication, she subconsciously always turns to him for comfort. But Ahmed is busy with Gulzar, engaged in a conversation that is seemingly intense. She wonders if he is avoiding her gaze on purpose.

Breaking away from the swarm of relatives, Laila rushes towards Ahmed.

'Father! What's happening here?'

Ahmed turns towards her and then hastily shifts his gaze to the floor. He is about to reply when an overly excited Aunt Helena interrupts him. Her aunts hold Laila by the shoulders and look at her with a love that never exists in a relative's eyes unless a girl is either being bound in matrimony or will soon have a little boy in her arms.

'We thought it would never happen, Laila, my jaan.'

'Yes, yes, and this is even better than expected. All those years of waiting turned out to be fruitful. Right, Ahmed?'

'Who knew Raymond Tony himself would ask for your hand?'

'Both father and husband in the council! Laila jaan, you will be the most pampered woman in this nation!'

eight

Jasmine

She didn't leave that night because Sabaar hit her. She left because the violence had become routine. Kaiza leaving had not only taken away her father but also her mother and her brother.

About six months after Kaiza had left, Jasmine was busy stirring lentils in the kitchen when Sabaar came home with his white shirt soaked in blood for the first time. The boys in his school had asked him where his father was. They had teased him mercilessly, called him a bastard. That's why his father never came back, they had taunted – because his mother was a whore.

As Nina cleaned the wounds where sand had already taken refuge, she told Sabaar not to pay any attention to the boys. His father was a coward for not returning, she said, and Sabaar shouldn't have to pay the price for that. But when all of his shirts started getting stained with blood and there was no more money to buy new clothes, Nina had him pulled out of school.

Jasmine remembers the day when the monster arrived. It was on one of Sabaar's last days of school. Jasmine had begun to grow out of her own clothes and so she was wearing her mother's old green kaftan, two sizes too big for her. She had begun to feel that Nina was feeding her less so she would still fit into her own clothes. Or perhaps their mother was simply ensuring that Sabaar had enough to eat. Jasmine couldn't decide which reason Nina had given herself.

Jasmine carried a tray with two loaves of bread and some watery chicken curry to Sabaar's room. Nina and Jasmine had to go to bed hungry that night. The boys had punched him hard and Sabaar needed all the food he could get so his body and his ego could recover faster.

'We must always put the men's needs before our own, Jasmine. They will in turn protect us in times of danger.'

Maybe that expectation had made Kaiza leave. He was smart, poetic, analytical and romantic even, but he was no warrior.

When Jasmine entered the room, Sabaar was lying on his bed with his eyes fixed on the ceiling. As Jasmine followed his gaze, she noticed for the first time that the pastel-green paint on the ceiling had started to chip off. Jasmine was only thirteen then, but she had no qualms about giving up her share of bread. She knew that her brother was hurt – hurt for no fault of his own – and that he needed all the support he could get.

She placed the tray beside him and lightly touched his hand. He shook it off and gave her a stern look.

'It's all right, Sabaar. They don't know about us, they don't know about Father.'

'And you, Jasmine, what do you know about him?' Sabaar shot the words at her like an arrow, questioning her defence of a man who had left them to fend for themselves.

Jasmine wanted to say that she knows that Kaiza loves them, that he will come back for them one day. But she didn't; she just looked down at the ground and listened as her brother insulted their father. Until it went too far.

'He just wanted to leave us, Jasmine! Why can't you accept it? Maybe he is living with another, younger woman, making new kids to take care of and leave behind for another. Maybe that's the kind of man he really is –'

'Sabaar, no,' Jasmine yelled. As she saw the expression on Sabaar's face change from anger to absolute rage, Jasmine shuddered. Should she have listened to her mother? Never questioned a man's opinion; never raised her voice?

Sabaar glared at his sister, and the next moment he slapped her face hard. His hands were shivering and his eyes were trying to understand this new sense of power building inside him. He could hurt her to mask his pain. He could hurt her to sew together his shattered ego. He could hurt her to take back what those boys had taken from him. He could hurt her to punish his father for deserting him. And no one would stop him.

Nina heard the cries from inside the room. She let a tear roll down her cheeks. She saw the red stains when Jasmine returned her green kaftan. She brushed out the stains and dried up her tears. She knew that from now on, only one of her children would be able to truly live – and she had already chosen which one it would be.

nine

Jasmine

Jasmine lifts the glass of water to confirm her suspicions by looking at the reflection in the glass. The moment she realizes it is him, stunned, she puts the glass back down. Her first instinct is to leave, to make herself invisible. She raises her hand to adjust her headscarf in a way that it covers her face but stops short. She doesn't know what she will say or how he will react, or whether he will remember her at all, but she does not want to hide her presence, so that he can initiate contact if he wants to.

She holds her thoughts back. He is not the reason she is here. For all she knows, he could drag her back to Mahlah and report her to the authorities back home. Sitting inside a jail cell is not going to help her find Kaiza. Four grey walls, tasteless food and sporadic slaps on the face do not scare her though. She has seen worse. But her mind refuses to see reason. Her heart believes that he will understand why she left. It believes, perhaps naively, that even if he sees her, he won't report her.

The spiced rice, mutton curry and chopped onion sit in front of her untouched as the dust dispersed by speeding vehicles settles on them. This street-side eatery is bustling with workers trying to get their midday meal, but Jasmine has eyes only for one.

Seeing him again has sparked a rush in her heart that she can't quite place, and knowing that he sits so close to her, that the air he breathes can touch her neck, sends her mind into a frenzy. What kind of sorcery has brought him to her again? She wants him to leave so she can breathe freely, without each breath making her cheeks flush. Yet she wants him to stay so she can continue to feel the rush of possibility. She wonders if he's found a girl yet. It can't be that difficult for him.

He sits alone, dressed in khaki pants, a light-blue cotton shirt that complements his eyes, and has a chequered scarf loosely wrapped around his neck. She wishes she looked more groomed herself. Her black hair is muddy and her eyes could use a week's worth of sleep. Her red top is wrinkled and she's not sure how well it matches the black pants she has on.

Jasmine's heart races as she hears the scrape of a chair sliding back. Then the sound of shoes walking away makes her heart sink. But soon, the two large feet, encased in brown leather, stop, hesitate, and turn around.

All Jasmine can hear is her own heart pounding in her chest. His feet stop right in front of her table. Jasmine resists the urge to sink into the floor. Maybe this is all just a mistake. But she's not wrong. It's the same strong voice with just a hint of huskiness. *I will marry Jasmine Mir, daughter of Kaiza Mir.* He looks at her as she hesitantly raises her head to acknowledge him.

'Hello. You're Jasmine, right? You might not… umm… I'm –'

She forgets all about the discernible blush on her face and the daze in her eyes.

'Amer, I…I do remember you.'

'May I have a seat then?'

The stout face of the head of state on the cream-and-purple paper stares back at her. She searches her pockets to see if she has any more notes left. Five hundred rehats in all; she can survive for five more days, perhaps a week. She tries to let the gravity of her situation sink in, but the chance encounter with Amer earlier in the day has left her elated.

She noted down the date, time and place carefully on a piece of paper, not that she would ever forget. As they were talking, Amer had lightly placed his strong, soft hand on hers and apologized for the way he and his family had behaved. She told him that no one was to blame but the circumstances. He ordered some coffee for her, which she went over to the counter and cancelled. She had already spent her allotted 20 rehats on the meal and she didn't want to ask Amer to pay. They sat in silence for a few minutes, she gulping down her rice and he grinning at the continuous flickering of her eyeballs from her food to his face.

There were histories, characteristics, minute nuances, and a lifetime of stories, all waiting to be shared, but words failed them at the moment they were needed the most. Or perhaps words know when to make room for silence, so the heart can speak, free of any misinterpretation.

Ten minutes that felt like a lifetime. Jasmine could have stayed there forever, looking into his clear blue eyes.

When he asked if she would like to meet him again, despite herself she responded with a strong nod in the affirmative. He is here on business and will be going back home to Mahlah for fifteen days. They are going to see each other the very day he returns to Rahat.

Jasmine is trying to drive the blush away from her face and concentrate on the problem at hand. She needs to find a way to earn money soon if she is to have any chance of surviving in this city and continue looking for Kaiza. She has not gotten anywhere with her search yet, and she is unable to trace Fern Tree, the company her father had come to Rahat to work for. But she knows she cannot, does not, want to return to her abusive home.

She is unsure about where she can start looking for a job and she cannot even read and write well, but she can perhaps start by enquiring at the railway station head office, in case they have any openings for women.

A job, a chance meeting with Amer; it feels almost odd to Jasmine that she is thinking about these things so far removed from her life back in Mahlah. Maybe there is more in this for her than just finding Kaiza.

ten

Laila

The wine-coloured silk gown is encrusted with the handiwork of the finest craftsmen in Rahat. The dress fits snugly against Laila's body till her waist and then balloons out in gorgeous ruffles. The skin on her neck is barely visible underneath all the diamonds. Chandeliers pale in comparison to the jewels dangling from her ears. Her shoes have been custom-made by Taf, the most renowned shoemaker in the nation. But beneath all the grandeur and luxury, behind all the beauty and blush, Laila's body suffocates in the skintight dress.

Laila stares at her mother's portrait hung up on the wall. There has never been a moment when Laila has longed for a mother as she does today. A loving touch, telling her that it is going to be okay. Maybe her mother would know of her arrangement, tell her that it is not worth a life full of suffering, warn her of how fickle a man could be.

Laila shudders as the realization dawns upon her. She herself is going to be a mother by the end of the day. Raymond's ten-year-old son is a bastard from a waitress in a local bar, who has not been seen in Rahat since the day she gave birth to the boy. Fortunately, the child was a boy and so he successfully avoided his mother's fate. Only Raymond and his son live in Rahat. The rest of Raymond's family lives in Mahlah, Raymond's home town. Laila has heard that in Mahlah women rarely step out of their houses without a man's company and that women are supposed to cover their heads at all times.

Ahmed walks into the room, snapping Laila's mind into attention. He takes her face in his hands and looks into her kohl-lined eyes. 'Thank you, Laila jaan. You have made a great decision for yourself and for our entire family.'

Laila remembers when she was only ten years old and had told Ahmed that she would never leave him. Ahmed had told her that one day she would find someone she would want to make her own home with, but until then she would not be forced into an arrangement. It is important for a woman to make something of her own life before she gets married, he had told her, so that if and when she does, she goes into the marriage as an equal, making sure that the man cannot use his privilege of being born a male to take his wife's life decisions.

Laila hides her face from him, thinking sadly of how the man who once said these things is now lost in a world where adhering to societal rules is not just important but necessary.

But Ahmed did not make this decision for Laila; she did.

As she walks onstage, Laila tells herself that this is her punishment for her own foolishness. Laila hadn't anticipated that Hooser would fail his promise and inform Thakur of their little chat, and that Thakur would be able to influence Hooser with such ease. She had Hooser's word, but she should have known that a word doesn't count for much these days. A short conversation with Thakur, and Hooser decided to reverse his vote. Thakur only had to feed Hooser's mind with what he already believed, while Laila had to attack the fundamentals of his entire system and hope for a win.

Her initial answer to Raymond's proposal was a clear no. Aunt Helena begged her to change her mind. 'You will never get an opportunity as good as this one again. Laila jaan, please don't let it go.' But Laila didn't have to think twice. Until Hooser came home and apologized to Laila, revealing to her his conversation with Thakur.

The day she made her decision Laila asked to meet Raymond in private. He was dressed in a turquoise kurta and matching pants. He wore a royal-blue vest, which made his light brown eyes look striking. His short black hair was slicked back.

Raymond is not a tall man and stands only an inch or two above Laila, but his broad shoulders and well-built muscles give him the appearance of being much larger than he is. Once he entered Laila's study, he asked his guards to leave.

Raymond made his way towards Laila and sat on the chair beside hers. When he stretched his hand out and lovingly stroked her face, caressing her cheeks like she was already his, Laila instinctively jerked away. An angry look settled on Raymond's face for a passing second before he regained composure and decided to open the conversation.

'Yes, Laila. I heard you wanted to meet me in private. I am pleased that you're considering this marriage. I'm sure you understand the value of a Tony–Jagir bloodline.'

Laila shifted further away from him, pierced his brown eyes with hers and said, 'I will marry you, but on one condition.'

Raymond looked on as Laila declared, 'You have to vote in favour of the bill that allows women to be elected into the national council.'

Raymond looked stunned. He was one of the most eligible bachelors in the nation; the thought that a woman would marry him as a barter never crossed his mind. He remained deep in thought for a few moments, then he then looked up at Laila, and said, 'All right, Laila. I accept your offer.'

He then proceeded to cup her face in his hands, caressing her cheeks, just as her father used to so often when she was a child. That was the first time Laila understood the true difference between lust and love.

Something in his eyes tugged at Laila's mind. A mistake she'd made before? She shrugged off the thought, and extended her hand for a firm shake, which Raymond took hold of and brought to his lips.

The sweet sound of the hymn fades as the priest stops singing and proceeds to place his calloused hands on Raymond's and Laila's intertwined palms. The priest then whispers a chant into their ears, telling them that they are being bound in holy matrimony and that breaking the fine thread of such a relationship is a sinful act that is condemned by God and the community. The priest then asks each of them if they accept, and they nod and answer yes.

For the ceremony, Laila and Raymond are standing on a stage which has been built at one end of the large ballroom, decorated in gold and white. This wedding, on Laila's insistence, is a rather small and private occasion. Laila thinks it might reduce her sense of shame if fewer people witness her compromise. There are about two hundred people in attendance, including a select few reporters. A seven-course meal and an unlimited supply of wine has been reason enough for most of them to be on time.

The priest is dressed in white cloth with gold borders. The cloth is loosely wrapped around his waist and falls till his feet. White; the colour of purity, the colour of peace. The white of Raymond's shirt subtly peeks out from under his perfectly tailored black silk tuxedo. His bow tie has his initials, R.T., stitched on it with silver thread. But none of his extravagance holds a light to Laila, who looks resplendent in her wine-coloured gown.

It is said that a girl never looks better than she does on her wedding day. The flush of red in her cheeks; the pink blush that Laila has brushed on. The sparkling light in her eyes; the reflection of the chandeliers in the hazel. The glow on her face; the two layers of a radiance mask that Aunt Helena had forced her to apply the previous night. Laila never knew that how you looked and how you felt had the potential of being a world apart. She wonders if that is the reality of the world, if hope is always made up of sacrifice, if you can never accurately perceive the layers underneath when you touch someone's surface.

Laila can feel her rising heartbeat, her clenching stomach. This is not her first step into the adult world of utter madness, where a plethora of masks are worn either to protect or to manipulate, the line between the two being very blurry. Laila was born into politics, but she is suddenly unsure if she can hold her own without her home, her comfort, her father, by her side.

The priest places Laila's left hand, full of delicate lines, a worrier's hand, in Raymond's calloused right palm. Acting on cue, they turn towards each other. A cloth is stretched and held as a screen between the newly-weds, to hide them from public view and allow them to take pleasure in their first kiss. It is neither Raymond's nor Laila's first. Anticipating Raymond's fat lips on her soft pink curves, Laila's heart drowns in agony. His eyes say it all; that she is his prize. Laila almost expects Ahmed to stand up and protest. But he wasn't the one who had cut a deal with the devil; she was. Her body stiffens as Raymond leans in; her mind rushes elsewhere to avoid being fully present in a moment she wants to have no memory of.

Laila finds herself behind the A block in Wallameri, a residential school in Rahat. Her body is pressed against the grey wall, her mouth gasping for air. She was there for a summer course on the nation's history and politics. It took a lot of convincing, but Ahmed eventually lost to Laila's tireless determination and agreed to send her away for a month. Laila was seventeen then. Omar was a year older. It wasn't much of a romance or maybe her distorted memories try to convince her now that it wasn't. He was quite a bit taller than her, and so she could always hear his heartbeat when she hugged him. His face was long and tanned. His dark hair was short and well styled. Every time his small brown eyes looked at her, it sent goosebumps down her right leg. It was not his gorgeous eyes though; it was the *way* he looked at her, like she was all that he could, and wanted, to see at that moment. The day before they left camp, he called her to their secret hideout, a narrow stretch of pathway between the rear side of the A block and the school boundary wall. They would often sit here and share their dreams, or talk about the council and discuss how the state was heading towards doom, or maybe even about how blue the sky looked that day; anything that caught their fancy. Sometimes they wouldn't talk. They would just lie there in silence, looking at the sky and searching for meaning in the secrets of the stars. But that day, as soon as he saw her, he held her by the hand and pulled her towards him, grabbing her waist and pressing her against the grey wall. Then he waited; both their hearts racing from the tension between their faces. Laila had fantasized about kissing those perfectly shaped lips, but never had she expected it to be a part of her reality. He held her chin up slightly and cupped her cheeks. The touch of his fingers sent a chill down her spine. They kissed with all their might, as though if they kissed hard enough, they would become one. Omar and Laila woke the next morning a smiling entangled mess. They quickly put their clothes on and rushed back to their dorms. Laila spent the afternoon with her cheeks swimming in crimson, but by the evening it hit her that they would not see each other for a long time as Omar was from Samin. They kissed a lot that day and promised to write letters. They were to meet in a month, when he would come back to Rahat to submit his university application, but she never heard from him again. Her tears dried up in a few months, and regret replaced sorrow in her mind.

As Raymond places his plump lips on Laila's, she is suddenly thankful for that summer romance. A negotiation is not her first kiss. A man who only sees the political benefits of joining his name to hers, a man in whose eyes she observes only lust but no warmth will not be the first person she will make love to.

A shiny long black car presents itself in front of the new couple. The car is decorated with colourful flowers and red silk bows; a customary present from the bride's family to the groom's. The chauffeur, dressed in white, opens the door for Laila. She turns around to look at Ahmed. His eyes are watery. Ahmed approaches his daughter and holds her by her shoulders. 'I'll always be there for you,' he says.

Laila immediately turns away, as if this is all in some way his fault. Laila knows that her mind often tries to fault others when the mistake is hers.

According to custom, one that Laila has always disapproved of, but now has to follow, a girl has to live with the man's family once they get married. Raymond nudges Laila to hurry. She has already spent too much time among crying relatives though she isn't sure why they are so sad at her departure. She will be living in Raymond's house, sure, but it is still in Rahat. They hardly ever see her anyway. She will understand later that they are not crying for her physical departure, but because her *ownership* has been transferred from her father to her husband. She now belongs to her husband's family, and her old life must come second to everything new.

The morning after her wedding, as Laila steps out of the shower, she notices a green kaftan and pair of pants laid out on the bed. Beside it lies a sheer scarf that matches the set. The dress is beautiful but not something that Laila would ever wear. The women from Raymond's family always cover their head with a scarf. Laila hadn't thought that

Raymond would expect the same from her. On the bed there is a small card with beautiful flowers drawn on it. He must have had it made; Laila knows from last night that Raymond does not have a steady hand. In it is a note: *You're a part of the Tony family now, Laila. You must dress like it. Welcome...*

Laila sits on the bed and lets out a deep sigh. She is exhausted from last night. Raymond had a little too much wine at the wedding party. As soon as they sat in the back seat of the car, he asked the driver to roll the partition up. With the windows heavily tinted there was no risk of public humiliation. As he leaned into her, she jerked away and tried to fight him off. Laila had observed Raymond's unsolicited sexual advances disguised as a brush on the cheek, as a slight touch of the hand, right from when he was only her suitor. She knew that marrying him would involve an aggressive physical relationship, but that he would try to force himself on her as soon as she was legally *his*, came as a shock, and her body reacted by stiffening up. His mouth reeked of alcohol. His perfectly ironed shirt had started to crumple. There was a spark of madness in his eyes as he put his lips onto all of her visible skin. Once they got to his house, he picked her up and threw her on his bed before ripping her clothes off. She was able to persuade him to put some protection on. She doesn't want a child, and he already has a boy of his own.

Laila didn't enjoy it. Laila didn't resist it. It hurt a little, but she knows that the pain will disappear with time. She took it like medicine, bitter but essential for her survival in this house.

Laila rises from the bed and puts on the green dress. She turns to the mirror and searches for a familiar face. She cannot find one. Every bit of the Jagir inside refuses to stare back at her. Instead, a wife looks up in despair. She quickly rushes to her bag and empties it. She looks at her denim pants, silk blouses, beautiful dresses and gowns. She grabs as many as she can hold and presses them against her chest, hugging them for a glimpse of her old life. In theory, this marriage is a negotiation that Laila orchestrated. And yes, she had always anticipated that her life would change drastically, but after living through only a single night of this negotiation, she realizes how much she has actually given up. She shudders as she imagines her life ahead, one of constant compromise and pain.

eleven

Jasmine

The assorted meats on the skewer have a slight char on their edges. They have been cooked well in the tandoor, and the aroma of the spices from their marinade fills Jasmine's senses. As she walks towards the table, she is careful not to tip over the tray in her hands. The butter on the naan jiggles with every step that Jasmine takes. She can feel her mouth water. She looks over at the round wooden clock on the wall.

It's 2 p.m. One more hour to go till it's break time.

There aren't many jobs that Jasmine can do. To begin with, even in Rahat, there are only a few areas where women are allowed to work. Magazines, restaurants, nursing, textile weaving and perhaps a few other handicraft industries. She has lost touch with reading and writing, and numbers had never been her forte. So, when the opportunity to work as a waitress presented itself, she took it. Jasmine loves the aroma of food. She likes how the smell of biryani takes her back to a happier time.

The restaurant manager is an old man named Ruff. Most of the little hair he has left on his head is grey. He is always dressed in his uniform, a white shirt, which snugly fits against his pot belly, a red bow tie and a pair of black pants fastened with a belt. His face has more than a few dents, marks left by small pox from his childhood. It is difficult to imagine that adults were once kids too. Mr Ruff is a kind man. At the restaurant, he doesn't yell much and always tries to fully grasp the situation before taking any action. What's unique about him are his eyes; his eyes are what led Jasmine to this small diner.

A couple of days after the chance encounter with Amer, Jasmine had been sleeping in the waiting room at Russel station, which is in a nicer part of the city. Her routine consisted of holding out Kaiza's black-and-white photograph and asking people if they'd seen him.

It had been almost a month since Jasmine had been in Rahat. She had spent every single day running around government offices, trying to look for any record of her father or the company he was supposed to be working for, and moving from one part of the city to another, asking people for help. But her search had yielded no result, no lead even. It seemed as if her father had disappeared into thin air. Had he even come to Rahat? Had he been lying from the very beginning? The constant cycle of hope every time a passer-by stopped to look at the photo, and the inevitable disappointment, was beginning to wear her out.

That's when she spotted those eyes in a swarm of office-goers. *Kaiza*!

With her heart racing, she started pacing towards him. As she got a little closer, she saw that the man was a bit plump, whereas Kaiza had always been scrawny. But he was about the same height and those striking eyes were unmistakable. She followed the man out of the station, into a busy street in Russel. Ten minutes later, he took a turn and vanished through the door of a small diner in one of the by-lanes.

She stood outside the diner which looked like it was closed. She wondered if she should knock on the door. For a few minutes, she paced back and forth, up and down the footpath, until a tall woman, possibly in her early thirties, came out of the door and placed a signboard.

'Open'.

Assuming Jasmine to be an early customer, she said, 'You can come in now, miss.'

Jasmine smiled at the waitress and followed her inside. She noticed that the waitress was wearing a full-sleeved yellow blouse, which was tucked into her knee-length black skirt, which left her legs bare. Looking at her bare legs made Jasmine feel uncomfortable. When she entered the diner, to the waitress's surprise, Jasmine didn't even glance at the tables as she walked straight to the manager's desk in the corner. Her heart sank as she reached him.

Barring the eyes, there was not an inch of Kaiza in his appearance. His nose was more like Nina's – shaped like a samosa – and his face was round and chubby. If she had to be honest with herself, a part of her knew even as she saw the first glimpse of the man, that it wasn't Kaiza. But those who are desperate never let go of hope.

'Yes, mam, what do you want?' Mr Ruff asked Jasmine politely.

The diner was a cosy place, with small wooden tables. With the beige curtains drawn back, the glass walls facing the road allowed plenty of sunlight to stream inside the room. It looked warm and beautiful.

Looking at Jasmine's lost expression, Mr Ruff continued, 'Did you see our ad in *Rahat Daily*? Have you come to apply for the waitress job?'

Jasmine paused for a moment, confused, but then realized the opportunity right in front of her.

'Yes.'

'Well, can you carry a tray full of food without tipping it over?'

'Yes, sir, I can.'

'Well, you have a pretty face and waitressing doesn't require much skill. I'll give you a one-week trial period. If you manage to deliver the right orders and not annoy any customers, you'll have the job.'

'Thank you, sir,' Jasmine said as she processed what had just happened.

'You can start from tomorrow. Report at nine in the morning. We open at ten, so you'll have to help get things ready before that. You get a break at three, once you clean up after the lunch hours.

You have to report back at six because we open at seven for dinner. You can leave at nine; we don't ask our female employees to stay for long after it gets dark outside. You'll be paid 7,000 rehats a month. If you miss a day of work, 200 rehats will be deducted from your salary. I'll get you a uniform tomorrow.'

There were two other waitresses in the diner. Both looked much older than her. The rest of the staff was male. As she looked at the skirts the waitresses wore, she visibly flinched. The thought of half of her legs being visible to strangers was frightening. Mr Ruff noticed the expression on Jasmine's face change.

'Is there a problem, miss?'

Jasmine gulped down the big lump forming in her throat as she continued to look at the skirts.

'Umm, also, about the uniform…only the colour combination and the restaurant badges are compulsory; you can also continue wearing your head scarf if you want to,' Ruff said with an understanding smile.

'Thank you, I'll see you at nine tomorrow,' Jasmine replied, relieved.

Jasmine places the kebab platter and the naan on table number two. She now waits on tables two and four. Both of them are placed near the glass wall, so they are usually the first to be occupied, even though the deserted street outside doesn't make for a great view. It has been eight days since she joined. Mr Ruff did not hesitate to make her a permanent staff member. Jasmine is a polite and good-looking girl. She did have a little problem writing down the names of the dishes when she initially took customer's orders, but the names are short and Jasmine is a fast learner.

The job gives her only a few hours in the day to carry out her personal investigation. Surprisingly, she doesn't mind it. She can feel the main reason for her travel to Rahat slowly slipping to the back of her mind.

Jasmine hardly interacts with anyone at work; she hasn't yet learnt how to make conversation with strangers. The two other waitresses, Janie and Lara, are the best of friends. Janie is the taller one, who had mistaken Jasmine for a customer the other day. She has light golden hair and pale skin, with grey eyes. She is in her mid-thirties and her age shows on her face. Lara is a few years younger than Janie. Like Jasmine, she has dark hair and dark eyes, but her skin is much paler. They both have young kids: Janie, a boy who is ten, and Lara, a girl who is six. She has often overheard the two talking about their kids and how they've been saving; for the boy's education and the girl's marriage.

Then there's Hugo and Amir, although Amir comes in only post six in the evening. They are both in their mid-twenties. The head chef is a man in his early fifties. He has been cooking at this diner since its inception almost a decade ago. His sous chef and his line cooks are all men. So is the pastry chef, who works alone and has earned quite a reputation for his warm cinnamon caramel cake.

When she takes her round badge off at the end of the day, she feels a sense of pride. *Karen's* it says in bold letters.

twelve

Laila

Laila stares at the long empty marble table in front of her. Most of Raymond's house is fitted with marble. The white makes the house look bigger than it is. The two-storey mansion is shaped like a castle, with a dome in the centre. The upper floor has bedrooms, while the ground floor comprises the dining area, the kitchen, the visitor's lounge, a small office room, and a game room, where Raymond and his friends often play cards. Laila's breath stops short as she realizes that this is now also *her* house.

She looks at the servants in discomfort as they bustle around her, trying to fill her plate with the dinner that has been prepared. For starters, there are curried potatoes and vegetable samosas. There's a yellow dal, a minced mutton kofta curry, an aubergine curry and a variety of naans and rotis for the main course, and cold thickened sweet milk with jalebi for dessert.

But Laila has lost her appetite. It is not because of the wedding or because she has to eat alone or because she hasn't left the house in the last three days. It's the taste of the food that she can't get used to. The Tony household likes putting sugar or jaggery in all of their dishes. The only flavour she can taste is sweet. Laila has been eating naan with some mint chutney to fill her stomach. One of these days, she will hopefully be hungry enough to eat the rest.

Raymond and his son, Jai, have already eaten. They begin their dinner at exactly seven in the evening. Once they finish eating and the table is cleared, it is Laila's turn to eat. A wife always lets her husband and children eat first in the Tony household.

It has been only a few days since Laila entered this house as a bride, but she has quickly understood the duties expected of a wife. The responsibilities of overseeing the servants, ensuring the upkeep of the house, deciding the menu for the day, looking after Raymond's and Jai's needs – are all slowly being transferred to her. To keep herself occupied, she has, on an occasion or two, stolen books from Raymond's shelves to read when he's not around. She also tries to steal moments for herself, away from the constant gaze of the servants or Raymond. Laila is trying to get by, by giving in to this new way of life as little as possible, but enough to not displease Raymond before the council vote. Though she feels stifled, especially in the headscarf which to her represents her new life, the hope for a better nation keeps her spirit from getting deflated.

That is all that's currently on her mind: that she will have played a part in a momentous decision for the nation. Though she does worry that life is going to be more difficult after the vote, without the council decision present to occupy her mind. Women in the Tony household are not allowed to work. In fact, they're not even allowed to leave the house without their elders' or husbands' permission. But perhaps after the council vote, Laila can work towards changing and questioning these norms; perhaps she can also make herself useful by taking advantage of the fact that she is married to a council member. Maybe she can find a way to influence Raymond's decisions. She prays though that the nights will get easier, that somehow, later in the marriage, they're not as painful.

Although she tries not to, she also despairs sometimes, thinking about Shadow, who she could not bring with her because Raymond would not allow it. She longs for freedom as she reminisces about her midnight meals. Her heart longs for the familiar so much that she can feel a certain uneasiness, a hollow in her chest, as she pictures what she would have been doing if she was at home, *home*, at this moment. She grieves for all those years that she and Ahmed didn't see eye to eye, and even misses the wrinkles around her grandfather's nose because she knew she could raise her voice to match his. Laila often thinks about how easy it was for her to get her way in her house. No one had owned her. And here she is, in a house where no decision of hers is allowed to be independent, where a man does to her what he pleases every night.

Apart from the nights with Raymond, she hasn't been able to spend much time with either Raymond or his son Jai alone. Raymond is at work all day and Jai at school. Jai comes back at around three in the afternoon and then takes a nap for a few hours, after which he goes down to the garden to play games with his caretakers.

Raymond returns only at six, after which he spends some time with Jai. Once he finishes his dinner, he goes into his home office to work and drink his whisky. He comes back out at ten, reeking of alcohol, after which he fucks Laila, and then, finally exhausted, he goes to sleep.

Raymond and Laila have had only a few conversations, mostly regarding the household and what is expected of Laila.

'Laila jaan, here, take this key. This is your house, your family too now, and you must take care of it.'

'Why did you ask the servants to prepare gram flour pakoras today? I told you that I'm allergic to gram flour. My lips were swollen all day.'

It has been difficult for Laila to gauge Raymond. He is polite to her through the day, but in the night, he wants his way. He spends his mandated half an hour with Jai, but doesn't pay much attention to the kid's needs. The kid is mostly left with the caretakers all day.

With a new life that she doesn't want to adjust into, there is only one thing that keeps Laila going. She has been counting down the days. Twenty days till the councilmen vote.

One evening, a maid knocks on the door as Laila is resting in her room. When Laila gives her permission to enter, she announces, 'Raymond sahib wants you to get dressed and come down. He is taking you and little sahib out for dinner.'

The maid blushes as though the invitation had been directed at her and not Laila. These little treats are taken as a sign of affection between a husband and wife, and the maid is happy to be the messenger.

Laila carefully sifts through her dresses. Raymond has got her a set in every colour. She picks out a short blue kurta with wide flowy pants. The kurta has beautiful flowers embroidered on its sleeves. There is a white scarf to go with it. But Laila doesn't notice its aesthetics; to her it is just a uniform.

She ties her long hair in a bun and wraps the white scarf around her head. As she walks down the stairs, Raymond's eyes spot her and widen immediately. A silent compliment.

Raymond is still dressed in his work clothes, a white kurta and matching pants. Jai is standing beside him, wearing a blue kurta set. Jai looks very much like his father, the same light-brown eyes and dark short hair. She wonders what his mother was like and where she must be now. But she knows that bringing it up is taboo.

Raymond takes them to a very beautiful restaurant called Hibana. She remembers coming here as a kid once with her father. As Raymond places the order, despite the uncomfortable company, Laila's mouth starts to water. She will finally eat food that is to her taste.

When the tandoori chicken arrives, the waiter walks towards Raymond to serve him. She thinks of how Ahmed would make sure that her plate was always full before he began eating. Raymond suddenly stops the waiter and directs him towards Laila first. The sweetness in Raymond's action surprises her. Laila begins by eating slowly, but as the meal progresses, she starts gulping down her food. The food is delicious and she hasn't eaten well in a long time.

Jai smiles at Laila as she serves him an extra piece of the kebab. Even though he doesn't know her well yet, he seems to have taken a liking to her. She doesn't mind the kid either. He's a burst of energy, and she feels sorry that his father doesn't pay him much attention and that he doesn't have his mother around.

As they sit, quietly eating their dinner, Laila tries to bring up the council elections, 'The council elections are due in fifteen days. I am so glad you are doing this; it is for the betterment of the nation…'

'Oh Laila jaan, why bring this up here? Let's enjoy this meal…'

'Umm, actually I was thinking I should come watch too. I mean, I want to, if you're okay with it…'

'But what will you do there?'

'Please, I would like to. Watching my husband and father both taking this decision, together, will be a privilege for me,' Laila coaxes, 'plus, it could be my father's last council meeting. You know his term ends soon.'

Raymond sighs, 'All right, if you insist –'

Their conversation is interrupted by a young man in his early twenties. He walks up to Laila. As she recognizes the man, Laila stands up to greet him. It's Saman, one of her friends from school. They were never very close, but have always been cordial.

'Laila, it has been so long. It's so good to see you!' he exclaims as he opens his arms to go in for a hug.

Raymond immediately stands up and sternly responds in a loud voice, 'Sir, is this any way to approach a lady? Laila is my wife and I do not approve that you have approached her directly for a conversation, without seeking my permission first.'

Jai looks scared, and Saman and Laila are both taken aback.

Raymond continues, 'Please leave. I am politely asking you. Do not make me do it by force.'

Laila intercedes, 'Raymond he is my classmate from school. He was only...'

'Laila,' Raymond shouts, 'this is not a matter for you to interfere in. I am talking to him.'

Laila looks at Saman with guilty eyes. Saman apologizes and leaves.

As they sit back down, Laila can suddenly make sense of all of Raymond's actions, his softness and harshness. He is behaving how he thinks a husband is supposed to. He has to ensure that his wife is always protected, always pampered. He believes it is his duty to keep her safe from the eyes of other men, but he can do whatever he pleases to her, because she belongs to him now. Her voice doesn't exist, because he doesn't see her as having an independent identity. She is his wife. She is *his*.

thirteen

Jasmine

'Mam, if you're looking for something mild yet flavourful, you must try our dahi kebabs. They are full of spices, but still light on the stomach. Plus, the mint chutney that is served with them is delightful.'

Jasmine is surprised at her fluency in restaurant lingo. In the few days that she has been here, she has tasted almost all the dishes. It was her idea to let the servers eat the restaurant dishes for lunch. She said that if they know what the dishes taste like, they'll be able to help the customers better. It took a little convincing but eventually Mr Ruff agreed.

The chef is brilliant and Jasmine is actually proud to work at a diner that serves such great food. Nina's food, though, doesn't fall too far behind. Her kebabs were almost as good as these; her biryani was definitely better. She wonders if they would have owned such a restaurant today if Nina had paid heed to Kaiza's advice and started a catering business. Perhaps Kaiza wouldn't have felt the need to find work elsewhere if that business had been established. In that moment, she suddenly longs for her father, for a time that was. Whenever her heart aches for those memories, an anxiety catches her unawares, because she realizes that even if she finds Kaiza, it is never going to go back to being the way it was.

The cheerful voice of a man shakes her out of her thoughts.

'Sure, get us a plate of your dahi kebabs, miss.'

Jasmine smiles in triumph as she walks away. She looks over at Mr Ruff, who gives her a nod of approval. It reminds her of when Kaiza used to give her assignments. *Name the birds that cannot fly. What is the speed of light? How do plants reproduce?* Mr Ruff has the same look of pride in his eyes that Kaiza used to when she answered correctly.

As she trots her way to the next table to take their order, Mr Ruff stops her and asks Janie to cover the table instead. Jasmine stares at Mr Ruff in disbelief. He used to ask Janie to wait Jasmine's tables for the first few days, but Jasmine's been doing really well lately. There is no reason for Mr Ruff to do that any more. She walks over to Mr Ruff's desk to demand an explanation.

'Getting a little too settled here, aren't you, girl?' Mr Ruff grins.

Jasmine narrows her eyes causing small crinkles to form around the top of her nose.

Mr Ruff laughs. 'Don't you have to leave early today, Jasmine? Stop staring at my face and go change out of those clothes.'

Jasmine laughs heartily, unexpectedly. Her plans for the rest of the day had completely skipped her mind. She is going to meet Amer on the other side of town. She rushes into the washroom to get ready.

The shadow of a girl fills the archway. As Jasmine enters the garden, she draws eyes from both men and women alike. She is dressed in a white blouse, a matching ivory scarf and blue denim pants. Her neck and ears are adorned with counterfeit pearls. She has borrowed this outfit from Lara. The sleeves of the blouse fall loosely on her arms, making her look elegant.

She spots the large dolphin-shaped fountain. Amer is already sitting by it. He is dressed in a turquoise shirt that deepens the blue in his eyes. He stands up as he sees Jasmine. They wait awkwardly, both anticipating a hug, but neither of them brave enough to make the first move.

'I'm glad to see you,' Amer breaks the silence. 'For a second there, I thought you weren't coming.'

'I wouldn't miss this for the world.'

'I thought we could go on a ferry. There is one from here every thirty minutes. It travels the bay for an hour before dropping passengers off at Lasale Street. Maybe we could eat something there. Only if you're not in a hurry.'

'No,' Jasmine says almost too eagerly, 'I'm in no hurry.'

Amer waves goodbye as he drops Jasmine at the station, wishing that he could steal some more moments to be with her. He would prefer to drop her home, but she refused his offer quite vehemently. As she disappears from his sight, he makes his way back to his hotel room in Lasale. Jasmine sits on the cold metal bench at the station and stares at the empty ice cream cup. Her cheeks turn red every time she thinks of that moment. It had been perfect. The warmth of that bench, the chill of the ice cream, the light breeze and the slight drizzle.

The evening had unfolded wonderfully. As the ocean slapped its waves against the white wooden ferry, Amer told her about his childhood, about how his mother would bake him apple pie as a reward for doing well at school and he would finish three servings worth of it in one sitting because it was his favourite thing to eat. His favourite subject in school was economics. He loves the way trends can predict behaviour.

He laid his life out in front of Jasmine, never once fearing that she would judge.

Day Shine was the name of his school. When Jasmine laughed a little at the name, Amer laughed with her. Maran, his neighbour, was his best friend growing up. They used to meet every evening to play games. Their fathers would often have to come out, pull the boys away from each other and drag them inside. Once, Amer and Maran hid because they didn't want to go back home. Their fathers searched for them for hours before finally finding them hidden amongst a few large rocks. Amer let out a little laugh as he said this.

The sound of his chuckle made Jasmine's heart flutter. The boys had not been allowed to leave their houses for a week after that.

After slight hesitation, Amer also spoke about the day he had come to seek Jasmine's hand and how it had impacted him, 'I apologize that I didn't know any better. After we went back home that day, I suggested to my father that we try to find out more about the situation, that we talk to your family. But my father stayed put. That's when I started thinking about how the entire process assessed an individual based on the family's wealth or social standing. Yes, I want compatibility in a life partner, but I also want a connection that I can explore. We had a huge argument at home, but I managed to convince my parents to put the process of trying to find me a partner on hold.'

Jasmine spoke very little. She didn't know how she could explain her situation. *When the time comes,* she said to herself, but admitted that Amer's rejection had also caused her to move to Rahat, 'I, I decided to come here to look for my father.'

Amer didn't ask her about her father's disappearance, didn't question her further. He just listened.

'You should know that your mother has told everyone that they got you married to a man in Baugh. I found out when I went back this time. Of course, because of our chance meeting, I knew better.'

Jasmine smiled, then said hesitantly, 'No one knows I'm here actually. Please don't...'

'I won't tell anyone; please don't worry about that.'

Amer also talked about the cinema. He loved watching movies. His favourite one was about a group of retired special agents who get together to take down a drug lord. When Jasmine said that she hadn't ever watched a movie, Amer first gasped in disbelief and then suggested that that's what they could do when they met next. There was a film about an eccentric detective and his wise sidekick. They could watch that.

As they got down from the ferry at Lasale Street, Amer slowly moved his hand towards Jasmine's. When she responded by bringing hers even closer, he took it in his. Then they held hands and walked. The tenderness of his touch made her feel shy, yet at home.

They ate butter chicken and naan. He mentioned how he'd loved the food she had cooked for him the day he'd come with the proposal. Jasmine wanted some ice cream, so they took a cup of caramel with walnut crumbs and sat on one of the many benches overlooking the ocean. For almost half an hour, they sat there in silence, hand in hand, looking at the waves hitting the rocks.

'Jasmine,' she remembers the sense of serenity in Amer's voice when he said her name. As she looked towards him, Amer lifted his hand and placed it on her cheek. Jasmine felt her stomach twirl and goosebumps travelled down her spine. He slowly moved his face closer, giving Jasmine the confidence to do the same. They kissed, softly, until a disgusted police officer spotted them and shooed them away with a warning.

fourteen

Laila

The red light refuses to turn green. The school is only a little more than a kilometre away, but the traffic light at the junction is proving to be a pain. Laila impulsively starts shaking her right leg and tapping her fingers on the soft cream leather of the car seat. Raymond has asked her to start picking Jai up from school, engage more in her motherly duties. Laila feels extremely uncomfortable being called a mother. She has never had a mother of her own. She does not know how mothers are supposed to behave and is not ready to be one. She feels alien in her own skin and cannot bring herself to call Raymond and his son family yet. But picking Jai up gives Laila an excuse to get out of the house.

She fears that she is going to be late on her first day. She hopes that the school doesn't let a child out before his parent arrives. Laila is getting anxious. What if the ten-year-old gets lost in the streets?

Laila breathes a sigh of relief when she sees Jai sitting in the school lobby. His white shirt tucked into grey pants; a grown man's attire on a child. He is the only child left in the waiting area and looks slightly lost. Worrying, though, hasn't entered his emotional system yet. He still has a few more years left for the wrinkled forehead to take form.

Jai spots Laila and runs towards her. He hugs her tightly, his tiny arms circling her just below her waist. Laila unwittingly giggles at his reaction.

On their way back, he tells her about his English teacher, Hamish sir, and how strict he is about maintaining silence in class. He tells her that to talk, they write on pieces of paper and pass them around. Hamish sir likes Jai though, because he usually answers him in class correctly. To her surprise, Laila enjoys the conversation with Jai.

A few minutes later, Laila spots an ice cream vendor on the street. She asks the driver to stop as they near the vendor. Laila and Jai both have a chocolate scoop with cookie crumbs each. As they lap up the cold treat, they are careful not to spill any on the seats. They've both learned from experience that Raymond is very particular about these things.

As they enter the driveway of the house, Jai looks at Laila eagerly. 'Are you going to come to pick me up every day?'

'Yes,' Laila smiles.

'Are we going to have ice cream every day?'

She lets out a laugh. 'No!'

The black ink bleeds on the yellowish paper. Multiple concentric circles with hints of a floral design. Laila often doodles in her journal while she is thinking.

She writes down names of all the women who would be suitable for the council. The council members are due to vote next week. The last date for nomination requests is only a little more than a month away. The Rahat election is just three months down the line. Not a lot of time, but maybe just enough.

Laila has come to the conclusion that to have a genuine chance, an aspiring councilwoman must run from Rahat because it is the only district where all women above the age of eighteen have the right to vote. Baugh and Samin allow only married women above the age of eighteen to vote, and that too, only in the presence of their husbands. Mahlah and Attara don't allow women to vote at all. Hopefully, that law will be changed soon too.

It's almost ten at night and Raymond must be getting done with his work. She shuts her journal and quickly hides it in a bag inside her cupboard. As she waits for Raymond, a name starts to appear in her mind.

Naya Roben

A few years ago, Naya Roben founded an organization to teach women skills such as writing, sewing and nursing, so they could take up jobs in areas that were opening up employment to women. Naya is also the wife of an ex-head of the Rahat police, which means her family is well respected in the region.

Laila has interacted with Naya a couple of times at parties. She is articulate, elegant and smart. There aren't a lot of women who exude that kind of confidence in public. Laila thinks she has her councilwoman. Convincing Naya might not be very difficult, but Laila will need to do her homework, find Naya's motivations and know more about her as a person before she tries.

Laila quietens her mind when she hears footsteps climbing up the stairs, as though Raymond will snatch her thoughts and rid her of them. She positions herself in front of the dressing table and takes off her jewellery. A good deception.

Raymond enters the room and surprisingly, instead of going straight at her, he sits down on the bed and signals for her to sit beside him.

'Laila, there's something I want to talk to you about.'

Laila glares at Raymond. He has one hand on her stomach, while the other cups her cheek.

'Laila jaan, please don't say no. This is the best way ahead for both of us.'

Laila knows that his decision is final and this is only his way to trick her into believing that it was a choice they both made. Together. Also, with the council vote looming, she has to make sure not to offend him or anger him in any way.

Laila knows that if she directly refuses, he will force her into it. She has to delay the inevitable in a bid to find a permanent way out. Laila can be a daughter. She can be a sister. She can be a friend. She can even play the role of a trophy wife. But motherhood, no. Motherhood is not for Laila. Having a child with Raymond will set their relationship in stone. Laila hadn't realized it yet, but in some deep corner of her heart, she still has hope that one day this will end.

'I am not ready for it, Raymond,' Laila says softly.

'But, Laila, this house needs a legitimate heir. What if people question Jai's claim in the future? We need a pure breed.'

Breed? Laila mentally spits the word out and throws Raymond's hands off her body.

'I will give you a son, Raymond. But you need to give me some time. I will not do this right now.'

'Laila jaan, I cannot allow you to have a say in this matter. This child will be for the good of our family. We need to have a child as early as possible. What if we don't have a boy? We'll have to try again. It's better to start now.'

Laila has no choice but to be firm, 'Raymond, if you give me a child today, I will have no choice but to end its life while it is still in my stomach.'

Raymond's face first turns pale before morphing into the heat of crimson, as if he cannot believe that Laila had the audacity to say what she did. He picks Laila up and throws her face down on the bed, rips her clothes off and makes her bleed. The only mercy is that he has still put on protection.

fifteen

Jasmine

He was wearing a red shirt underneath his favourite blue jacket. Even though it is a black-and-white photograph, Jasmine remembers every single colour that should have been in it. It was one of the colder evenings in Mahlah. The desert is as cold in the night as it is hot during the day. Rahat, on the other hand, doesn't experience such harsh temperatures. It is humid and warm almost all year round barring the nights when it rains.

They had gone out to watch a play. Mahlah has very few amphitheatres and none of them are near their house. But Kaiza was very keen on watching this play. The play was about a maverick, who the world identified as an absent-minded introvert. Jasmine is sure that Kaiza related to this character.

The picture was taken by a photographer stationed right outside the theatre looking to earn some quick cash. Jasmine had insisted on getting her picture clicked and put her hand on her hips and smiled. They all lovingly laughed at her attempt to strike a pose. When Nina discovered the photographer was talented, she insisted they all get their photos taken. This ended in a family picture. Sabaar put his hands in his pant pockets and gazed into the distance. Nina sat on a bench and flashed a wide, toothy smile at the camera. Kaiza stood shyly, as if telling himself a joke, trying to get himself to smile. The photographer caught the purest reflection of Kaiza, that shy smile, with a glint of light in his eyes. Kaiza had a moustache then, which suited his narrow face very well. Jasmine wonders if Kaiza still has it and if it is still black. She remembers he used to dye it. The simple Kaiza had his own set of whims.

Jasmine runs her hand over the photograph and contains the small tear trying to slip out of her eye.

Mr Ruff's voice startles her out of her nostalgia.

'Is that your father?' Mr Ruff asks as he puts a hand on Jasmine's head, 'Sorry, I didn't mean to intrude.'

Jasmine looks up at Mr Ruff and smiles. Her eyes can't hold the tears any more.

'He would be very proud of you, Jasmine.'

Mr Ruff holds Jasmine's hands, and for the first time since she left her house in Mahlah, she allows herself to break down. Her tears wet Kaiza's photograph. Mr Ruff slowly takes it out of her hand and shakes it dry.

The small square window looks out onto a grey wall. The room is a closet-sized extra, built into the ground floor of a building; it was initially meant to accommodate the servants. Its walls have been freshly painted white; the floor is grey. The room is not as good as the others she has seen, but it's the only one she can afford. It is located just a few lanes away from the diner, and it shouldn't take her more than twenty minutes to get there if she walks fast enough. Jasmine is at the diner for most of her day anyway. She only needs a place to come back and have a good night's sleep, and she reckons that this room will do.

As she takes the key from the owner, she feels something tug at her chest. The constant whirr of the engine, the chatter of the crowd, the rush, the noise, make her feel safe at train stations. They made her feel like she was a part of something greater. Chaos has always been her escape.

As Jasmine enters the room, which is now her house, she feels like she is visiting a stranger. She wonders if she will ever call the room home. Kaiza's books – home. Games with Sabaar – home. Nina's constant nagging – also home. Jasmine doesn't want a new home; she just wants her old one back.

She doesn't know yet that home can be found in the unlikeliest of places, and family in the unlikeliest of people.

Jasmine keeps her belongings in the room, locks the creaky blue door and steps out. Amer will pick her up from the diner at three. They meet often these days. Once, when it was very sunny outside, he even came inside the diner for a sip of water, attracting curious glances from Janie and Lara, and a wide grin from Mr Ruff. Jasmine thinks one of the girls might have even winked at her. *What did they think she was doing?*

It came as a surprise to Jasmine when Amer didn't think of her job as unacceptable. He only smiled as she carefully revealed more parts of her story, his mind unsure how to react, but sure not to judge.

sixteen

Laila

The soft leaves brush past her fingers as she walks down the footpath. She breathes heavily and slowly as though it is freedom itself that has taken the form of air. Laila glances at her wristwatch. There are still thirty minutes to go. She will definitely reach the school in time.

Laila has grown fed up of spending all her time indoors. She decided to convince Raymond to let her walk Jai home instead of picking him up in a car to give her some time with herself, away from the eyes of the servants.

'A Tony, even if not of pure blood, should not have to walk back from school. What will people say?'

Laila had her excuse ready, 'They will say that Raymond's son is bonding with his mother and that he is already mature enough to not call for a car over such a short distance. It will give him some exercise and fresh air too.'

He explained the route to her at least five times, even though she already knew it. He doesn't trust her sense of direction. Laila wonders how Raymond will react if he finds out that she even knows how to drive – *Laila jaan, your father has had no control over you!*

She remembers those driving lessons very well. She was only sixteen years old. Ahmed would wake her up at four every morning. She can still hear his voice. *Leave the clutch slowly as you press the accelerator.* He made her circle around their driveway till she got it right. She didn't take much time though. Within a few weeks, she was already very good.

Laila reaches the school ahead of time, and as she waits for Jai, a strange feeling catches her unawares. She is actually looking forward to seeing that little boy.

Jai walks home nonchalantly, as though he hasn't even noticed the change in his daily commute, all the while holding the hand of his partner in crime.

They make their way through smaller lanes. Laila doesn't want to risk walking in the traffic. Jai is a hyperactive kid, and she's noticed that he always runs more than he walks. When Jai's feet suddenly stop, Laila sighs. She knows what he wants. Chocolate will be the death of this boy. She tries to ward off his gaze whenever he looks at her lovingly, waiting for an answer. She tries to deny him his chocolate, but more often than not, she gives in.

All the walking has made Laila quite hungry, so today she doesn't need much convincing. Jai has a surprised look on his face as she agrees without even giving him a chance to persuade her. He is slightly disappointed even. He likes their little game.

'All right, Jai, what do you want to have?'

Jai doesn't even take a second to think. He already has his heart set.

'Cake. I want some tasty chocolate cake.'

'Okay. We'll have some if we spot a bakery on our way.'

Jai's finger points towards a small diner at the corner of the street. It's not a bakery, but Laila reckons they might get some cake there. Once she gives him her approval, Jai takes her hand and almost drags her to the diner. Laila walks fast, but this little bundle's energy is unmatchable.

They walk into the diner to see most of the tables empty. It's past lunchtime, and the diner must have been getting ready to shut down for the afternoon. Laila and Jai take a table by the glass walls. Laila likes looking at cars passing by, though not many use this small street.

A young waitress walks up to the table while Laila is still going through the menu. Her dark eyes linger on Laila for a moment. The girl smiles and asks them in a pleasant voice, 'What would you like to have, mam?' then turning towards Jai, 'sir?'

Jai squeals, 'I want a chocolate cake.'

'Are you going to finish the whole cake by yourself or would you prefer a slice?' the waitress teases him.

Laila laughs, while going through the menu once again.

'And you, mam?'

'Could you suggest something?'

The waitress thinks for a moment. Laila notices that the yellow blouse really suits the waitress's olive skin.

'You should try our cinnamon caramel cake. It's the best one you'll ever –'

Another taller, older waitress interrupts her mid-sentence.

'You can give me your order, mam.'

The younger waitress pats her head with her hand. Her cheeks turn red and she immediately runs into the restroom. As the cakes arrive, a small blue car comes to a halt outside the diner. Laila watches as the waitress, now dressed in a blue blouse and white pants, runs outside. A good-looking man, perhaps in his mid-twenties, comes out of the car and gives her a hug before they both drive away.

Laila finishes her slice faster than Jai finishes his. It is one of the best cakes she has had. The moist interior, the crispy crumb, the salty-sweet sauce. Perfect. Both of them lick their plates clean and smile in contentment.

As they walk out the door, Jai gives Laila the widest smile she has seen from him yet. *Thank you.*

seventeen

Jasmine

The man in the pointed hat passes a cigar to his stout friend. Walking down the footpath, Jasmine looks at them and wonders if they run a criminal organization. She shakes herself out of her stupidity and slides her hand into Amer's. Her eyes are dazed. She and Amer finally managed to catch the detective film. Jasmine's first cinema experience. Never had a fictional world appeared so real to her. She felt like she knew the detective and his sidekick in real life. Jasmine laughed when the sidekick slipped on a banana peel. She cried when the detective's mother met with a car accident. She blushed when the detective and Miss Aprie kissed. She felt like shouting out loud when the detective and the criminal passed each other on the street. *Come on, look a little towards your left. He's the one who's been robbing all the banks!* But, for most part, Jasmine just looked on amazed, completely lost in a story that was never intended to be real.

They held hands through much of the film. After the movie, Jasmine let Amer walk her to her small one-room house. She has slowly started trusting him with parts of her she doesn't even let herself see often.

A few days ago, she finally told him about her father's disappearance, about her relationship with Nina and Sabaar. Amer looked into her eyes and sandwiched her right hand in his palms. He kissed her forehead and enveloped her in his arms. He didn't say much. He didn't need to.

A large man walks over to a baby girl who is crying in an abandoned crib. Someone has left her to fend for herself on the footpath, out in the rain. He picks her up in his arms and she gives him a magical smile. Just as he turns to take her home, three men in black masks attack him. As they knock him unconscious and drag him away, the little girl starts to cry.

Jasmine wakes up with an ache in her chest. She looks around the unfamiliar white walls, suddenly uncomfortable on the hard mattress she is sleeping on. The air inside the tiny room is suffocating, and the small window doesn't help with ventilation. In some way, she still misses the hustle and bustle of the railway station. Silence has always been uncomfortable to her.

Jasmine thinks of her room back home. She had decorated it with little string lights. When she was young, her bedside table would always have one of Kaiza's books on it, with a ruler becoming a makeshift bookmark. Her bed was small and circular, and made of polished wood. But after Kaiza's disappearance, Nina sold off all of Jasmine's things one by one. The heaviest books were the first to go.

Hand them to me, laado. The scrap dealer down the street will give a very good price for them. Don't make me snatch them from you. Jasmine! Hand them over.

The birds begin their morning chorus and Jasmine tries but is unable to go back to sleep. She wraps a scarf around her shoulders and decides to take a stroll outside. There is a slight chill in the morning air. Monsoon will be here soon and she cannot wait; the rains in Rahat are supposed to be magical.

Rahat, even in the morning, is busy. Jasmine's morning walk is a welcome change, and her mind calms down, almost, but is interrupted by a whiff in the air.

The aroma of garlic being tossed into hot oil can never escape her. Jasmine's nose leads her to a roadside kulcha stall.

A short dusky man, with dark-brown hair and blue–grey eyes, probably in his mid-thirties, is the culprit. Jasmine is surprised to see the man cooking this early in the morning. As she approaches him, he smiles.

'Do people actually eat kulchas this early in the day?' Jasmine asks, in the spirit of friendly conversation.

The vendor laughs, crinkling his little nose and flaring his chubby cheeks in the process. 'No, miss, I am just getting the masala and the stuffing ready. Soon the office-goers will hound me for breakfast.'

'I've tasted many kulchas. Dare I say, I usually prefer buttery naan instead.'

'I can guarantee that you'll change your mind once you taste mine. Kulchas can be eaten on their own. They're a meal contained in one piece of bread. Naan always needs a curry.'

'All right!' Jasmine says. 'I'll come by on my way to work. Let's see if you can convince me on behalf of the kulcha tribe.'

'I've convinced many others, *sahiba*!'

Jasmine involuntarily smiles at this show of respect.

The vendor then points towards a mansion down the road. Its large dome is visible over all the houses and trees scattered in between. 'That is the house of a councilman. Even he stopped at my stall once. He ate a mutton kulcha, I remember. He said that it was one of the best he'd ever had. I hope he brings his new wife here. She was a Jagir. It will be an honour to feed someone who has Jagir blood flowing in them.'

Jasmine remembers seeing a picture of the newly-wed couple in a newspaper. That's when it strikes her that this was the same woman who had come to the restaurant yesterday. No wonder Jasmine felt like she'd seen her somewhere before.

'Oh! What's her name?' Jasmine asks the kulchawallah.

The small man looks at her, surprised she doesn't already know.

'Laila Jagir,' he says, and then corrects himself. 'Sorry, Laila Raymond Tony.'

eighteen

Laila

As soon as the tail of the black car comes into view, it sends a shiver of unease down Laila's spine. Jai and Laila have just reached home. Sometimes they turn into random lanes to discover a new route back home. Laila has grown fond of their time together. When she sits in the school waiting room with the other parents and caretakers, even though she is neither Jai's mother nor nanny, she can understand how they feel; she understands their anxious wait before seeing the only person who has the ability to light up their day. She has been helping Jai with his schoolwork as well; a rather satisfying activity. His language skills are great, but he is weak with numbers. Jai has begun to love Laila.

As Laila gets closer to the black car, she looks at the number plate to make sure. 1010. It is him. She stops outside the door to take a deep breath. The anticipation on her face is difficult to hide. She slowly takes a few steps inside. She is not sure what he will think of her attire. Her father cannot ask Raymond to let her wear what she wants, but maybe he will sympathize with her. They can talk, just like old times, about how pointless these traditions are. They haven't done that in years, but she hopes that the time away from her has made him miss the time when they used to be on the same side.

Ahmed is sitting in the living room. He shakes hands with Jai, who has run up to greet him. When he spots Laila, who enters a few seconds after, he smiles. His daughter looks different, a girl become a lady, the spark of rebellion in her eyes dimmed.

Laila asks a servant to take Jai to play in the garden outside. As soon as he leaves, both father and daughter embrace in a long, overdue hug.

'We miss you, Laila jaan,' Ahmed says.

They sit down on the sofa and Laila asks him about Gulzar and Thakur. She asks him about Shadow and learns that he is quite sedentary now. The doctor says he is depressed. Apparently Shadow misses Laila more than she misses him. All of a sudden, she feels guilty about enjoying her walks with Jai. Shadow used to be her companion. Memories fade away quite easily though, or rather, they become blurry, coming back into sight only with reminders – the bark of another's pet, a carton of chocolate cereal on a shelf.

'How are you, Laila?' Ahmed asks.

The words comfort her for a brief moment, and Laila almost lets her worries burst out. But she holds herself back and tells Ahmed that she is fine, hoping for him to probe further, so that she can prove to herself that he truly cares, so that she can allow herself to delve deeper into her emotions as well.

But instead, Ahmed shifts the topic, 'Laila, Aunt Melina is looking for a husband for her daughter. She is a good-looking, intelligent girl. Plus, she prepares the most delicious meat samosas –'

'Get to the point, Father,' Laila says with irritation. Ahmed usually never involves himself in these matters.

'Raymond's mother has always been very close to the Bethen family of Mahlah. They are quite well-to-do and their youngest son is well educated.'

'And unmarried,' Laila adds.

Ahmed nods. 'Yes, yes. I have a favour to ask of you, Laila jaan. If you could ask your family to put in a good word –'

She rises to her feet with so much force the sofa shivers. *Your* family. She can hardly believe her ears.

'I thought I was *your* daughter. A part of *your* family. All you had to do was say you wanted me to ask *them* to do you a favour. Instead, you come and talk to me like I'm an outsider to a family that I share blood with.'

'That is not what I meant, jaan.' Ahmed starts to explain.

'Then what did you mean, Father? It has been only two weeks since I got married, and you call this, this my family? That's how you have always looked at me, isn't it, like everyone else does…a daughter, who is to be given away at marriage, a burden to be relieved of?'

Her words seem too harsh, even to herself. She can hardly believe it is her tongue that said those words. Somewhere inside, she knows that her father doesn't look at her as a burden, as someone else's property. That somewhere, he is still the same Ahmed he was before he became a councilman, before he had to keep up appearances. But years of disappointment have finally broken through her defences. The times when discussions turned into heated arguments. The day he stopped standing up for her. Everything boils inside her. She subconsciously blames him for her reckless decisions, for her marriage.

'Laila jaan, listen to me. You will always be –'

Laila doesn't want to reason any more. 'You break my heart, Father. Please leave.'

Laila's heart sinks as she watches her father leave, without any apology, without asking for another chance.

Laila takes the gold bangles off her arms. What if they make too much noise in the council meeting? She is wearing a yellow embroidered kurta with flowy pants. Her scarf is a mix of gold and white. Her heart is beating fast, as if a decision about *her* future is going to be made.

It is difficult to believe that the day is actually here; she couldn't be more relieved. Raymond has become more agitated and the nights have been rough, but Laila has made sure not to raise her voice, so as to not anger him before the vote.

The voting process is cumbersome and takes very long. Anyone can come and witness it but usually no one chooses to. The meeting begins with arguments put forward by the council members on the current bill, after which the floor opens up to the audience. Anyone who has anything to say is given a minute to present their case. Then, on the Speaker's cue, the votes are verbally cast.

All she can think about is the joy that will flood her once the meeting is over. Women will be allowed to be elected to the national council. Laila's arrangement will be justified. Laila will not just be a trophy wife. She will have silently brought forth a revolution.

The session will start in an hour. She wants to get there early so that she can have a front-row seat to the biggest change in the history of the nation. She wonders if Naya Roben will be there; maybe Laila will get a chance to talk to her.

Laila can hear her heart thumping in her temples, in her fingers, and all over her body. Once she sits inside the car, nervousness and excitement fill her, yet she is completely still. The silence before the storm.

nineteen

Jasmine

Jasmine stirs the chai she has just prepared for herself. Then she picks it up and takes a sip. Delicious. After closing the diner for the afternoon, Jasmine and the others have all stayed back because Mr Ruff has an announcement to make. Jasmine doesn't mind waiting. The diner now almost feels like home. While they wait for Mr Ruff to finish the accounts, they start to talk amongst themselves. Lara, Janie and Jasmine sit at one table, sipping tea and munching on leftover tikkas.

'You won't believe what I heard on the radio today!' Janie exclaims.

Jasmine and Lara throw curious looks her way. Janie continues, 'That the councilmen are going to vote today on the issue of letting women stand for elections.'

Jasmine has not been exposed to the world of politics much, but this seems interesting, and she remembers Amer talking about going to the council house today to see some voting process.

'What kind of elections?' Jasmine enquires.

'Elections to be voted into the national council,' Janie answers.

'Oh wow, so any woman can stand for elections?' Lara asks.

'I'm not sure…' replies Janie, 'but imagine if we could. Imagine if we could be in a council and make decisions for ourselves!'

'I am a councilwoman and I vote yes; yes, to never washing the dishes again!' Lara stands up, waving one hand in the air. The three girls break into laughter.

Mr Ruff looks up from his books to observe the merrymaking. The diner has become a much happier place since Jasmine's arrival, and more profitable too. She always manages to get customers to eat dessert and it shows in the accounts.

Mr Ruff walks up to his staff, taking with him some kulchas and butter-chicken curry. Lunch first, meeting second. As Jasmine sinks her teeth into the stuffed kulcha, she is disappointed. It pales in comparison to the one she had at the kulchawallah's stall a few days ago.

Once the empty plates are collected and stacked, Mr Ruff stands up and gathers everyone's attention.

'The diner has been doing very well and the profits are rising, largely due to your efforts. Starting next month, you will all get a 20 per cent increment on your current pay.'

The announcement is received with applause and loud cheering. Jasmine claps along but is simultaneously engrossed in an idea starting to form in her mind. As everyone disperses, Jasmine walks up to Mr Ruff. 'I need to talk to you about something. There's this kulchawallah I know, who I think should come work for the diner.'

twenty

Laila

Not one of the fifty chairs is empty. A full house is unusual for council sessions. Most of the seats are occupied by men. As Laila looks around, she sees that Councilmen Hooser's and Briggs's wives are present. There are only two other women in the audience and Laila doesn't recognize either. Both are accompanied by their husbands. Naya Roben isn't here. It has been two years since the council voted on letting women attend its meetings. But hardly any ever show up.

Laila, though, has attended many such meetings ever since Ahmed has been part of the council. From a young age it inspired her to see how laws were made – the debate, the suspense, the outcome. Laila believes that law has the ability to change mindsets; that the everyday lives of an entire nation can be affected, potentially bettered, by a single sentence.

Laila's grandfather, Thakur, is sitting three seats to the left of Laila. Councilman Hooser's wife, brother, and Laila's uncle Gulzar sit between them. Gulzar gives her a bright smile as their eyes meet. Thakur doesn't even acknowledge her presence.

The audience settles down when the councilmen enter the room. Councilmen James, Hooser, Briggs, her husband, Raymond Tony, and her father, Ahmed Jagir, are seated at the semicircular podium, in clear view of the audience. Laila catches Ahmed looking at her and averts her gaze quickly.

The Speaker of the house walks inside and takes his seat facing the council members. As the Speaker introduces the bill, Laila takes a deep breath. These past few months and more importantly, the future of women in the nation, all come down to this decision: 'The Women Counsellors Bill to Permit Women to Be Elected into the National Council'. The entire courtroom listens intently. The split in the audience is polar, and both sides are waiting for the final votes with bated breath. After the Speaker finishes reading out the bill, he opens the floor to the audience.

First, a woman with a blue scarf tied around her head approaches the stand. Laila sees this with pride; the bill is already making a difference, already giving women a voice. The woman's face is covered, leaving only her hazel eyes visible. She positions herself in front of the microphone and begins to recite what sounds like a memorized speech: 'If women are allowed to be elected into the council, soon they will start being allowed into other fields of work as well. This additional pressure of performing at work will divert our attention from the household. Do I want to hire someone to take care of my child? To cook food for my husband? To make sure my house is neat and clean? No. Those are my duties and I am happy to be performing them. If society compels me to work, then I will not be able to do the things that I must as a woman. Of what use is such change?'

The woman turns to look at a man who Laila presumes to be her husband. He nods approvingly. Half the audience nods in approval; some even clap. Laila feels her anger rising and has to hold herself back from getting up from her seat and confronting the woman. *Giving women the right to work gives them a choice. Do you understand the meaning of choice?* But she knows that the words that were just spoken are not the woman's, but even though they are not the woman's, she probably believes them, a chain of realization that makes Laila even sadder.

A few more people stand up and present their views, both sides speaking to convince the voting councilmen. Laila would have liked to voice her opinion as well, but as the daughter of a councilman and the wife of another, both of whom are going to present their votes, she believes it is best to keep quiet so that later their votes are not questioned as being influenced.

Laila knows, through years of watching Ahmed's process of deciding on a vote, from everything that she has done to secure Raymond's vote, that the audience's words will not add much weight to the councilmen's decisions. The councilmen have all already made up their minds. Going by the knowledge that Laila is privy to, her father and her husband will both vote for the bill, and the bill will become a law by the end of the day.

The Speaker finally announces, 'As there are no more members of the audience who want to voice their views, I announce the floor for opinions closed. The councilmen are now required to vote. As Councilman James has proposed the motion, his vote is taken as an affirmative and he does not have permission to change it. All the other council members must answer when called upon with either a "yes" or "no".'

The councilmen nod to show they understand, and the audience falls silent. The Speaker looks at Councilman Hooser and states,

'Councilman Hooser, you have one minute to announce your vote.'

He takes only a few seconds.

'No.'

He hasn't seen her since the day he spotted her outside Councilman Hooser's house. In the little time that has passed, he cannot believe that she got married. She looks different today, much older, tired and more subdued.

He has made sure to seat himself somewhere in the back. Even though he is here for her, he knows that this is going to be a monumental day. He wishes he could hold Laila in his arms, and give her the comfort that she needs and deserves. He wonders what it would be like if he revealed his identity. But he knows he cannot enter her life and turn it upside down. It's not like she would even believe him. He watches as she shuts her eyes when the Speaker declares the floor open for voting. He watches as Ahmed looks at his daughter and wipes away the tears forming in his eyes.

As Councilman Hooser votes no, Laila's eyes remain shut. The Speaker notes his answer down and moves forward to Ahmed.

'Councilman Jagir, you have one minute to announce your vote.'

'Yes.'

Laila looks up at her father with pride.

Only two votes left and only one more affirmative needed for the motion to pass. As he looks at Raymond, he starts to fear. He has an inkling as to why Laila might have agreed to marry him. He hopes she hasn't given away her life in a deal.

Laila's face turns red. Raymond's voice reverberates in her mind. 'No.'

Laila wants to shout. '*NO, NO, NO, NO, NO, NO.*' She feels helpless. She wants to cry out loud. Turn back time. Do something. Do anything. But her body is unable to move. As she looks up at the podium, the faces of the council members start to blur. She can't hear anything any more. The Speaker's voice is distant and his words are mere murmurs. Her body feels weightless and in a few seconds her vision turns black.

Two hands pick up Laila's body from the floor and take her outside the room. Ahmed fidgets in his chair. He wants to run to his little girl and make sure that she is all right. The entire room erupts in whispers. She must be carrying a baby, most say. Ahmed listens to those rumours and turns to Raymond, whose expression neither confirms nor denies them.

The Speaker brings the room back to order and the voting continues.

Ahmed's face resumes its shape as she opens her eyes. Laila is in the clinic at the council house. Ahmed is seated beside her. Slowly surveying the room, she sees that Raymond and Gulzar are sitting on a couch across from her. At first, she's not sure where she is but then recent events replay in her mind and anxiety begins clawing at her chest again. In an attempt to avoid blacking out once more, she reaches and grasps Ahmed's hand tightly. Ahmed squeezes her hand and asks Gulzar to bring her some water. She takes a few sips. Then she looks at the three men in the room and feebly mouths, 'Please leave.'

The doctor signals the men to clear the room. Once they leave Laila allows herself to break down. Her mind is unable to process any thoughts; she can only feel a stinging pain in her chest. The doctor leaves the room, perhaps to give her a moment alone, or to get some help. Laila doesn't know, nor does she care. Her sobs echo through the room until she is interrupted by a knock on the door.

Gulzar enters the room without waiting for Laila to respond. Laila's face is hot and wet. He puts his hands on her shoulders. The gesture eases Laila into speaking and she says, 'It's all over, Uncle. Every sacrifice, all the effort, everything gone in vain. How many years will we wait for this chance to come again?'

'Laila jaan –' Gulzar tries to get her attention, but Laila turns her head on the pillow.

'How could this happen? No, I refuse to believe it –'

Gulzar shakes Laila's shoulders.

'Laila, listen to me! The bill has passed. Briggs voted yes.'

twenty-one

Jasmine

Festivity surrounds the diner. Jasmine begins her shift with a hop. All the girls are extremely chirpy today. Today, they feel valued. Not one of the three women working in the diner is actually going to stand for the council elections, but it thrills them to think that if they wanted to, they could. It's not even just about the elections. Lara has been saving up for her daughter's wedding, but she now wonders if she should send her little girl to school. *If women are capable of running a country, they can definitely study, work with numbers, do anything that they like.*

Amer attended the council meeting, and Jasmine can't wait till her break time to hear all about it. It was heartening for Jasmine, when Amer mentioned how he supports the bill and thinks it is high time that such a law was made. In fact, he mentioned his disappointment with himself for not doing enough when he could, for falling prey to a system that inherently treats one gender better. They discussed how Amer initially agreed to look at girls to get married to, giving in when his mother said she needed help in the house, when he himself has never believed that women must only be restricted to household duties.

When she was in Mahlah, she herself had not questioned these constructs, but being in this city, being on her own, is bringing out a sense of perspective in her that she didn't even know existed. If she was still in Mahlah, she might have never even known about the vote, or even the fact that such a bill existed.

Jasmine decides that she wants to watch one of these voting sessions. Perhaps she will ask Amer to take her the next time he goes. She imagines it must have been thrilling for Amer to witness such an important decision being made. Even the audience is allowed to speak and pose questions during council meetings, Amer had said. Jasmine wonders if she would ever have a political opinion strong enough to express in front of the council members. She'd also heard that someone fainted during the meeting. She makes a mental note to ask him about that too. Most of her morning is spent daydreaming of the conversation that will take place with Amer. They talk to each other about everything that goes on in their lives now.

Mr Ruff is having an exasperating day with all three of his waitresses lost in their own worlds. He smiles though, letting them enjoy the moment. It is not often that women triumph in this nation.

Jasmine gets more and more impatient as the afternoon arrives. The clock is taking too long to strike three, and she hopes that Amer won't be late. When he arrives, they decide to drive all the way to Lasale Street. As they drive through the wider lanes, Jasmine puts her head outside the window to feel the wind on her face. Amer places his hand on hers. As Jasmine turns, she notices that he looks worried.

'Is everything all right?'

'There is something that I have to tell you, Jasmine. Something that I found out a few days ago from friends in Mahlah...'

Jasmine's stomach tightens. She nods and asks him to continue.

'A few officials recently went to Mahlah to look for men to stand guard at the border. The troops on the other side have been causing more trouble lately.'

Jasmine thinks she knows where this is going.

'They took Sabaar with them. He hadn't done any years in the army as a teenager, so they were allowed to take him by force. He's gone for a minimum of two years, Jasmine.'

Jasmine looks at Amer, feeling relief course through her body. It is perhaps better for Sabaar to be with the army, fighting people who have the ability to fight back. It is Nina she is worried about. She has lost her husband, her daughter, and now her son. A lonely woman in a world that doesn't need any reason to point fingers at her. Jasmine begins to feel guilty for abandoning her mother.

With one hand on the wheel, Amer stretches out his free arm and pulls Jasmine into a hug. As she lays her head on his chest, he says, 'It's not your fault, Jasmine. There is a reason that you left that house. I am proud of you for standing up for yourself. I am proud of you for leaving, Jasmine.'

Amer stops the car near the sea and they stay there, sitting in silence for a little while.

They walk around Lasale Street, eating ice cream. Amer tries to divert Jasmine's attention to something more pleasant.

'You haven't asked me anything about the council meeting yet. You were so excited about it.'

Talk of the council meeting lifts Jasmine's mood. Amer tells her about the entire proceeding. His favourite councilman is Ahmed Jagir.

'He's really intelligent,' Amer says fervently.

Once he finishes describing the hour-long session, they decide to get some kebabs. Sitting on the same bench where they had first kissed, they begin to munch on the tasty meat. They steal kisses all the time, now – on the lips, on the cheek, on the forehead.

Suddenly, Jasmine remembers, 'We heard someone at the restaurant talk about a woman fainting. Did that happen?'

Amer gulps and answers, 'Yes, it did.'

'Do you know who it was?'

'Yes, it was Councilman Tony's wife.'

'Oh! Laila sahiba?'

Amer's eyes shift at the mention of Laila's name, 'Do you know her, Jasmine?'

'No no, but she had come to the restaurant a few days ago, with Raymond's son,' Jasmine explains.

A little dog comes running towards them. As she gets busy playing with the canine, Amer stares into the distance, lost in thought.

twenty-two

Laila

The yellow street lamps flicker to life as the orange sky fades to black. Laila's legs begin to ache so she sits down on the footpath. She is not sure why she is crying and whether her tears are of sorrow or joy. *The motion passed. The motion passed!* But her chest is still heavy. It's late and the roads are empty. She's sure that Raymond is searching for her.

Laila was discharged earlier this afternoon and Raymond had sent a car for her but she had left before the car got to the hospital.

After his betrayal, Laila doesn't want to even look at Raymond's face any more, certain her mouth will hurl insults as soon as she lays eyes on him. She doesn't want to touch him, even if it were the blow of her fist. If she can help it, she wants to avoid going back to that house for as long as possible. Her slouching frame stares at the ground a long time, and when she looks up, she notices tiny drops of water have started to fall from the sky. Monsoon has arrived. Tired and stifled, in one swift action she unties her scarf and takes a deep breath as she lets loose her hair. Running her hands through her hair, Laila realizes that she has forgotten what it is like to be herself.

The bright headlights of a long black car grab her attention. Raymond has sent his servants to look for his wife. How considerate. The chauffeur steps out of the car and walks up to Laila.

'Mam, sir has asked me to get you home safely.'

There is no use resisting. Raymond will send more men if she doesn't agree to go back with this one. Once inside the car, she lets herself sink into the back seat.

Raymond sits beside Laila on the bed. Her body is as stiff as a stick. The maids have given her a bath and have fed her some sweet lentil soup with rice. She had refused to go wash herself and Raymond wanted her to be clean.

As Raymond stretches one hand towards her face, Laila backs away.

'Come on, Laila jaan. Don't behave like a child. What I did was for the betterment of the nation. Yes, I changed my decision after our marriage. But Jai finally has a mother; this house finally has a lady. I understood the value of a woman in a household. Men are able to work so well only because women support them from home. If they start to leave and go to work, become councilwomen, who will take care of the house, of the man's needs? The entire system will collapse, Laila jaan. I'm sure you will understand once you give it some thought.'

Laila doesn't respond. She doesn't believe him; she doesn't care if he changed his mind before or after their wedding. She doesn't care what reasons he gave himself. All she can think of is how naive she was to believe his words, to give her life away for a false promise. She was brought up by politicians. How could she have trusted so easily?

Raymond continues, 'Talk to me, Laila. Tell me what the problem is. You should be thankful. No other man would allow his wife to behave this way. You came back home with your head uncovered. You have been walking the streets of Rahat alone every afternoon. Have I said anything? No! And you treat me this way?'

A man like Raymond will always believe that he is right. When he commits a wrong, he will convince himself that it was necessary, for the betterment of the world. For the betterment of *his* world.

'I don't understand. You're the best-kept wife in Rahat. All the luxury, the dresses, the parties, the food. And yet, this attitude?' Raymond holds Laila's jaw tight between his fingers. 'It's true what they say; don't marry a woman with a liberal father. She's lost her way even before she has entered the world. Maybe if you had a mother, it would –'

Laila slaps Raymond's face hard to stop him from speaking. He stares at her in disbelief. 'Don't touch me,' she says.

She gets up to leave the room.

Furious, Raymond grabs her from behind, holds down her neck and pins her to the floor. Laila screams and tries to escape, but his hands are too strong for her. Raymond puts one hand on her mouth and strips her naked with the other. He makes a fist and pounds her stomach, her breasts, her face. As Laila cries, he pushes himself inside her, sliding in and out until she starts bleeding and blacks out.

The final school bell goes off, and Jai runs towards Laila and hugs her tight. He hasn't seen her in the last few days. When he sees her, he hugs her tight.

'Where were you, Laila? I missed you so much.'

Laila can't get herself to look at the boy. There's a big blood clot on her cheek and she is sure he will notice.

'I had gone to see my father, Jai,' Laila tells her first lie of motherhood. She hated it when she was a child and Ahmed lied to her. She always caught on. But as Jai stares at her bruise with uncertainty, she realizes that in some situations a parent cannot afford to be completely honest with their children.

Laila and Jai make their way towards the car. Raymond has forbidden her from walking the streets any more. Her hands are stuck to her sides, her body alert. Each step she takes sends a sharp pain through her stomach.

They sit down in the car and Jai looks at Laila peculiarly, as if he is trying to make sense of the marks on her face. He looks at her, then looks away, then looks back at her before asking if she wants to have something sweet to eat.

Laila smiles, 'Your teeth will develop cavities if you eat so much chocolate, Jai.'

'I promise I won't eat anything. But please, will you eat something nice? You liked the cinnamon caramel cake that day, didn't you? Let's go have that.'

Laila's eyes swell with tears.

'All right, Jai, let's go.'

Jai smiles and then hesitates.

'What happened?' Laila asks.

'What happened to your face?' he asks.

Laila looks at the floor. 'Oh, I tripped and fell down the stairs.' A common excuse. She tries to fake a laugh. 'It hurt a lot, but it was quite funny.'

On the way, Laila spots the lamp post by which she had been sitting the night the motion passed. She touches the scarf on her head and unwraps it to let her hair loose again.

twenty-three

Jasmine

As Jasmine serves a piece of the cinnamon caramel cake and a scoop of chocolate ice cream, she can see a bruise on Laila's cheek.

Since she wears no scarf today, Jasmine notices that Councilman Raymond Tony's wife has beautiful, long and wavy hair. But Jasmine can also see a sadness in the woman's eyes. The little boy looks at her all the time: for her approval of his order, to see if she's eating her cake.

Behind the counter Jasmine overhears Janie and Lara talking in whispers.

'It's a pity how she looks. Once upon a time her confident pictures were plastered all over the newspapers.'

'I swear, she was the only woman who had the grit to do something like that. To be honest, I was proud of her spirit.'

'But I guess they all fall in line some time or another. Never thought she would though.'

'What do you mean?' Jasmine interrupts them.

'Oh, she used to be all over the place. I've heard that she used to protest at weddings, stop the ceremony if it was being held against the wishes of the couple. She used to openly urge women, and even men, to wear what they liked and do what they wanted to,' Lara says.

'She was the first woman to start attending council meetings. I think I saw her once outside the council, on my way to work. She was dressed in a silk white blouse and white pants. She walked with so much confidence. It's funny how circumstances change people.'

Jasmine hurries as Raymond's wife calls for the bill. When Laila walks out of the diner, Jasmine looks at her with both admiration and pity.

There is no mistaking the brown spots on the envelope. Everything from Mahlah carries with it the symbol of the desert. When Amer hands over the envelope to Jasmine, she hesitates.

Amer had suggested that Jasmine write a letter to Nina. Even though it was not easy, she built up the courage and wrote one. Most parts of her are relieved that she is finally free from an abuse that went way beyond the physical. But a part of her also grieves for her mother. In her letter, Jasmine apologized for leaving and informed that she was doing fine. Hesitantly, she asked Nina to come live with her in Rahat. If they sold their house in Mahlah, they would be able to afford a single-room apartment in Rahat. Jasmine earns a decent amount of money and it should suffice for the both of them. Nina wouldn't have to live alone any more.

The letter was short. Jasmine wanted to write more but realized that the longer she went on, the sourer the letter would get. She hasn't forgiven her mother yet; she hopes she will one day. She does not think she will ever be able to forgive Sabaar though. She doesn't want to. Yet, she thinks she has a duty towards her family. A duty towards her father, to keep his wife safe. But Nina's reply to Jasmine read differently.

I'm surprised to find that you're still alive, Jasmine. You turned out to be exactly like your father. Betrayal runs in your blood. I told all the neighbours that we got you married. At least they look at me with some respect now. The day you left, you ceased to be my daughter. There is no reason for you to be concerned about me now. I have only one child, one person who I can call family, and I will wait for him to return. I will stay right here, in my home. I will not betray it like you and your father did.

Jasmine is unsure how she should react. Distance had dulled the impact of her mother's previous actions. But this letter has brought those memories right back. Jasmine reads it one more time, then crumples it up and throws her mother's letter in the dustbin.

Nina sits on the sofa, with her front door slightly ajar. She looks at the empty house around her. She runs her hand on the once cream-coloured sofa and remembers the many nights when she would lie there with Kaiza after they had put the children to sleep. Kaiza would always have a joke or two up his sleeve. He knew how to make her laugh.

She looks at the torn carpet, where the children would play their games. Sabaar would always be in a terrible mood when Jasmine refused to play because she'd found a good book to read. Nina would worry about Jasmine's future. Men don't like to be with women smarter than them. Yet, she would always be a little proud of her girl; secretly hoping that she would someday do something great with her life. She made sure never to say that to Jasmine though. There was no point in putting useless thoughts and frivolous dreams in a little girl's head.

Her favourite part of the day was when her three kids, Kaiza included, would sit at the dining table, waiting for Nina's freshly prepared food. They would all eat together. Kaiza used to insist it be that way. It made no sense to him that the women of the house eat after the men.

The whiff of biryani would get Kaiza and Jasmine salivating, but Sabaar liked her samosas the best. Regardless of what she had cooked, the dinner table would always erupt with praise.

Oh, Ma, this is so delicious.

Nina, you've outdone yourself.

Kaiza wanted her to start her own food business. She always thought it was an outrageous idea. All Nina ever wanted to do was cook for her own family. To see their happy faces swallow every bite with a smile.

Nina creates the outline of Kaiza's face in the air with her fingers. She still remembers every detail of it. His narrow jawline, the pointy nose that she always teased him about. When she used to put her lips to his, his moustache would scrape against her upper lip. But she loved it. She loved every part of Kaiza. Even if their last few years together were not the most pleasant, she would do anything to have those back too.

Jasmine had always taken after her father. And when she left, every essence of Kaiza was wiped from the house. She cursed the girl that day, for abandoning them, even though she knew that Jasmine had no other choice but to leave. Though the letter from her daughter made her feel relieved, she didn't let one bit of that relief seep into her reply, each word of which was filled with spite. Nina can't seem to express much else these days.

She lies down on the sofa, dreams of Kaiza, the feeling of his body against hers. Her children are peacefully asleep inside their rooms, she knows it. After all, Nina's tasty food fills their stomach. Everything is fine; everything is as it was. Slowly, Nina falls deep into slumber, not bothering to shut the large wooden door. Maybe a man will return on a camel. Or maybe all three will.

twenty-four

Laila

She turns the knob and shuts the door. Since the incident, Laila has been locking herself in different rooms of the house before Raymond's return at night. He is almost always intoxicated. If it is a lucky day, Raymond gives up early and goes to sleep. Some days he persists until he finds the right key. Once he even broke down a door in a fit of rage.

Laila's old bruises have healed, though Raymond manages to give her new ones often. She's been taking pills in secret to make sure that she doesn't have Raymond's child. Every night, she wonders for how long this will continue; she shudders because she doesn't know. She has thought about going back home, but the one time her father came to the Tony house to check on her after the council vote, she told him that she isn't expecting a child and asked him to leave. She cannot bring herself to seek refuge with her old family, in her father.

Even if she does manage to find another place to go to, if she is caught attempting to leave, Raymond will never let her out of his sight again. If she is to escape Raymond's house, she has to plan it carefully. Perhaps she could apply for an official separation, but it will be near impossible for her to get Raymond to agree. A long legal battle will require resources and independence, and she lacks both in this house.

For now, there is nowhere to go.

During the day, Laila has been keeping herself busy by trying to find out as much about Naya as she can. The Rahat election is only a couple of months away, and despite her personal troubles, she cannot give up her work for the nation. Not many people agree to meet with her though. As a councilman's wife and another councilman's daughter, and with bruises on her face, she is a sure sign of trouble.

Laila's heart stops as she hears the first knock. The knocks slowly turn into loud thuds.

She backs away from the door and shuts her ears. Still, she can hear Raymond's voice. 'Open the goddamn door, Laila. You're a whore of a woman, I know it. Women whose fathers lose control over them turn into whores; then what problem do you have in fucking me?'

He has definitely had more than his usual share of alcohol today. Raymond's incessant howling grows louder by the minute. Laila tries not to react and give this monster any more fodder. She presses her palms tighter onto her ears.

Raymond starts punching the door, and Laila fears that he is going to break this one too.

A few minutes later, the banging on the door stops and she hears footsteps receding. Laila has been spared for today. She lies down on the bed, praying that the night passes quickly. Sleep is hard to come by these days and the skin under her eyes has been growing darker and darker. She shuts her eyes, hoping that the devil doesn't catch her in her sleep.

After a long time, there's another knock on the door. Laila hopes it is just a nightmare. But the knocking continues and shakes her out of her half-asleep state. She sits still, trying not to respond. Raymond waits for a few minutes; then he starts to speak slowly, loudly and clearly, 'Jai is standing right beside me. If you don't come out, I will beat him up, Laila.'

Laila freezes. It is his *own* goddamn son.

'I don't believe you,' she says. She doesn't believe him.

Raymond doesn't reply, but Jai does.

'Father is holding me by my shoulders, Laila. Really tightly. It hurts, Laila.' She can hear the little boy crying. Still, his own father wouldn't hurt him. Then she remembers what Raymond had told her. *I want a legitimate heir.*

Before she can respond, she hears the sound of a slap. 'Aaaaah!' One cry is enough to make her run towards the door and unlock it.

The door opens to the sight of Jai lying on the ground. His face is red. Laila runs to pick him up. He hugs her tightly and refuses to leave her when she asks one of the servants to take him to his room. She pulls him away from her by force and sends the crying child away.

Once Jai is out of sight, Laila stands up and looks at Raymond. He is smirking, basking in the power he thinks he has. Over her. Over everyone. Finding the strength hidden within her, with a sudden uncompromising tone, she says, 'You have no shame, Raymond. Do what you want to. I am done hiding. Not because I've given up. But because I'm not afraid of you any more.'

He pushes her down to the floor and drags her by her hair. Once they reach his room, he doesn't even undress her. He only takes her pants off and pounds her hard while slapping her face. Once he finishes, he leaves her on the floor and falls asleep on his bed. Laila gets up and looks at Raymond. She doesn't see a monster any more; she is looking at a filthy animal who is about to get hunted down.

twenty-five

Jasmine

Amer walks into the diner, immediately catching the attention of all the girls inside. He is dressed in a white shirt and denim pants. It is a little after three in the afternoon. The diner is empty and the staff is about to leave for their midday break. Jasmine looks up from her desk as she sees Amer approaching. As always, her cheeks turn red as soon as she spots him.

Jasmine can't leave for her break today. Mr Ruff is unavailable for the day because the owner of the restaurant, Mr Karen, has called him for a meeting. Mr Ruff made her the makeshift manager before he left. When he asked Jasmine if she could do the job, she jumped at the chance.

'I know you're going to do your job well. But don't do it so well that you end up taking away mine,' Mr Ruff teased her before leaving.

Mr Ruff has been encouraging Jasmine to come up with new ideas for the restaurant. Since she got the kulchawallah on board, the sales of kulchas have skyrocketed. She even suggested some changes to the menu when she noticed a few items were completely getting ignored.

'Almost nobody orders the stuffed masala pomfret. I've seen only one order for the starter since I've started working here. The fish gets spoiled so fast that new batches have to be bought every two to three days. There is no other item with pomfret on the menu. There's hardly any seafood on the menu. You're wasting so much fish and so much money. Seafood dishes are not what people come to this restaurant for.'

Mr Ruff passed on this advice to the owner, and a few days later, new sets of the menu were printed. The owner personally sent thanks to Jasmine and even asked Mr Ruff to give her 1,000 rehats as a bonus.

Jasmine has been handling her makeshift responsibility well. At times she finds it awkward to give instructions to Lara and Janie but they don't seem to mind it. Jasmine is glad that the excitement of this new position keeps her busy, because Amer is going back to Mahlah for a while. He often travels between the two districts to manage the business. He says he should be back in a week but Jasmine is afraid these few days will stretch forever. Time always seems to slow down when Amer is not around.

Once the rest of the staff leaves for their break, Amer wraps one arm around Jasmine's waist and brings her closer. They caress each other's faces, feeling every turn, every edge, etching the details in their memories. Jasmine moves closer as Amer tilts his face. They kiss passionately and then Amer moves both his arms to Jasmine's waist. He smiles suddenly. 'Yellow really suits you.'

Jasmine realizes that this is the first time he has seen her in her uniform. She always changes before meeting him. She stiffens for one second, but as Amer's fingers trace the bend of her knee, she relaxes. As they kiss again, his hands slowly work upwards and reach her blouse. Before he proceeds to cup her breasts, he stops kissing her and looks at her. *Is this okay?* Jasmine pulls him in tighter and continues kissing him as his hands caress her breasts. He makes his way towards the buttons on her blouse and starts unbuttoning them. She tenses for a few moments. The crack of the whip and the blows from Sabaar's fist have left scars on her body, memories on her skin. As Amer runs his warm hands on her bare body, it relaxes. The first step to her body forming new, kinder memories.

twenty-six

Laila

The kurtas have been rolled tightly and tucked inside. Laila has managed to fit three sets of clothes without making the bag look bulkier than usual. She has also sealed and put in a few packets of dried fruits and nuts. She opens Jai's three-tiered steel tiffin box and packs naan and samosas in the topmost container, chicken curry in the middle one and 2,000 rehats in the final one. Laila has been stealing from Raymond by taking notes of small denominations out of his wallet when he isn't looking, and by inflating the household expenses. She has managed to collect about 4,000 rehats so far.

She hesitates, and reopens the tiffin box and replaces the 2,000 rehats with some more minced meat samosas that Jai loves. If anyone spots the money, they will be ready to harm Jai just to make him part with it. Instead, she hides the money in her little purse. Laila asks Jai to keep the rest of the items in his locker at school. Bit by bit, they have accumulated enough supplies to survive a few weeks. She has no idea what conditions they might have to live in once they leave. Or how Raymond might react and what his next move will be. There is only one thing she's sure of – they're leaving. If they don't, not only hers, but a little boy's life will be in danger.

Raymond is due to attend a conference in Mahlah sometime next week. He will leave in the afternoon and only return the next morning. If Laila and Jai escape right after Jai's classes that afternoon, Raymond will not find out until the next day, which should give them enough time to get a safe distance away from him.

Laila picks up her journal to place it amongst the clothes in Jai's bag. Before she puts it inside, she opens it for a quick glance. *Naya Roben. The first councilwoman.* For the first time, her hopes and dreams for the nation have taken a back seat. Jai comes first now.

Jai finishes his breakfast and comes running to Laila. He shoulders his bag and looks at Laila for instructions.

'Remember what I told you, Jai? Make sure that no one is looking when you empty your bag, and lock your locker carefully.'

She runs her hands over Jai's head. She knows she is asking a lot from him. He nods before hesitantly asking, 'Isn't lying a bad thing, Laila?'

She smiles. He is nothing like his father.

'It is, Jai. But some circumstances require that you break the rules. This is very important. I promise I will explain everything to you one day. For now, will you please promise me that you will do what we talked about and not tell anyone?'

Laila extends her hand towards Jai. He puts his tiny palms on hers and holds it as firmly as he can.

'I promise, Laila.'

'Okay then, hurry up now. I have packed your favourite mutton samosas for lunch. I want your tiffin empty when I see it next.'

Laila watches as the little boy takes off. She thinks of Raymond, and how he is incapable of being a parent. She feels a sudden pull in her chest as she thinks of Ahmed. How he never raised his hand or his voice even when she accused him of being a terrible father.

twenty-seven

Jasmine

Jasmine stabilizes the tray in time, helping the lamb curry stay put in its bowl. Everybody is putting in extra effort to make these last few days perfect. They shut the restaurant at three, after which they all silently sit together in a circle.

They can't believe that in a few days the order slips in the kitchen will cease to exist and that Karen's has probably already served its last kulcha. She's only been here a few weeks, but this diner has become home. How she wishes Amer was here right now.

Jasmine lays her hands on the table and feels the wood, mentally saying goodbye, thanking it for all the wonderful memories. Then she holds Mr Ruff's shaking hands. It is harder for him than for anybody else. This restaurant has been his life for over a decade.

Jasmine had rushed over to greet Mr Ruff as soon as he entered the room earlier this morning. While she had enjoyed handling the restaurant, there really was no better restaurant manager than him. She dangled the keys in front of him to tease him. 'You have to fight to reclaim your fortress, sir.'

Mr Ruff tried to chuckle but his eyes told another story.

'What's wrong, Mr Ruff?' she asked.

'Round everyone up. I have some news.'

The restaurant was being taken over, he told them. The buyer intended to convert the restaurant space into a grocery store. The location is prime, just off the main road, and the profits would be great. He told them that this would be the last week of operation for the restaurant, and that Karen has decided to give each of them an amount worth two month's salary as severance pay. As he explained these points, Mr Ruff observed the unconvinced looks on his staff's faces.

'Karen and I, we could do nothing to stop this. This restaurant is his life and his livelihood, and he knows how attached we are to this place. But really, he didn't have a say in the matter either.'

'How?' the staff cried out. And then, individual protests start rising. 'It's his restaurant. No one has control over it, but him.'

'Yes, if he didn't want to sell it, why did he?'

'No, no. Karen is a great man and my friend. He does not want to give this place up. He loves it with his heart and soul. Plus, it's been earning him good money –' Mr Ruff starts to explain, stopping to swallow the lump that has formed in his throat. 'But some people are powerful enough to get what they want. They don't care about the needs of people like us, or even a man like Karen.'

Jasmine asks, 'Who has bought the diner, Mr Ruff?'

'It's a company called Private Foods Limited. It is owned by the powerful Jagir family.'

A group of eleven people assembles outside the white mansion. They shout slogans: 'The Jagirs don't care, the Jagirs aren't fair, if Karen's isn't saved, we're looking at our graves.'

From his home office, Ahmed listens to the commotion outside and asks his accountant if he knows why the people are so agitated.

'Sir, we bought a restaurant named Karen's recently. Looks like it's related to that.'

'Have the papers been signed?'

'Yes, sir.'

'So, the owner and you came to an agreement, right?'

'Yes, sir.'

Ahmed asks the accountant to go address the situation outside. The manager doesn't tell Ahmed about the threats he issued to the owner. 'I will make sure your restaurant is caught with a health code violation. I will make sure it shuts down. I will make sure that your staff is starving and that you and your manager are in jail. Don't forget, Ahmed sahib is a councilman...'

Jasmine watches the stout man open the gate. His face is round and chubby, just like his belly. He has a thin moustache that does nothing for his already overly circular face. He smiles and lets the restaurant employees into the property. In this short span of time, he has managed to arrange the exact number of plastic chairs for them. A few servants come with glasses filled with orange juice.

No one drinks the juice. No one takes a seat.

'I don't understand the problem here, sir.' He looks at Mr Ruff, who is standing at the back. Mr Ruff had given up on the protest even before it started.

'We want Karen's back. You can't force someone to sell it to you!' Jasmine steps up and glares at the accountant. She is in disbelief at her own show of bravery.

'Miss, we bought the diner fair and square. Mr Karen's and Jagir sahib's signatures are on the agreement. I have brought along a copy for you to have a look.'

He hands over a thin booklet to Jasmine, identifying her as the leader of the pack.

'We know that you forced or, rather, threatened Mr Karen into signing the deal,' Jasmine says, unruffled by the accountant's dismissal of their claim.

The accountant walks up to Jasmine. He brings his lips close to her ears. 'Miss, the deal has been signed. You can do nothing about it. If you care for yours and your little troop's safety, you should leave immediately. There is a lot that can be done to pretty girls like you...'

Mr Ruff walks forward and pulls Jasmine away from the accountant. She is shaken by how he has the power to publicly threaten her and get away with it. She goes numb and her face flushes.

Mr Ruff calls out to his staff, 'Turn around, we're leaving immediately.'

He looks at the accountant and says, 'Sorry, we all have been terribly disturbed by the news. That restaurant was like our home. We won't cause any more trouble.'

As Mr Ruff drags her out of the gates of the Jagir mansion, Jasmine turns and looks at the sly grin of triumph on the accountant's lips. She recognizes her own helplessness as she holds Mr Ruff's arms tight to stop herself from turning back and landing a punch on that man's round face.

The white plates and bowls, all embossed with a golden-coloured 'K', are washed clean and put to dry on a rack. It is ten past eleven and the diner has just been closed for the night. Jasmine takes the white paper from Mr Ruff's hands, sticks it on the door, and then drags the metal 'Open' board inside the restaurant. The notice reads, 'This establishment has been permanently closed. The property now belongs to Private Foods Limited.'

In the next few days, as she walks down this road to try and make herself feel at home, she will notice another sign.

A white aproned cartoon character, the mascot holding a milk carton in one hand and giving passers-by a thumbs up with his other hand. Beneath it, in red letters, '*Food Mart. Coming soon.*'

She remembers that girl who used to come with the little boy. The only Jagir she has seen in person. She had been in awe of her back then, but now she knows *how* she is able to stand up for what she believes in. Powerful families do indeed get away with everything. Respect has soured into disgust, and Jasmine suddenly regrets looking up to her for those few moments. It is because people like Jasmine look up to people like Laila that they become powerful enough to snatch everything away from the people who actually made them.

They have to hand over the keys to Jagir's men at eight in the morning. Till that moment arrives, they have decided to stay in the diner, standing by each other. Jasmine is not only grieving for the loss of her job; she is grieving for the loss of another family. She watches as the chef goes back to the kitchen and announces, 'Karen's deserves one last meal, doesn't it?'

Faint applause fills the room. They are trying to enjoy every bit of their final moments in the diner. The chef rings the bell. *Food is ready*. The three waiters run inside to collect the dishes. They carry plates of mutton chops, dahi kebabs, naan, lamb curry, and some of that famous cinnamon caramel cake for dessert. They spread the feast on the counter and one by one, they fill up their plates.

All night, they sit around a table and share their fondest memories of the restaurant, and bond over their recently developed mutual hatred for the Jagirs. They promise that they'll stay in touch. They laugh at how Mr Ruff once had bird dropping on his shirt the entire day and didn't notice; how Jasmine always forgot what the time was. They talk about Janie and Lara's little gossip sessions and tease the boys for always being shy around the girls.

Just as the sun comes up, they fall asleep with their heads on the table. Jasmine looks at Mr Ruff before dozing off. There is more of Kaiza in him than just his eyes.

The sound of loud knocks on the door wakes them up. They quickly clean the place and give it a long last look before heading out. There is not one pair of eyes that is not moist that day. Once they clear the area, Mr Ruff hands over the keys to the two men in suits. The men don't smile; they don't even give him a look of acknowledgement.

The staff steps out of the restaurant and go their separate ways. Mr Ruff walks Jasmine home. He hugs her goodbye and plants a kiss on her forehead. He promises to meet her as often as he can. Then he heads home, turning back again and again, till Jasmine disappears from his sight.

A farewell can never be perfect when no one really wants to say goodbye.

twenty-eight

Laila

Laila tries to stay calm but the constant whirr of the engine only worsens her anxiety. She hopes that the driver can't spot her fidgeting with her fingers, breathing through her mouth.

She has carried one of her bigger purses today. Inside it resides a folded handbag and a small cloth wallet with all the money that she has been able to steal.

The cold leather back seat doesn't do much to comfort Laila. She wishes the chauffeur would drive faster. But he doesn't sense any emergency, which means that Laila is playing her part well. Laila can feel her heart speed up. A moment of guilt. *Is she doing something wrong?* She is taking a child away from his father. Then she remembers Jai, lying on the ground, helpless because his father refused to stop playing the big bully. In a moment, any doubt regarding her decision vanishes. *This is the only way.*

As they approach the school building, Laila masks her nervousness and tells the driver, 'You will have to wait longer today. Jai's teacher has called me in for a meeting.'

She gets out of the car, gripping her purse tight. In the lobby, Jai runs towards her.

'Jai, we are not going back home today. You have to do exactly as I say.'

Jai nods.

They head over to the guard at the reception. Parents are usually not allowed inside the school premises unless they have specific work, or a teacher has asked to meet with them. Laila makes a face that signals urgency to the guard, and says, 'I really have to use the lavatory; is it all right if I go inside?'

The guard nods. Laila and Jai both head inside and slip away towards the corridor. She asks Jai to lead him to his locker. All the supplies, the dry food packets, the clothes and other necessities are hidden in it.

They plan to leave from the back entrance, so that they don't come in sight of the driver waiting outside. Just as Laila finishes stuffing her handbag, a teacher, Mr Hamish, comes up to them. Laila's already tense shoulders tighten further, and she hopes he will leave quickly.

'Jai's mother? Laila sahiba, good afternoon,' he greets them.

'Good afternoon, sir,' Laila replies, without looking Mr Hamish directly in the eye. Her hands tightly clench her bag. She tries to smile at the teacher but is only able to manage a slight purse of the lips.

'I'm so glad to actually meet you in person. Your son is one of the most intelligent kids in my class –'

Laila doesn't pay attention to what he is saying. She is proud of Jai for performing well, but more pressing matters require her attention at this moment. If Mr Hamish doesn't stop talking soon, their window of opportunity will close. Raymond's drivers have been asked to keep a close watch on Laila ever since the council vote, and despite her excuse of having to meet Jai's teacher, the driver will get suspicious soon. The plan is to already be quite a way to the old guest house that she has rented under a false name with the help of one of Raymond's kind female servants, before the driver's suspicions are aroused.

Mr Hamish finally ends the one-sided conversation. 'Were you just about to leave?'

Laila should have said no. She should have said that she wanted to use the washroom. She should have said anything but yes.

'Yes,' she says, unable to think clearly in her nervousness.

'Oh, then we can discuss Jai's performance on our way out.' He starts walking to the front door, signalling Jai and Laila to follow him. They hesitate, but there is nothing they can do, so they give up and walk with him.

'Jai is great, but lately he's been mixing with the wrong bunch of students. They write chits in class and pass them around. Now, which child from a good household would do something like that…?'

Laila is rethinking their exit. The guard will not let them back into the school, so their access to the back door is lost. If they leave from the front door, they will have to cross the parking lot. But the chauffeur usually chats with other chauffeurs while Laila waits inside for Jai, and the parking area is large. They could still get away.

Mr Hamish leaves them in the lobby, his attention turning to something he'd forgotten in his office. Laila heaves a sigh of relief. Laila tells Jai to stay close to her and walk quickly. In the parking area they make their way through the maze of cars, and almost make it to the entrance gates when, suddenly, a voice calls out to them from behind.

'Laila sahiba?'

The driver is at the other end of the car park, but he can see them clearly. He waves to them, thinking they've forgotten where the car is parked, and starts calling out to them. Laila ignores the driver's calls. The driver calls out to them louder, 'Laila sahiba, the car is here. Jai baba, look here.'

Jai instinctively turns towards the driver and then, quickly realizing his mistake, turns back ahead. The driver, confused, starts walking towards Laila and Jai, who begin pacing out of the school gate. He keeps calling out to them. The driver notices the large red bag on Laila's arm and as they continue to pace and ignore his calls, he puts two and two together and stops trying to get their attention. Realizing that they are planning to escape, he quickens his pace and starts running towards Laila and Jai.

The bare concrete walls brush against Laila's arm as she tries to peek into the adjacent lane. They are hiding between two rows of houses pressed closely together. Laila can hear the sound of a mixer churning, the smell of masala, spices being ground together, a man shouting at his kid for losing a toy, a lady singing softly while cooking in the kitchen. 'Oh, come to me, dear, hold me in your arms.' Laila hasn't heard this song before.

Jai and Laila are both crouched on the ground. She straightens up slightly to see if she can spot the driver.

The driver chased them for a long time, but he is not a young man. When he started to run out of breath, Laila and Jai gained some distance. At first, he stopped and turned back, and they thought they were in the clear. But he had only decided to take the car to come after them, and so they ran straight into the closely packed slum area. Laila knows they aren't going to be safe for very long. As soon as the driver reaches home with news of the attempted escape, there will be scores of men looking for a cinnamon-haired girl in her early twenties with a ten-year-old boy.

There is a commotion in one of the houses. 'Have you seen a girl in a blue kurta with a white scarf around her head? She is with a small ten-year-old boy.' Even though the voice is faint, Laila realizes that they have already waited too long. The men have already traced her to the slums. The sun is on its way down and she hopes that once it gets darker, slipping away will be easier.

Laila unties her scarf. She holds Jai's hand and decides to make a dash for the street. Once they catch a cab, they should be able to get away with ease. But as soon as they step out of their hiding spot, one of Raymond's security guards spots them. They start rapidly moving through the narrow pathways lined with grey concrete back walls of one-room houses and try to make their way through the slums, turning whenever they can. Whatever they can do to lose him. But Laila can't run any faster because Jai has trouble keeping up. She drops her bag of supplies in a bush to gain speed and they make a sharp turn into one of the smaller lanes. Laila tightens her grip on Jai's hand as they walk one behind the other because, sandwiched between grey walls, there is no space to walk side by side. She spots the brick-and-tar boundary wall and realizes that she has hit the end of the slum compound. As she hears footsteps close by, she starts to panic. They cannot turn back, and here in this narrow lane, they are trapped. Jai pants excessively, turning to look at Laila with his eyes as slits. She says nothing. Her hands get sweaty and she instantly recognizes the feeling from the day of the council vote. The lanes of the slums start to blur and the commotion becomes a thick but distant buzz. No, she can't allow herself to collapse again. If it was just her, she might have even given up. But she is not going to put

Jai's life in danger. Laila takes a few deep breaths. *In through your nose. Out through your mouth,* her father's voice echoes in her head. He had taught her that technique to calm her down before her school examinations.

As shapes and objects start to form in front of her again, she notices there is a small wooden carton, used as a flowerpot by one of the houses. Laila turns it upside down and climbs on top of it, and holding the wall hoists herself up to a sitting position. She struggles to balance since the wall is thin. Jai climbs on top of the carton and stretches his arm out to her. She manages to grasp Jai's hand and pull him up.

On the other side it's a steep jump. Jai is frozen in place. She holds his hand and jumps, but they slip and have a disastrous landing. Her forehead starts bleeding and Jai has scraped his arm. Laila tries to get Jai to walk but he remains frozen with fear. With great difficulty, lifting Jai up in her arms, she runs across the road, and disappears into one of the lanes.

Jai is heavy and Laila is not very strong. She puts him down after covering some distance in the small lane. She can see a few buildings around her but doesn't see anyone on the street. She spots a large tree and decides to hide behind it till either she can convince Jai to run or till she regains the energy to carry Jai again.

She looks Jai in the eyes, 'Jai, I know this is scary, but you have to run. Please don't give up on me now, Jai. Please listen to me.'

She shakes him by the shoulders, but the little boy has gone numb. He refuses to react. She kneels on the footpath, trying to think of where they can hide. It is not safe for them to travel the distance to the guest house any more. Raymond's men must be patrolling the streets, and they could have already questioned all the servants in the house. She doesn't think her help will give her up, but she cannot take that chance. Still hidden behind the tree, Laila turns back to see a simple cream-coloured five-storeyed building. Fortunately for them, the watchman of the building has dozed off. Laila thinks there's no one around and decides to sneak into the building compound till she can figure out her next move, but she is startled to find a girl peeping out of a room on the ground floor. She can't see her face clearly. She stares at Laila, who doesn't know if she should run. What if that girl makes a sound, calls other people from the building to take note of their uninvited visitor? If there is too much commotion, she is sure that Raymond's men will come running.

The girl peeping through the room's door quickly pulls her head back in and then a few seconds later, peeps out again. She slowly holds out a hand. She signals towards Laila and then points at the room she's in. *Come inside.* Laila picks up Jai and enters the small, stuffy room. The girl locks the room. Laila looks at her. 'Thank you!'

The girl doesn't respond. She doesn't even look Laila in the eye. She just says, 'You can stay the night here. But please leave as soon as you can.'

twenty-nine

Jasmine

Jasmine had opened her room door to use the common lavatory outside, but the image in front of her made her completely forget her bodily needs. It has been only two nights since the restaurant shut. Jasmine has had trouble sleeping. Even if she does manage to fall into slumber, when she wakes up in the morning, she feels a pang of emptiness in her chest. Amer hasn't returned yet. She longs for someone to understand her pain, to comfort her.

Jasmine looks twice to make sure she's seeing what she thinks she's seeing. It *is* her. In a blue kurta that has almost turned brown, she is on her knees talking to the boy. Both their faces are covered in dust. She is shaking the kid out of his stupor, but she definitely looks more shaken herself. It takes Jasmine a few minutes to realize that both the woman and the child are deliberately crouched behind the tree.

They are trying to hide.

Jasmine tries to make sense of the situation she finds herself in. Laila *Jagir*. Or Laila Raymond Tony. Her family stole Jasmine's entire life and the lives of everyone in the restaurant. Receding back into the room, Jasmine shuts the door and proceeds to sit on her mattress, trying not to think of the young woman and little boy hiding in fear. *She is a Jagir; she can help herself.* But her mind refuses to obey, and she wishes she hadn't opened the door at all. *If I help her, I will be betraying everyone from the restaurant.*

Jasmine shuts her eyes tight but her mind is bustling with incessant chatter, conjuring up a world full of gruesome possibilities. *What if someone is after their lives, maybe a gang of thugs? What if they are unable to call for help? What if I hear tomorrow that Raymond's wife and son had been brutally murdered right outside my house?*

Jasmine brushes these thoughts away. There is no need to imagine danger when there probably isn't any. She can't bear the thought of having a Jagir anywhere close to her, let alone spending the night in her house. She opens her eyes and shuts them again, but the picture of the terrified-looking boy and woman does not leave her mind.

She finally, unwillingly, opens the front door. They are still there, crouched behind the tree. Laila turns to survey the area and spots her. Jasmine is caught off guard. When Laila turns to look at her again, Jasmine signals for her to come inside. She hesitates for a second, then picks up the boy and rushes in. Jasmine locks the door, hoping that the night will pass quickly.

Laila

Up on the first floor, someone places a disk on a record player. The slight hum of music is enough to wake Laila up. She can only faintly hear the song but she recognizes the tune. It is difficult to make out if the sun has risen. The tiny box of a window on the rear wall doesn't let much light in. Her muscles are sore. She must have slept a long time.

Jai is curled up in a corner of the room. There is hardly any space for even one person to live comfortably among these four walls. The walls are white, too white, perhaps newly painted. The girl is asleep on a thin mattress. Laila doesn't know her name yet; she didn't seem eager for interaction last night. But Laila recalls seeing her at the diner she and Jai had visited.

When Laila stands, she can see a thin line of the sky above the grey wall outside the window. She has seen too much grey in the last twelve hours. A tinge of gold appears and starts melting with the blue. The sun has just come out of hiding.

Laila unties her bun and runs her hands through her hair. It feels greasy because of all the sweat and dust. She ties it back into a loose braid and then both of Laila's hands instinctively go to her stomach. It has been growling ever since she woke up. She regrets ditching the bag with all the supplies. Luckily, she had tucked her cloth wallet inside her pants.

She walks up to the flimsy blue door but then decides against venturing outside. For all she knows there might be 'Missing' posters stuck on the walls with her picture. She worries that Raymond will even file a legal complaint against Laila, for abducting his child. Or simply, for running away. It is a punishable offence if a wife leaves her husband without an official separation and the act of separation is considered taboo.

Laila notices an earthern water pot lying beside the mattress. She quietly helps herself, to a glass. With her hands still on her stomach, she lies back down in the corner, as she waits for the woman of the house to awaken.

The wind knocks violently on the blue steel door, bringing with it warning of an impending storm. Laila unwraps the crumpled newspaper the waitress has placed before her to find hot, crisp samosas with fried green chillies and a sweet tamarind sauce. She looks at the waitress, who is trying to cover the small window with a blue plastic sheet. Laila still doesn't know her name.

Laila hands a samosa to Jai, who has just woken up. She takes one for herself then, holding the rest of them, extends her hand towards the waitress. Seated on her mattress, the girl is folding her clothes, seeming busy.

'They're all for you. I already ate at the stall.' The girl doesn't bother looking up at Laila.

So far, the girl hasn't asked them any questions about last night. Or anything at all. Taking a bite of the samosa, Laila tries to make some small talk.

'You don't know how grateful we are to you –'

'It's all right, really.'

The dark-eyed girl is stiff, but Laila pushes for a conversation.

'If you hadn't taken us in, who knows what would have happened to us? Maybe we wouldn't even have survived the –'

'Please don't make me sound like a saviour. The only reason I took you in is because my conscience didn't allow me to leave a scared-looking woman with a child out on the street. Quite honestly, I wish I hadn't opened the door and seen the both of you at all.'

The girl's olive face turns red. Laila senses that she would have stormed out if she had anywhere to go. But this little room has her trapped just a few feet away from Laila. So instead, she just turns and faces the window.

They are not welcome here. But this is perhaps the best shelter that they could have found. Even if someone comes to look for them, knocks on every door in every building, they are never going to look for her in this closet-sized extra room, probably built for servants or guards to sleep in at night. Laila has decided to stay here till she figures out their next step, whether their host likes it or not.

It has been two days since their escape. Laila lays down the two sheets that their host has bought from a nearby store. Her name is Jasmine. Jai refused to let her move until she accepted his gratitude and told him her name. Laila thinks she even saw Jasmine try to hide a smile.

Jai lies down on one of the sheets and Laila pats his head to put him to sleep. This must all be especially hard for Jai, being away from his home, from his life, without completely understanding why. Jai had even had a slight fever yesterday; Jasmine bought some medicines and helped ice Jai.

Laila knows that her escape means her research about Naya Roben, her plan to convince her to run for the Rahat elections and subsequently planning her campaign to help her win, will all have to be paused; unless she finds a way which doesn't involve her presence, which allows her to work from behind the scenes. Their situation is such that Laila knows survival needs to be her top priority. But since the elections are near, she cannot postpone talking to Naya Roben for much longer.

Laila slowly withdraws her hand from Jai's head when his breathing evens out. She looks over to see Jasmine lying on her mattress, but her constant tossing and turning tells Laila that she is not asleep yet. Laila wonders if Jasmine works at that diner, if she has another job or a husband. She hasn't gone anywhere other than to get supplies in the last couple of days that they have been here.

As Jasmine sits up to take a few sips of water, Laila decides to make conversation.

'Jasmine,' she whispers, making sure not to wake the little boy up.

Jasmine is slightly drowsy and thus, less cold towards her. 'Yes?'

'I want to thank you once more. I know that we're an inconvenience to you, and I promise we'll leave soon. But we really don't have a safer place to be right now. I cannot tell you exactly what has happened to me, but Jai and I cannot go back home for a while for the sake of our own safety.'

Jasmine only nods her head and then lies back down.

I remember seeing you at a diner in Russel. You work there as a waitress, right?' Laila asks, determined to know more about Jasmine.

'Not any more.' Jasmine's reply is short.

'Oh, how come?'

'No one works at the diner any more because it was shut down. One of your father's companies bought it forcefully from the owner to convert it into a grocery store.'

Laila is taken aback. Her father was never a ruthless businessman, but Laila doesn't feel like she knows her father any more.

She understands Jasmine's reaction towards them now, and appreciates her kindness even more.

'I'm...I'm sorry, Jasmine. I had no idea. Once I am out of this situation, I can perhaps talk to father...'

'I am going to look for another job soon. I don't need your sympathy or your help.'

Laila is still shaken by the impact a simple business decision can have on the lives of so many people, but as her conversation with Jasmine continues, an idea forms in her mind.

'Jasmine,' Laila continues cautiously, 'I cannot claim to understand your loss, but I am genuinely sorry. But since you are looking for a job, perhaps we can help each other out.'

Jasmine doesn't reply, but her eyes are open, so Laila knows she is listening.

'I don't know if you've heard, but women are now allowed to be elected into the national council. It was such a monumental moment when the bill passed. But this is only the beginning. If we –' Laila pauses to check if she still has Jasmine's attention. '– manage to get a woman elected in the council, imagine the impact it will have on women in all walks of life. Imagine the kind of bills that might get passed, giving us our rights after all these years.'

Laila waits for Jasmine to respond. Nothing comes from her.

'No woman has applied to stand for the election yet. But I have one in mind. Naya Roben. She is the founder of an organization that trains women with skills so that they are employable. I reckon she is perfectly suited for the role. But I need to find out everything about Naya if I am to convince her to run for the council. As you must have figured by now, I have to stay in hiding for a while. It's dangerous for me to even be seen in public, leave alone trying to approach someone or scout the public library for information. But I have an idea. If you agree to work for the cause, perhaps you can do the research for me, get me everything I need to know about Naya –' Laila pauses. 'Once I'm out of here, I'll find a way to compensate you. The Rahat elections are only two months away, and...'

'No,' Jasmine cuts her short.

'Jasmine, at least give it some consideration. I'm not asking you to do this for any personal gain. And I promise to compensate you fairly as soon as I can.'

'No.' Jasmine turns away from Laila. 'You cannot buy me like your father bought our restaurant, our home. You cannot always get your way, just because you have the money and power.'

thirty

Jasmine

Soft knocks on the door wake her up. She opens her eyes to see that Laila is already awake. She is still dressed in the blue kurta from two nights ago. *I should lend her some clothes.* Yet, Laila looks so different from any other woman that she has seen so far. It's not her cinnamon hair or her hazel eyes. It is the look that she has on her face. The undersides of her eyes have become dark due to sleepless nights, but the light in her eyes refuses to fade. Laila is a woman who demands what she deserves. Jasmine is surprised that even in this dire situation, Laila is thinking about the nation, about the elections.

Jasmine hasn't been able to ease up since they arrived. Laila goes to sleep after Jasmine and wakes up before her, giving Jasmine no time to herself. Laila mostly spends time looking outside the little window. Jasmine has avoided talking to her despite Laila's apology on behalf of her family. But Jasmine now also feels like she has a responsibility towards Laila, towards both of them. She took them in, so she must protect them.

Another knock. Laila looks at Jasmine, asking who it might be.

The possibility that anyone knows that Jasmine has hidden Laila and Jai in her closet-sized room is slim. Still, Jasmine doesn't open the door. Both women continue to stare at the door in anticipation.

The knocking stops and a man's voice comes from outside. 'Jasmine, it's Amer. Are you in there? Open the door.'

Jasmine doesn't notice when Laila glances curiously at her. She springs from her bed and rushes to open the door. As soon as Jasmine spots Amer, not caring that there is another set of eyes looking at her from inside, she runs into Amer's arms. He holds her tightly, releasing her only when his eyes open to see the Jagir girl staring at him from inside the small room.

'Let's go somewhere and talk,' Jasmine tells Amer. 'I'll explain.'

Amer watches as Jasmine instructs Laila to keep the door locked. She tells her about the leftover kulchas that she and Jai can have for breakfast.

'I'll be back soon. Please try to not get yourself into any trouble,' she says.

Two hot cups of filter coffee are placed on the plastic table. Sitting at the small roadside stall, Jasmine observes the traffic that's passing by, rushing as always. Her mornings also used to be the same. She misses this hustle and bustle.

She looks into the blue eyes in front of her and smiles, trying unsuccessfully to hide the blush in her cheeks. Amer extends his right hand and she slides hers into it. He is wearing a white shirt, perhaps the same one that he had worn the first time she had seen him. Amer hadn't given her the time to change out of the blue blouse she had worn for the night. She hasn't even washed her face. Still, since he's come back, he hasn't stopped telling her how beautiful she looks. Jasmine looks at the skin visible around Amer's neck and grins because she now knows how his body looks beneath his layer of clothing. She can't wait to touch him, even though he's right in front of her. Amer holds up her hand and brushes his lips across her fingers. The stall owner's lascivious glance puts a halt to their flirtation. They start to sip on their coffees, not taking their eyes off each other.

'I think you should help her, Jasmine,' Amer's face suddenly becomes contemplative.

She has just finished telling him about Laila and her proposal but all she expected was an understanding nod, not an outrageous suggestion.

'What? Amer, you know I can't! Her family is the reason all of us from the restaurant are suffering.'

Amer holds Jasmine by her shoulders. 'Jasmine, listen. I understand the pain you're going through. Believe me, I feel it too. But it's not her fault, Jasmine. You can't punish her for the wrongdoings of her father.'

Jasmine notices Amer's voice shake. *What was done to me was unfair. Why should I bother treating the Jagir girl fairly? And why are you trying to defend that girl anyway?*

Amer shifts closer to Jasmine and takes her in his arms. She tries to resist in childish vexation but she can never deny herself the pleasure of his warm embrace.

'It's not even about her, Jasmine. What she is asking you to do is in your interest as well. It's going to be a huge step for all the women of this nation. Not only women, for all the men too. Wouldn't you want to be a part of this?'

'But –' she begins.

Amer smiles at her. 'Jasmine, you took her in. You helped her when you had no obligation to do so. Deep inside, you know as well as I do that what happened to you is not her fault. Of course, if you don't actually want to do this, don't. I don't have the right to invalidate your anger. But think about her offer once again?'

Jasmine remains quiet. She nods and burrows her head into Amer's chest.

The curves of the black ink have smudged, and the edges of the yellowing paper have frayed. Most records were still handwritten back then. Amer brushes his fingers on the paper, able to read every word clearly.

'Bernad Hospital.'

This record had been tossed into the trash, only to be recovered by a four-year-old boy. The memory of his tears still haunts the paper; it has inscribed his sorrow into itself. A blot and a light smudge on the words 'female' and 'Moran'.

It was going to be a boy. His parents were sure of it. He was going to have a baby brother to play with. He sat outside with a nurse while the delivery was taking place. The nurse was a slender man, dressed in blue pants and a blue shirt, the only evidence of colour in an otherwise predominantly white setting – the floors, the walls, the chairs – giving the space an illusion of brightness. After all, it was one of the only hospitals that mostly saw people both come in and go out happy. It was a maternity hospital that ensured that the cases they took were already happy with the gender growing in the mother's belly. Mostly they delivered only boys. Amer, his mother and his father had travelled for over a day to come to Rahat. Bernard was considered one of the best hospitals of the nation. Amer was born in Bernad too.

Amer still remembers the nurse's name. Wyan. They sat outside. Or rather, the nurse sat while Amer jumped around, discussing names for his little brother. Amir. He really wanted the baby to be called Amir. It was a lot like Amer, but slightly different; exactly how his baby brother would be. But his mother had grown very fond of the name Salzan, after the ancient conqueror who had united the land of the five districts and set its slaves free. His father refused to budge from Dil. It was simple and its meaning was direct; *dil* means heart. None of their preferences really mattered though. First an astrologer would look at the time, date and month of birth, and then suggest one or two alphabets for the beginning of the baby's name. Only then would a name be decided. If 'A' turned out to be the letter of the astrologer's choice, it would be Amer's turn to rejoice.

A few hours had passed when the doctor finally walked out the door with a sweaty forehead and shifty eyes. He tried to look at anything else but the anticipation in the little kid's blue eyes. Once the doctor left, Amer rushed into the room. The lights were dim, and his father and mother were both tied in an embrace. And there he was, the little boy, wrapped in a blue blanket, asleep in a cradle, right beside his mother. His hair was muddy brown, very different from Amer's black locks. His cheeks were chubby and his mouth was smiling.

Amer remembers asking if he could touch him. He didn't pay attention to the tears in his parents' eyes. They said he couldn't, and asked him to wait outside. Wyan came a while later and explained that his brother had passed on into a better world. The nurse embraced the crying boy until it was time to go look after another, happier delivery.

Later, Amer watched as the doctor walked out of the door with his baby brother. *I want him in my arms.* Even if his little brother was no more, Amer wanted to hold him, at least once. Amer followed the doctor as he took the baby to the next wing. The doctor stopped at another delivery room. This area of the hospital was much bigger. The waiting seats were not plastic chairs but cushioned sofas. The hallway was air-conditioned, and there were beautiful paintings of mountains that hung on the walls. Tall, golden-coloured metal vases with floral designs lined the edges of the carpeted floor. Amer hid behind one of them.

The doctor knocked and waited as a young man walked out the door. The man was tall, dressed in a white kurta and a blue sweater vest. His square face was dull, and his brown eyes were red and swollen. He looked at Amer's brother and then took him in his arms. Amer was confused but furious. *He is my brother. I want to hold him.*

'Such a sweet girl. Are you sure the family doesn't want her?' The man had tears in his eyes as he looked at the baby lovingly. *Her?* Amer froze. The little boy couldn't comprehend it. He wanted to shout, but all he could do was cry. His arms ached to hold the little baby girl. *His sister.* He was almost overjoyed as the baby started crying, though he had already got the hint that his sibling was still alive.

He could only watch helplessly as the doctor threw out the old record and made a new one, erasing all proof of her association with Amer. But they would always have the same blood in them.

'No, Ahmed sahib. Not many can bear the burden of a girl child. And don't worry. They don't want to know who is adopting the child,' the doctor said, and looked down at the record sheet. 'What should I mention in the records, sahib? Once you give her a name, I will make a certificate for her.'

'I already have a name for her.' The man looked at the baby girl. 'Laila, Doctor. She will be called Laila Jagir after her mother,' he kisses the girl's soft cheeks.

'And I will love her better than anyone else could have.'

thirty-one

Laila

On most nights, Laila can hear thunder. Sometimes the flashes of light coming through the window disturb her sleep. During the day, the air is dewy and the sky is dark. Laila has opened up to Jasmine over the last few days and told her about the circumstances of her running away.

Right now, hearing the faint drizzle outside she longs to step out and feel the drops on her skin. Ahmed never let her play in the rain. She would always sneak out when no one was looking and sit on the swing in their garden, until an unsuspecting servant found her, sent her inside and arranged a tub of warm water for her to sit in. Laila's punishment would be a half-hearted, wide-eyed glance from Ahmed, like he knew the joys of getting drenched in fresh rainwater but his duties as a father didn't allow him to explore those joys any more, or let his daughter do so either. Laila later realized that his notion of duty often stopped him from listening to his heart.

Laila tries to divert her attention back to the list. She doesn't know what convinced Jasmine to change her mind, but she has decided not to dwell on the inner workings of the girl's mind. Jasmine will pose as an aspiring journalist, writing an article on non-conformist women, with the hope of selling the article to a big magazine. To Laila's surprise, Jasmine herself suggested the guise. Of course, it would introduce some form of bias in the research, but years of living with a political family has taught Laila to look past it. She has decided that she will need to find out what Naya's daily routine is, details of how she grew up, information on all of her projects, her characteristics, what motivates her, what discourages her, her relationship with her husband and anything else that Jasmine is able to dig up. Everything will contribute towards Laila's final proposal.

Laila watches as the handle on the door turns. Jasmine hasn't yet been able to let go of her resentment towards Laila, but she's really taken to Jai. She had taken Jai out for a walk, as she does very often these days. They covered Jai's face with a scarf and dressed him in a pair of pants and a shirt bought from the nearby market. Jai's health has been deteriorating from being locked up inside all day. He needs some fresh air, and evidently, ice cream. Jai hands over the pistachio ice cream cone they brought for Laila. Jasmine and Jai laugh as she laps it up in no time. They had wagered on how long it would take for her to finish it.

Jai walks up to Laila as she finishes her ice cream and settles himself on her lap.

'Next time, you should come out with us too, Laila.'

She longs for fresh air.

'Yes, Laila, you should come out with us too. I can give you my clothes and you can cover your face with a scarf. We can go in the night...'

Laila is surprised by Jasmine's sudden display of camaraderie.

'No, it's too risky.'

'Raymond hasn't made anything public yet. If we stay in this area, there's a very slim chance that one of his men will spot you. Laila, look at you. You're suffocating yourself by staying inside these four walls, and your mental state has such an effect on Jai as well.'

'Jasmine, you don't understand. Raymond hasn't given up. I'm sure he has men canvassing the entire neighbourhood day and night. People like him may give up when you hurt their emotions, but they never give up when you hurt their pride.'

Later that evening, Jasmine finally convinces Laila to walk with them to the end of the street. Jasmine hands some clothes over to

Laila, along with a blue scarf. 'It's not as nice as what you must be used to, but it's decent. Wash yourself, change your clothes, cover your face with this scarf, and walk with me to the kebab stall at the end of the street. It's only a few metres away. Please, Laila, fresh air for you will be good for all three of us.'

The white blouse is short-sleeved, revealing the bruises on Laila's skin. Jasmine had said that it was a gift from one of her friends at the diner, but that she wasn't comfortable enough herself to wear it yet. There are long blackish-green marks slashed just above Laila's elbows. Laila has watched the bruises turn from red to blue to black. Now that they are out in the open, she is embarrassed.

How could I let a man do this to me?

She tries to hide her arms behind her back as they walk towards the kebab stall.

Laila bursts into a wide smile when the wind hits her face. She can breathe again. Jasmine was right; staying inside for so long has not done her much good.

The kebab vendor slides the meat off the skewers and wraps them in a flatbread with some tangy mint sauce. The smoke from the coal helps dispense some warmth into the cold, dewy air. As Laila takes a bite of her kebab roll, she is reminded of the feasts she sat through at home. She'd never taken a moment to cherish a single bite, always rushing to taste everything on the table.

'Well, food does taste better in fresh air,' Laila proclaims.

Jasmine laughs. 'Maybe you just like your food with a light coating of dust and rain.' She gives Laila a slight nudge, which makes Laila chuckle.

They make way for a Labrador to pass. Quite a few dogs are out on walks with their owners. Laila looks at them and suddenly longs for Shadow, for the warmth in his eyes whenever she returned home even after a short period of absence.

On the way home, Laila lets her arms hang down by her sides. Jai walks between Laila and Jasmine, holding both their hands, swinging every few steps. Before they sleep Jasmine hands a tube to Laila. 'It's a gel, to help the wounds heal quicker.' Laila looks down, instead of at Jasmine, ashamed of the marks on her body. She takes the tube and shifts her gaze.

'Thanks,' she says quietly.

Laila watches as Jasmine lifts her maroon kurta to her chest to reveal her stomach. Four red lines, the kind that won't fade with time. She pulls her kurta back down and looks out the window, towards the thin sliver of sky bathed in the moonlight.

'Laila, we escaped. We stood up for ourselves when no one else would. I think that's something to be proud of. I think that's a victory.'

thirty-two

Jasmine

The white leather upholstery makes the living room look brighter than it is. A marble statue of a horse with a glass top serves as the centre table, set upon a marble floor. The ceiling is high, high enough to comfortably fit another storey. From it hangs a three-tiered chandelier. The walls are decorated with framed medals and pictures of Naya Roben's family.

Jasmine has never been in a room even half this luxurious before. As a servant comes up to her and serves her water in a silver glass, she realizes that this is how Laila must have lived all her life. Silver spoons. Crystal chandeliers. Silk clothes. Marble floors. Servants with dress codes. And now she has been living in Jasmine's small hole in the wall without making a fuss.

Jasmine involuntarily stands up as Naya enters the room. Her presence demands attention, and respect. Naya Roben is a tall woman with broad shoulders. She is wearing a white pencil skirt that ends a little below her knees. Her cream shirt is tucked into the skirt. Her hair is permed to perfection and ends just below her ears. Her grey eyes look mysterious and the maroon stain on her lips makes her look authoritative. Her nose is very small, but like everything else, it looks good on her.

Naya holds out her hand and gives Jasmine's a firm shake. She takes a seat and signals Jasmine to do the same.

'Jasmine, right? I hear you want to write an article on my life. Tell me, what do you want to know about me?'

Jasmine fidgets. She tries to search for the right words but her vocabulary fails her. 'Umm, everything. The more I know about you, the better. I want to lay your life out as an inspiration to all the young women out there.'

Naya laughs. She has a perfect laugh. Not loud enough to offend, but loud enough to be heard. Jasmine already understands why Laila wants this woman to stand for the election.

'Well, I'm glad that you're taking this initiative. That's what our organization is all about, helping women stand for themselves.'

Jasmine smiles. She has never met a more striking woman. Without needing to be asked a second time, Naya tells Jasmine about her life. She wakes up every morning with a glass of fresh juice. Her favourite fruit is kiwi, but it is very difficult to get them at this time of year. She has a pet rabbit. It has pink eyes. She started her organization when she wanted to become a writer but no one would let her join their publication.

'To be honest, I wasn't that good a writer. How will women be good at something if they're never exposed to it?' she says.

Naya tells Jasmine about how she and her husband, Ayen Roben, met through their parents, but how it was also love at first sight. It reminds Jasmine of a particular afternoon when her dark eyes collided with Amer's blue. It was as if she'd met the ocean itself. Vast, full of life, and ready to become one with her.

Swimming in Naya's charm, Jasmine has wandered so deep that she has almost forgotten why she is here. As she regains her sense of purpose and time, she decides to bid farewell to Naya. It is almost seven in the evening. Laila and Jai must be starving.

'Run the article by me once you're done writing it. If it's good, I could convince a magazine to publish it. I don't mean to discourage you, but honestly, without the right connections, it's very difficult to make a name for yourself these days. Especially as a woman.'

Jasmine replies politely, 'Sure. Thank you very much.'

She walks out of the Roben mansion, exhilarated. Maybe Laila has done her a favour by introducing this phenomenal woman in her life.

Jasmine stops at the kulchawallah's to pick up dinner for the three of them. She longs to see a familiar face, and this stout man is the only memory of the diner that she has around.

'Jasmine sahiba! So good to see you!' the kulchawallah exclaims. 'It has been a long time, no?'

Jasmine nods with a smile. 'Hope you've been keeping well?' she asks politely.

'Yes, sahiba, family is good, I am good,' he replies cheerily. 'Hope you, your parents, your family are well too?'

Jasmine feels a jab in her chest as she nods to answer the question. Family. She had come here for family. She had came here for Kaiza, but life has taken her in a completely unexpected direction. Even though she has no leads and doesn't know how to actively look for her father any more, she often wonders if she will run into him while walking on the street someday. *What will I say? What will I do? Will he recognize me?* Then, *Will I recognize him?*

'How's the business going?' she asks the kulchawallah, as he hands over her order of six stuffed kulchas.

'Fine. I don't make as much as I used to at the diner. But I survive. Thankfully, most of my old customers have returned. There isn't any kulcha like mine,' he says in his usual jovial tone. Some people are just difficult to bring down, however hard circumstances try.

'I can't deny that. You are credited for shifting my loyalties from the humble naan to the lip-smacking kulcha,' Jasmine chirps. They both share a laugh.

It starts to drizzle. Just then, Jasmine notices a long black car pass by. The kulchawallah points at it and exclaims, 'Oh, that's Raymond sahib's car. Did I tell you that he once ate at my stall?' Jasmine nods quickly, hoping that the kulchawallah doesn't start narrating the same story again. 'I've heard rumours that his wife, Laila sahiba, ran away,' he whispers. Then he leans closer to Jasmine and adds, 'With his son.'

Jasmine clenches her jaw as he continues, 'I wonder why anyone would do that. Raymond sahib is a great man. I thought Laila sahiba would be a good woman, an understanding woman, coming from the Jagir family. People say that she was having an affair; some say that it was with one of his servants, and that she took Raymond's son to blackmail him into providing for her rich lifestyle. Some even say that she tortures his poor kid so that he doesn't disobey her.'

The kulchawallah shakes his head in disgust. He has no doubt in his head that Raymond, the noble man, is a victim.

Jasmine takes a step back. She understands immediately why Raymond isn't actively looking for Laila. He is spreading false rumours to gain sympathy. He is defaming Laila so if she is ever seen in public again, leave alone found trying to run a campaign for someone, people will refuse to listen to a word she says. They will take Jai away from her, they will pelt stones at her, chant slogans to get her arrested. As Jasmine imagines these possibilities, her face turns pale. With her heart racing, she clasps the food close to her chest and runs home. Laila has to come clean. She has to apply for an official separation before it's too late.

thirty-three

Laila

Wooden bookcases line the walls of the room. There is a matching desk in the middle. Next to Laila is a metal chair, identical to the one she is sitting on. Across the table is a much more comfortable-looking black armchair. The table is stacked with piles of books. Some are journals while others prescribe the laws that each citizen of the nation must abide by. There is a metal nameplate placed on the desk.

Ruff Junior

There are photos on the wall. A family; two men and a little boy. A framed law degree keeps them in good company. There's even a poster of a famous cricketer. Jamin. Laila remembers meeting him when she was younger. He had been invited to one of her father's parties.

Getting here was not easy. Laila covered herself in a maroon scarf, leaving only her eyes visible. It is easier for Laila to leave the house now that she knows Raymond's men are not actively looking for her, but it's still dangerous. Laila is dressed in Jasmine's clothes. A blue buttoned blouse and pants. Her long hair is pulled back in a braid. She doesn't know what the proper attire would be to meet an attorney.

The attorney is Jasmine's ex-boss, Mr Ruff's, son. To look for a lawyer for Laila, Jasmine spoke to her friends from the diner and her lover Amer, and this is the closest and the most trustworthy connection they could find.

Laila is not sure about the separation. She believes that it is not what she should be concentrating on right now. If Naya isn't convinced soon to run for the elections, there won't be enough time left to build a successful campaign. But on Jasmine's insistence, and keeping Jai's safety in mind, she has decided to apply for it.

As Laila watches the attorney enter the room, she is quite amused. She remembers that her father's lawyers always dressed formally. Always in a suit and tie. This man definitely hasn't followed suit.

The attorney smiles at her and places two cups of coffee on the table.

'Miss Laila, right?'

She nods. He looks just a few years older than her. His dark curly hair ends at the beginning of his neck. He is tall and lean. His eyes are small and coloured a beautiful shade of dark brown. His face is long and dons a light stubble. He is dressed in blue pants and a white, untucked shirt. The sleeves of his shirt are rolled up to his elbow. She looks at his unbuttoned collar and wonders if that is why no other clients are lining up to see him.

He clears his throat to signal for Laila to slip out of her reverie. She smiles in embarrassment. Then, without another thought, the words slip out, 'Is your name *really* Ruff Junior?' She immediately presses her hands against her mouth in embarrassment and signals with her eyes. *I'm so sorry.*

Laila almost never loses control over her tongue. She is a Jagir; diplomacy runs in her veins. Fortunately, the lawyer laughs.

'Well, my father was quite adamant about it.'

He points towards the older man in the photograph, with a triangle-shaped nose, and says, 'This is my father, Mr Ruff Senior.' Then pointing to the other, taller man, he says, '*This* is also my father, Seth. And he's the one who insisted I be called Ruff.'

Laila smiles at Ruff, unsure how to react.

He smiles back and continues, 'My fathers adopted me soon after I was born. They've loved me and each other so much, but can never step out in public together.'

As Laila listens to Ruff, she remembers the time a few eunuchs had come to their house after her father's victory to celebrate, and how her grandfather had called them names and not allowed them inside the gate. Laila realizes that having a woman in the council is not where her work will end if she truly wants to see everyone in the country have an equal chance at life.

Ruff clears his throat again to direct her attention towards him. 'Anyway, so my father, Ruff, told me your story. I'm ready to help. I must admit that this will be my first big case out of law school. But I promise that I will give it my all.'

Laila serves him a polite smile. She knows she has nowhere else to go. No attorney will agree to see her, and even if one does, she can never be sure where his loyalties would lie.

When Ruff asks, she tells him about her marriage, carefully skipping the part about her deal with Raymond. As she narrates the incidents, she lives through them all over again in her head; the betrayal, the carnage. Her heart suddenly searches for Ahmed.

Is he even worried about me? Is he looking for me?

She realizes suddenly that her eyes are watering and her hands are pressed tightly against her thighs. Ruff tries to comfort her with a smile.

'I'm not going to sugar-coat it. If a woman wants a separation without the man's consent, she needs an infallible case. Your running away with his child doesn't make things better. We need to prove in court beyond doubt that living with Raymond any longer would have harmed you. Then, the court might grant you a separation and forbid him to come anywhere near you. Difficult, but possible.'

'And the child? How will I get his custody?'

Ruff looks up from his book. His eyes are wide with shock. 'You want the child's custody?'

'Of course. What did you think? I'd let Jai go back to that filthy animal?'

'But he's not even your biological child. He is Raymond's blood. It's going to be next to impossible to get custody. Or even a separation if you demand custody. Your best bet would –'

Laila slams her fist on the table. She is furious even though she knows that he is only trying to help her.

'If I ask for a separation, it will be with Jai's custody. If you can't do it, I will fight for it myself.'

Ruff takes a deep breath.

'Please take your seat, madam.' He sighs before continuing. 'I'll do it. I think that laws should help people and support those who are right.'

Laila calms down and takes her seat again. She apologizes for her sudden uproar.

'What will be your fee?' she asks.

'Father has specifically requested me not to charge you.'

'I want you to do your best work. Money might just be your motivation.'

'I want to fight for people's rights. And let me put it bluntly, mam. If you had the money, I would ask you for it. But you don't. You don't have money and I don't have a case. It's a win-win for both of us.'

Ruff gets up and shakes Laila's hand. Just before she exits, she turns back and says, 'And Ruff, please, you can call me Laila.'

thirty-four

Jasmine

The long wooden shelves have hundreds of books stacked in them, first according to subject and then in alphabetical order. Jasmine scouts the area for magazines and looks for the month and year that Naya's organization was founded. Wings. It was started almost six years ago. Jasmine was twelve then. Kaiza was still with her in Mahlah.

Naya Roben was only thirty-six when she founded Wings. It must have taken immense courage and determination. Jasmine places the stack of dusty magazines on the dark, wooden table at which Amer is already seated. He is helping with her research.

Jasmine takes a seat beside Amer. She is happy to have him here, and as they quietly flip through the magazines, she wishes that they were sitting even closer. There is something uncannily romantic about the smell of old books and rustic wooden furniture. She knows that Amer is busy and appreciates that he takes time out to spend with her whenever he can.

A few months ago, Jasmine had come to Rahat with an emptiness in her chest and only memories of her father's books. And now she sits in a library where she can read about any topic she wants, and in the company of someone who deeply cares about her. Some things have a way of working out by themselves; you just need to pick yourself up and keep moving forward.

A lot of magazines have articles about Naya, some applauding her, some defaming her for her spirit. She used to be a famous face once upon a time, and magazine covers often carried her picture on them. But she seems to have kept a low profile over the last few years. Naya was not from a very well-to-do family but her parents were quite open-minded. She was one of the first women in the entire nation to go to college. She also used to look very different back then. Her hair was long and frizzy, and her lips were thinner. But the look in her eyes was the same, a look of steely determination. Jasmine has seen the same look in someone else's eyes too, another young woman.

Amer and Jasmine bury their faces in the books. Jasmine thinks it shouldn't take a lot to convince Naya to run for the council. She is built for the position, and she probably wants it as much as they want her to do it. Laila might not even have to form a concrete plan to convince her. It might even work if Jasmine casually brings it up during her next meeting with Naya. *What's your take on the decision to allow women into the council? Who do you think would make a good councilwoman? I think you would; you should definitely consider trying.* In an ideal world, Naya Roben will go deep in thought, already imagining Jasmine's words to be true, and then thank Jasmine for her life-changing suggestion.

Laila can at least concentrate on going through with her separation then. Jasmine suspects that Laila wants to play a pivotal role in Naya's campaign, see it through to victory, but that circumstances as they stood might not allow it. Jasmine is sure that Naya Roben is more than capable of emerging victorious on her own anyway.

Once they are done with the magazines, Jasmine and Amer decide to call it a day. As soon as they take their seat in Amer's tiny car, he leans over and passionately locks his lips with hers. She shuts her eyes and smiles. She never knew that a touch could feel so full of love.

thirty-five

Laila

Laila takes a sip of water to clear her throat. Still, words refuse to form in her mouth.

Instinctively, she touches the bruise on her arm through her sleeve. Despite the marks, despite the nightmares, despite the quickening of her heartbeat, her abuse still feels unreal, as if it was a distant dream, and she will soon wake up from it.

As Raymond walks in, the smell of alcohol fills her senses. Raymond reeks of his favourite whisky; she has learned to recognize his stench. He looks at her with disgust. He quickly sits in his designated seat beside Laila. Across the old wooden table in front of them is a long chair for the counsellor they are waiting for.

The room is small but well-lit. Laila shivers but tries to not let her anxiety show.

Within three days of their first meeting, Ruff prepared the necessary documents and helped her file for separation. Laila remembers the look on the filing official's face. Disgust. Shame. Disapproval.

Ruff told her that she will have to take at least one court-ordered counselling session with Raymond. The court does not allow parties to file for a separation without as much as a single try at maintaining the sanctity of marriage.

Raymond turns towards Laila, 'Hello, Laila jaan, you've shrivelled. Hiding hasn't done you much good, has it?'

Laila's breath is short. She does not answer. Ruff, who is seated at the back of the room, has advised her not to speak to Raymond directly. Laila had requested for her lawyer to be present during this session, and because Laila has accused Raymond of physical abuse the court has allowed it.

To Laila's relief, the counsellor enters and takes his seat. He looks at Raymond and then at Laila. 'I see that the wife,' he twitches his mouth, 'has applied for the separation. Separation is akin to a sin. The court gives you a chance for peaceful reconciliation. I'd like to know what is going on in both your minds.'

Raymond goes first. 'I think there's a lot that our marriage has left to offer. I don't know which of my actions have hurt her, but I am ready to give this relationship another chance.'

Laila turns back to look at Ruff. Ruff gives her a nod. They have discussed this.

Laila takes another sip of water. 'I refuse to reconsider my decision. This man has physically, sexually and mentally abused me. I do not want to live with him again or to call him my husband.'

The counsellor rubs his temples. 'Mr Raymond, is there anything that you would like to tell her that would change her mind?'

Raymond turns to face Laila. 'Laila, my dear. The acts which I and anyone thinks are essential to any marriage, you refused to be a part of. Yes, I did exert force, but only because you refused to fulfil your duties as my wife.' Raymond looks at the counsellor who nods in approval. 'But if it offends or hurts you in any way, I promise to never force you again. But Laila jaan, please come back to me. The house feels empty without you.'

Laila knows it's a lie. He wants her back so he can show her that it is truly he who owns her; so that he can heal his bruised ego.

Laila follows Ruff's instructions.

Stay calm.

'I refuse to reconsider my decision,' she says, turning away from him.

Raymond doesn't wait for the counsellor to intervene. Laila can picture the smirk that is hiding behind his deceitful show of concern and sorrow.

'Why, Laila jaan? Tell me, is it true? Are the rumours true? Is there another man?'

'There is no other man. But when I married you, I was promised a man and given a monster, and that is why my decision is final.' Laila's voice starts to quiver.

'What?' Raymond erupts at a higher pitch. 'Such accusations? And I haven't even blamed you for taking my child!'

He turns to look at the counsellor, who is trying to keep up with the sharp turn the session has just taken. 'I haven't seen Jai in so long. My heart aches to hear his sweet voice, Laila jaan. I decided to forgive you for running away without so much as an apology. This is what I get in return?'

Ruff tries to signal Laila to stay quiet. This is not the place to fight it out. Laila's face is red with rage.

'Your son? A son you don't even consider to be your heir? A son you beat up just so that you could blackmail me and rape me?' Laila's hands tremble as she stands up. 'I am more of a parent to him than you could ever be, Raymond. You don't deserve a son like him. You don't deserve him!'

Raymond gets up from his chair and makes a slapping motion with his wrist. He is careful not to touch Laila. Laila falls backwards in her chair. Raymond turns towards the counsellor. 'See, see, how any man would need to discipline a woman who talks like that? I am ready to give her another chance. *Her* reputation is on the line here. I will marry someone else, have a family of my own. But no one will take her. Still, she behaves this way. What is a man to do?'

Laila tries to hold back the tears in her eyes but her trembling legs and hands give her away.

The counsellor looks at the time and stands up. 'All right, I will write in my report that this case is beyond reconciliation. Though, Miss Laila, I wish you would have tried harder.'

As the counsellor leaves the room, Raymond stands up and walks towards Laila who is now near the door, igniting an involuntary reaction from Ruff, who stands up too. Raymond leans over and whispers, 'I will win this case, Laila. One way or another, you will be in my bed again. If you want to go easy on yourself, take back your demand for a separation.'

Ruff holds a shaken Laila up and helps her walk to the car.

Not a word is uttered during the drive back home. When they reach Jasmine's building, Ruff finally breaks the silence.

'You have to stay strong, Laila,' he says as he walks her up to the little room.

Laila nods her head feebly. Then, to her surprise, he takes her hands in his and says vehemently, 'Seeing Raymond in person has given me the determination to make sure that he pays for what he's done. I promise you that we will get through this. But you have to stay strong. I promise we will win this.'

Jasmine opens the door to bring inside a shaking woman. She thanks the attorney and shuts the door. Laila remains quiet. As Jasmine serves Laila some hot chicken soup, she rests her head on her shoulder and closes her eyes.

As they lay down their sheets to sleep, Laila notices when Jasmine counts the money in her wallet. Her search for a new job has been put on hold since Laila decided to stay and turn her life upside down. But something tells her that she didn't take the journey from Mahlah to Rahat to look for a job. She scoots over to Jasmine's side and whispers, making sure not to wake the sleeping child.

'Once Raymond and I are officially separated, we'll both start working. And of course, I also have to pay you for helping me with Naya.'

Jasmine looks up at Laila and smiles, 'You know you don't have to do that. I am happy to play a small part in getting a woman elected.' Laila decides to push the conversation ahead.

'Why are you here, Jasmine? In Rahat I mean. You said you have a family still living in Mahlah.'

Jasmine shifts her gaze, but soon turns back to look at Laila. A thin line of moonlight illuminates her dark, almost black eyes. She realizes she doesn't have to hide behind a veil of self-protection any more, that she has begun to trust Laila.

'A few years ago, things changed drastically,' Jasmine looks down as she narrates her story. She removes the black-and-white photo her father from her wallet. She brushes her thumb over his face, 'My father left us.'

Laila looks at the moisture in Jasmine's eyes. She remembers the time when Ahmed used to hold her in his arms. Softly, she says, 'That makes two of us then.'

Jasmine silently stares at her father's picture for a long time. Then she looks up at Laila with her eyes full of tears.

In a rare moment of opinionated advice, Jasmine replies, 'You know where your father is, Laila. You know he is alive. All I have is a memory. My heart doesn't want to accept that I might never see my father again. But I might not. I don't know how your relationship with your father has been. But I can see that you miss him. Maybe you should try to make things better. Maybe he hasn't given up on you yet.'

Laila turns away from Jasmine. Maybe Ahmed hasn't given up on her yet, but she has given up on him.

thirty-six

Jasmine

She must be in an alternate universe. In fact, she is sure that she *is* in an alternate universe. A woman, dressed in a blue uniform, with a small gun attached to her waist, lets her in. As she enters the well-furnished lobby, with carpeted floors and leather couches, a *female* receptionist greets her. She remembers Naya's words, 'It's not exactly in the spirit of equality that we fight. But since women are hardly employed elsewhere, we try to employ mostly women in our organization.'

Jasmine wonders how Wings is able to afford such a well-maintained, luxurious centre. Perhaps it has donors.

Jasmine walks over to the receptionist.

'I'm Jasmine. Miss Naya Roben said that someone would give me a tour of the place...'

'Oh yes,' the receptionist says. She is dressed in a white blouse and black pants. Her hair is tied in a tight bun. Jasmine soon notices that everyone employed at the organization is dressed in a similar fashion. The smile plastered across the receptionist's face never once fades. Naya Roben has trained her well.

She directs Jasmine to a second, smaller waiting room. It is furnished with white leather couches, and has a fridge stocked with water and chocolates.

'Your guide will be here soon.'

The receptionist shuts the door and walks back to the front desk. A few minutes and a couple of chocolates later, a young girl walks in. She flashes Jasmine another plastered smile. As she signals for her to follow her, Jasmine notices her perfectly manicured nails. *All of them are so well groomed*! She suddenly desires to be one of them. Maybe she could apply to work in Naya's organization once she convinces her to run for the council. As the girl leads Jasmine down a corridor, she sees a line of closed doors. They're numbered workshop halls.

'You're a writer, right?' the girl asks.

'Yes,' Jasmine replies. Lost in the wonders of this haven, she had almost forgotten about her subterfuge.

'Then I'm sure you'd like to experience our writing workshop. Gilbert Hunderman, one of the most famous writers of reportage, is conducting it today. It's going to start in about twenty minutes. I have arranged a seat for you.'

The girl stops and opens the door in front of them. Workshop Room 8. Inside, there is a large round wooden table, with about twenty chairs around it. Three women are already seated, busy jotting down something in their respective journals. One looks like she is about Jasmine's age. The other two seem older. They don't look up as Jasmine walks in. She notices her name tag on the table and takes the corresponding seat. In front of her is a folder with a notepad, some writing equipment and a few sheets bearing instructions from Gilbert Hunderman.

Jasmine tries to start a conversation with the woman sitting beside her. She must be only in her thirties, but her face has already started to wrinkle. She has a white scarf tied around her head.

'Hi, is this your first time here too?'

The lady looks up at Jasmine, her eyes wide and brows knotted, making it clear that she does not want to be disturbed.

'No. Now if you'll excuse me, I need to finish my assignment before the class begins.'

So that's what they're all busy doing. A few minutes later, another girl walks in. Her emerald eyes look slightly sore, a sure sign of a sleepless night, or a few. She must be a couple of years younger than Jasmine. Her golden hair is tied up in a simple braid. She takes a seat a few chairs away from Jasmine.

Jasmine waits for her to settle down, before asking, 'Are you new here?'

The girl turns towards Jasmine. She seems to be surprised that someone is making an effort to talk to her.

'No,' she says, and then turns away.

Jasmine persists. 'How long have you been studying here?'

The girl makes the effort to talk softly. 'You must be new here. Have you not taken the orientation? We are not supposed to interact with the other girls. It's a space for skill learning, not for chit-chat. And, if you must know, I've been here for almost a year now.'

Jasmine is surprised. It's an organization that is supposed to help uplift women. It's strange that it stops them from having conversations amongst themselves. Most of the women she has met today are exactly like one other. Different in looks, but clones in behaviour.

Ironically, the pens stop writing as soon as Gilbert Hunderman enters the room. He is a rather large man, slightly bent from his spine up. His hair is as grey as his eyes, and his long face is heavily wrinkled. He is dressed in a simple blue cotton kurta and matching pants. He takes his seat on the round table. A few more girls have walked in by now.

Jasmine follows the roller coaster of a class as Gilbert makes them think of a topic, then explains how they must carry out their research, and how thorough it must be. He helps them chart out their thoughts with the help of diagrams. All of this results in a page of wonderful writing. Jasminc reads her own work in disbelief. She never thought she was capable of creating such art.

Being absolutely spellbound, she doesn't notice the queasy feeling in the pit of her stomach as she is escorted out of Wings.

thirty-seven

Laila

I am confident that you will speak the truth and support me in your testimony. I have faith that you believe in me. Please, father, don't let me down.

Laila folds the sheet of ivory paper, and places it inside an envelope. Behind it, she writes down Ahmed's name and address – her *home* address. Ruff seals it shut with his stamp. It's a simple red circle with the engraving 'Ruff Jr' on it and a picture of the scales of justice.

Ruff made Laila add the word 'father' to her last line. And 'please'. Laila wants to believe that Ahmed will support her but she doesn't know any more. There was a time, when Laila was young and Ahmed was not a councilman, that Laila and Ahmed could never consider that any opinion of theirs could be in disagreement. Laila has also written a letter to Gulzar, expecting better odds with him.

Ruff is about to leave to post the letter but Laila snatches the envelope from his hand and breaks the seal.

'Sorry,' she says. 'But will it be okay if I put in a personal request too?'

Ruff stares at her.

'Is the request related to the separation?'

Laila tries not to grin. 'No.'

'I see, and if you would have asked me a minute ago, I wouldn't have had to waste the envelope.'

Laila opens the letter. 'Well, since we've already wasted it, might as well put in the request.'

Below the last line, she starts writing, as Ruff looks on.

Also, I want to see Shadow. I request you to hand him over to me. Please bring him to my lawyer's office at three in the afternoon tomorrow.

I know you have no obligation to do so, but it would mean a lot to me. I know Shadow misses me too.

'Really? You're going to risk the sanctity of this letter for a dog?'

'So, what if he's a dog? He's family.'

Surprisingly, Ruff breaks into a smile. His face shows a sense of understanding that Laila doesn't often expect from people. She notices his dark eyes. They are tiny, but they look like they have an entire forest residing in them. Her eyes then shift to his full lips. His upper lip is slightly curved. She shifts her gaze back to his eyes, to see they are still watching her. Breaking this uncalled-for intimacy, Ruff says, 'I'm going to go send the letter now. Let's hope you get your dog tomorrow.'

'There's another thing,' Laila says. She looks down shiftily.

'What?'

'If they do send Shadow, you will have to keep him with you for a while. I don't want to give Jasmine any more trouble.'

A roughened hand rings the doorbell. It is exactly three in the afternoon. Laila jumps out of her chair in excitement. She doesn't admit it, even to herself, but she expects to see her father on the other side of the wooden door.

There is something comforting about seeing a familiar face in times of distress.

The scene that greets her is a perfect contrast of colours. A chauffeur, dressed in white, is holding little black Shadow's leash. It takes Shadow a moment to realize that it is indeed Laila who he sees and smells. He jumps and licks her face as she holds him up, scratching her along the way but she doesn't care. Laila peeks at the car parked outside. Ahmed isn't inside it. The chauffeur hands over another bag to Laila which contains a few essentials like clothes, shoes and some money for daily use. And a note with two lines – *I will not let you down. Hope you are well, Laila jaan.* Laila wonders for a moment if she should refuse to take the bag, but she is reminded of Jasmine and Jai. She thanks the chauffeur and shuts the door. Ahmed hasn't tried to reach out to Laila since she left Raymond's house. Perhaps he did try to look for her, but couldn't find her? Somewhere deep inside, she longs for familiarity, for home, but knows that she cannot go back. It is a home that *was*.

Shadow continues to lick Laila's face. She is in no hurry to calm him down. His fur is longer than usual but he is still well groomed. He is wearing her favourite collar, the black one with golden paws on it. She is sure Ahmed got him ready for the welcome. She knows he will miss Shadow. Laila smiles. At least they still have something in common.

Ruff watches as Laila plays with her terrier. She knows how her dog will react to her every action. He hasn't ever seen her so – he searches for the right phrase in his head – *at home*. He wonders how different Laila would have been when she was a Jagir; how much of herself she has lost since then.

Once Shadow settles down, she tries to help Ruff befriend him. Shadow is not very friendly with strangers. He has hardly ever been outside their mansion's premises. Laila has brought his favourite treat with her; a bribe to help him spend the night with a stranger. Ruff holds out the treat but Shadow refuses to leave Laila's lap. Laila signals for Ruff to bring the treat closer. Ruff doesn't move.

'Well, you'd both better become friends, now that you'll be living together,' she laughs.

'I did not sign up for this,' Ruff says meekly. It's just something to say. Ruff can't think straight around the little furry creature.

'Ruff, are you afraid of dogs?' Laila asks, amused.

Ruff breathes heavily as he nods his head.

Laila laughs again. 'Why didn't you tell me yesterday?'

Ruff remains quiet. He didn't even realize he had agreed to it. *Because you looked so happy.*

'I can ask Jasmine to figure out a way to keep him...'

'No, no. I'll be okay.'

'Are you sure?'

Ruff nods to give a positive confirmation.

Laila decides to leave once it starts getting dark outside. She thanks Ruff and assures him that Shadow will not harm him. She kisses Shadow and hands him over to Ruff. Shadow barks as he watches her leave.

'I'll be back soon, Shadow. Don't worry.'

Then shifting her attention to Ruff, 'I know you aren't too happy about keeping Shadow. But you don't know how much I envy you right now.'

Ruff walks her to the door. 'Don't worry; I'll make sure he's safe. Can't say the same about me, with him around.'

'Well, I'm glad you've got your priorities right,' Laila grins.

thirty-eight

Jasmine

Sitting in their small white-walled room, Jasmine tries to calm Laila down. Today is the first court hearing. Laila's long tresses fall to her waist. She sits impatiently as Jasmine combs through her locks and trims the ends. Laila needs to look presentable in the courtroom. She must look capable of looking after Jai by herself.

Once Jasmine finishes her work with the scissors, she begins to braid Laila's hair. She starts from the top, weaving small sections, and then keeps adding in more. Jai sits beside them, intrigued by Jasmine's handiwork. They have to look for a school for him once Laila wins the case. Jai needs to go back to his classes. She knows he misses them, misses his friends. Laila hasn't said much all day; just breathing heavily and rubbing her fingers together in a continuous circular motion. Her numbness seems to intensify as the hour approaches.

Laila doesn't want Jasmine to come with her to the court.

If anyone realizes that you're with me, it could put you in danger. Plus, Naya might not agree to see you again.

Jai isn't going either. Amer said he would go watch, give Jasmine the details of the proceedings.

Jasmine has put together a meal of chicken curry and hot naan. The building recently fixed a community stove, and Jasmine has been cooking often since then. Jasmine has got the knack of mixing the right flavours from her mother. Nina would always say that every person cooks the same recipe differently, but if you put your heart into the dish, it can never go wrong. This chicken curry is Nina's recipe, the one she used after Kaiza left; the one with fewer, cheaper ingredients. Every time Jasmine lights a stove, it reminds her of Nina. Something kicks her in the stomach when she thinks of her mother living alone in that old, dusty, single-storeyed house.

There are two soft knocks on the metal door; the flimsy door shaking with each knock. Jasmine feels a sense of nervousness rush through her. Laila must be going through something similar, just multiple times more intense.

Ruff has offered to drive Laila to the court. As he stands outside, giving Laila a few minutes to let it sink in that the moment has actually arrived, Jasmine notices that his long hair has been swept back, and for once he looks elegant. He is wearing a crisp blue shirt tucked into black pants. A black silk tie hangs around his neck, perfectly complementing his black coat. He looks very much like his father, barring Ruff Senior's beer belly and samosa of a nose. For Laila, they've put together a pink kurta, white pants and a fuchsia scarf, the scarf a visual reminder to the judge that she conformed to the norms of the Tony household... When Laila steps out, Jasmine sees her shoulders straighten; her anxiety transforms into determination. Jasmine knows that Laila will be able to face whatever is thrown at her in the court today because she knows her friend believes that problems and solutions come in pairs. Laila's life is a testament to her resilience.

Laila

There are about forty people seated in the gallery. *No one usually comes to watch divorce proceedings*, Ruff had told her. A thin wooden partition separates the onlookers from Laila, who is seated beside Ruff, behind a wooden table. Behind a similar table, to Laila's left, Raymond sits with his attorneys. He hasn't looked at her once since they entered the courtroom, probably on his lawyers' advice. Facing the courtroom, the judge, an old man with greying hair, sits on a pedestal, in a raised wooden enclosure. Ruff says that he is one of the more progressive judges. There is no jury present for the proceedings, only a balance resting in front of the judge, anticipating justice.

As she turns around to look at the audience, she hopes to spot a familiar face; maybe Gulzar, preferably Ahmed. Instead the only person she recognizes is Amer. Laila has not interacted with him much yet, but is grateful he is here to support her. She catches his eye and smiles. *Thank you.*

The trial is set to start in five minutes. Laila looks at Ruff. They are both concerned about their lack of witnesses, especially since Raymond could have bribed and created false witnesses.

If the judge does not come to a decision today, there will be two more sessions. If, by the end of the third session, the judge still does not make a decision then by default the marriage stands. If the separation comes through then the clauses put forward by both parties are addressed. If there is a disagreement on either the issue of property or children, another trial takes place. If the person that asked for the separation loses the ensuing trial for the clause, he or she can ask for the separation to be revoked.

Laila starts to sweat as the judge announces the session as open. Ruff glances at her and signals her to stay calm, before he walks up to present the opening of the case. *I've got this*. Just before the courtroom doors shut, there's a collective gasp from the gallery. Laila whips around to see the entire Jagir family walk in and take seats in the front row.

Standing on the witness stand, Ahmed's eyes are locked onto Laila's.

Why didn't you come to me, Laila? Why didn't you tell me about your pain, they seem to ask.

Even though she has not yet been able to forgive Ahmed, she hopes that he will not disappoint her today. Seeing her father feels surreal. He reminds her of a world that was; of a home that was, that will perhaps never be again. He reminds her of herself back when she knew what that meant. Ahmed looks different now, much older; his eyes look tired.

Ruff walks up to Ahmed to begin the questioning. He has done a really good job so far. His opening statement was so touching that Laila swears she almost saw the judge's expression become compassionate. For those few minutes, the audience felt her pain. They could picture the violence that Raymond had subjected Laila to every single night. But she doesn't only want them to feel bad for her; she wants them to be angry at what Raymond has done.

'How often did you see your daughter after she got married?' Ruff asks Ahmed.

'I saw her only three times. The first was when I visited her at their house just a few weeks after the marriage. The second time was at the council house on the day of the vote to allow women to be council members. The third time was at their house a few days after the vote.'

'And how did Laila appear the three times? What was her emotional state? What was she wearing? What was she doing? Describe everything for us please.'

'The first time I met her was at Raymond's house. She wasn't home when I arrived. She had gone to pick Raymond's son, Jai, from school. She was dressed how she is dressed right now. She wore a kurta, pants, a scarf on her head. In our house, we had no dress code in place, but she seemed to have started following the rules set in place by the Tonys. From her expression, I could see that she was uncomfortable, perhaps sad about something. As her father, I should have asked why. But I didn't...'

Ahmed turns to Laila as he speaks, as though asking for forgiveness.

'And the other two times?' Ruff prompts.

'The second time, at the council house, again, she was in similar attire. We didn't speak that day. She fainted during the session and had to be rushed to the clinic. A while later, when my brother Gulzar, Raymond and I went to see her, we found her crying. The third time, a few days after the council session, I met her at their house. I had gone to check on her health. She assured me that things were fine, but her face looked pale and her eyes sore.'

Ruff turns to the judge. 'So, your honour, both the times that Ahmed saw his daughter, she was dressed exactly as Raymond had asked her to, conforming to the norms of the Tony household; she even went and picked Jai up from school, suggesting compliance and obedience. And every time, she was not in a state of well-being.'

All she wanted her father to do was tell the truth, and he did. Laila smiles. As Ahmed leaves the witness stand, Raymond's lawyer stands. He walks up to the judge and announces, 'I would like to ask Laila Raymond Tony, my client's wife, to please come to the witness stand.

Laila stands white-faced as Raymond's attorney repeats his question.

'Did you refuse to bear my client an heir?'

She nods her head. 'Yes.'

The attorney turns to the judge. 'Yes, my client did hurt his wife a few times. But what is a man to do if not get furious when his wife does not do the one thing that is expected of her after marriage? He got angry, and he apologizes for hurting her. But he had his reasons. Later in their marriage, she even refused to get intimate with my client.'

The judge nods.

Ruff looks concerned.

As Laila leaves the witness stand, the judge calls for a break. Standing at the witness stand, Laila felt as if she was being sucked into a whirlpool. She felt helpless but also angry. How can she be expected to answer a question which itself stems from a system she doesn't believe in. She was questioned over her refusal to give this man an offspring, a decision Laila believes should be made by both parties in the marriage. But a husband's will is all that matters, the law gives the husband the right to an heir. Laila recalls why she had got into this mess in the first place – because this system is unfair. How can a woman expect justice when the laws are based in prejudice?

Laila walks out of the courtroom and finds Ruff sitting on a bench in the corridor, with his head bent over his journal. He looks up as she sits down beside him.

'Why did you marry him, Laila?' he asks, realizing that there is more to the story than she has allowed him to see.

Laila takes a deep breath and tells Ruff about the deal that she made with Raymond, about how she exchanged her life for a vote. Ruff stares at her blankly.

'I don't mean to be patronizing, but you do realize that it was an incredibly foolish thing to do, right?'

Laila smiles and places her hand on Ruff's. He doesn't want to lose her this case, but he is on the brink of thinking that he just might. Laila whispers, 'Please, call Raymond to the witness stand.'

Ruff nods. They need to prove him wrong before he catches Laila on the grounds that his actions, even the physical abuse, are justified because of the emotional turmoil *he* was going through because of *her*.

Ruff looks into Raymond's eyes, ensuring he returns his gaze.

'So, you admit that you physically hurt Laila, Raymond?'

Raymond's face clearly shows that he thinks the question is obsolete.

'Yes.'

'Because she denied you an offspring?'

'Yes.'

'Do you remember the conversation you had that day? My client said she was not comfortable having a child *at that moment*. You hadn't even been married for a month then.'

Taken aback, Raymond remains silent for a few moments and then nods. Ruff looks at the judge who has noted the affirmation.

'You beat her up because she couldn't give you the pleasure of instant gratification?' Ruff signals Laila to fold her sleeves up to reveal the marks that remain.

'You didn't just slap her or hit her once or twice. You incessantly tortured her every single night.'

Ruff continues, 'My client did not refuse to give you an heir; she only asked for some more time. Even if a woman refuses to bear an heir, the law gives a man the right to a separation, not the right to abuse. Your honour, Mr Tony beat my client up every single night, to a point where she would bleed. We have reports and lacerations on my client's body to prove the assault. Mr Tony's attorney also admitted to Mr Tony hurting my client. My client refused to get intimate with Mr Tony only after he started physically abusing her. Marriage, according to law, does not give a man the right to physically abuse a woman, but Mr Tony did, every single night. In view of my client's safety, I request your honour to grant my client this separation.'

Ruff takes a second to breathe. 'That will be all, your honour.'

As Ruff takes his seat, he thinks about how the fact that Raymond sexually abused Laila could not be brought up in this case because the concept of sexual abuse after marriage does not exist in the eyes of the law. Justice is truly blind.

Laila clenches her hands into tight fists. Her breath is slow and shallow. She stares at the judge's face but can only see blots of colour. Cream. Grey. Black. The judge addresses the room. She can hear Ruff's voice chanting softly, 'It'll be all right. It'll be all right.'

The judge speaks in a loud and clear voice. 'After listening to both sides of the story, I have come to the conclusion that it will be dangerous for Laila Raymond Tony to live with Raymond Tony any longer. Thus, after much deliberation, this court grants Laila Raymond Tony separation from Raymond Tony.'

As the tears fall, Laila makes no effort to stop them. It will take a while for it to sink in that she doesn't have to roam the streets with her face, her identity, covered any more. She is officially Laila Jagir again. A few members from the gallery cheer, a few cuss. She knows that only half the battle has been won, but she has tasted victory after so long that she believes she deserves to swim in its sweet waters until the day of reckoning comes once again.

Laila and Ruff begin gathering their things as the judge indicates he has another announcement.

'There has been a request by Councilman Raymond. The court has pondered upon it and considers it appropriate. Until the time that a decision about the custody of the child in question, Jai Raymond Tony, is made, the boy will stay in a foster home.'

All the blood rushes out of Laila's face. *No, no, no, no, no, no*, she screams in her head. Raymond's strategy suddenly becomes clear to her. Raymond had never targeted the separation. His aim had always been to win Jai's custody. After all, Jai has Raymond's blood flowing through him. Raymond also knows that not having Jai by her side while she prepares for the custody battle will weaken Laila emotionally. It was wrong of her to think that this victory would stump him. He knows that Laila will take the decision to revoke the separation if she doesn't have Jai's custody. He never wanted to win her this way; he always wanted her to beg to come back.

thirty-nine

Jasmine

The little blue backpack is a parting gift from Jasmine. Jai is dressed in his favourite white kurta.

The rain has decided to show some mercy on them. There are hardly any clouds in the sky today. In fact, the sun is shining brightly enough to light up the entire room. Their little silver lining has turned golden, a stark contrast to their gloomy faces. Jasmine watches as Laila packs Jai's clothes in a bag. She also tucks a few hundred rehats in one of his shirts. She's told him very clearly, 'If they don't treat you well, don't be afraid to leave. You know the way back home. We'll always be here for you.'

Jasmine doesn't say much. There is already a house full of emotions and she doesn't want to add to it. The trial for Jai's custody will be in two weeks. Until then, they cannot do much. Ruff and Raymond's lawyer were both called to inspect the foster home. Ruff says that the family seemed very warm.

Amer has also come to say goodbye. He has brought a little red toy car for Jai to play with. Amer seems different; his cheeks have a flush of embarrassment in them as he glances nervously at Laila. Jasmine tells herself that it's nothing.

She watches as Laila combs Jai's hair and recalls when Nina used to tie hers in a braid. Nina would yell at Kaiza when he would tell Jasmine that one day she would carry that thick braid of hers right into school. Jasmine had wanted to go to school. She always wanted to *go*, go somewhere, see the world and learn everything about it.

As Jai comes over and takes her hand in his, she understands the importance of staying. Jai and Laila have made this tiny room a home. That's what family does.

When Ruff arrives to pick them up, Jasmine kisses Jai's forehead. Jai is trying his best to smile; Laila is doing her best to assure him that they aren't parting for very long. But she chokes every time she gives him her word. Jasmine rubs her palm with her thumb and takes a few sips of water to contain her own tears. Laila picks Jai up and walks towards Ruff's car.

Amer takes Jasmine's hand as they watch the three of them leave. Jasmine realizes that Jai might never come back to live with her. Once Laila gets custody, she and Jai will go to live on their own, build their own family. Loss is a familiar pain, and Jasmine is now adept at dealing with it, but that does not mean that she finds comfort in its familiarity. As Ruff's car disappears behind the bend of the lane, Jasmine's heart aches for a home built in stone.

Later that evening Jasmine asks Amer to drop her at Naya Roben's house.

forty

Laila

Ruff brings Laila a cup of freshly brewed coffee. Shadow is sitting on her lap. The dog's excitement refuses to wear down and he tries his best to lift Laila's spirits. She instructs Shadow to sit on the floor and places her head on Ruff's polished wooden table. She knows that Jai is away only temporarily, but she can't get herself to relax. Her mind inevitably goes to the extreme.

What if I lose the case? What if the foster family abuses Jai? What have I done? He should have been with me. I'm to keep him safe.

The pain of parting threatens to engulf her chest once again. She feels helpless. When she goes back home tonight, there won't be two tiny eyes to put to sleep.

Ruff takes a seat beside her. 'Laila, like you said, regardless of what the court decides, neither of you is going back to that house. We'll find a way.'

Laila takes deep breaths and tries to vacate her mind of her fears. She lifts her head up from the table to see Ruff's dark eyes locked into hers. He is still in the same blue shirt that he'd worn yesterday. The coffee stain below his collar is proof of his lethargy. Ruff's hair is also back to its usual unruly self. She's surprised to find that she thinks it suits him better this way.

Laila isn't looking too well either. Her large eyes appear to have halved from their usual size. She is wearing a loose, crumpled red blouse and worn-out denim pants. She notices her braid has come undone and proceeds to loosen her tresses.

Keeping her gaze fixed on Ruff, she expresses her heartfelt gratitude. 'Thank you, Ruff,' she begins and then stretches her lips into a weak, but teasing smile. 'Well, I did most of the thinking; I was just thanking you for the support.'

Playfully, Ruff points to the door, 'Sure, mam. You don't appreciate my help; I don't appreciate you being here.'

Laila walks to the door, the smile now a grin plastered in place, and then stops and turns around. 'I would leave, but I don't want to leave you stranded. I know you need me here.'

Ruff makes his way towards Laila and whispers, 'Maybe I do.' Then, he extends his hand towards the doorknob, taking their game a little further. 'Maybe I don't.' But instead of the doorknob, his hands find Laila's soft red blouse. He holds her waist lightly making all the hair on Laila's body stand up. His soft eyes question her, ask her if she is okay, if the touch feels okay. The strongest memory she has of touch is rooted in violence. But she does not want her body to carry the pain of her scars, of being powerless, of belonging to someone else. She slowly and deliberately, looking for herself in her own body, moves closer to Ruff. The comfort she finds in this intimacy is alien. They swim in the intensity of the closeness for a long time, allowing her stiffened body to slowly breathe. She wants to take back control of her body. It will take time, but slowly, she knows she will ensure that she heals. She delicately, hesitantly, lifts her hand and cups his stubbled chin with her palm, her face a couple of inches away from his. She notices the perfect curve of his upper lip. As she brings her face closer to his, her eyes closed, suddenly his hands drop from her waist and her lips taste air instead of his lips.

Laila opens her eyes wide, and they embody as much fury as the red in her cheeks display her embarrassment. As Ruff extends an arm to caress her cheek, she lightly slaps it away. He rushes to clarify. 'Laila, I want this. I want to hold you right now and kiss you. But if the court finds out that you're seeing someone, the chances of you claiming Jai's custody will be close to nothing.'

But how would anyone know, her eyes say, surly as ever.

'Maybe no one will find out. But one thing I've learned is that secrets are difficult to hide. Your tongue doesn't narrate them, but your eyes always do; loud and clear.'

Laila's heart flutters when Ruff looks down at the floor to hide the blush on his cheeks.

Laila smiles too, at another unexpected reason to win the case.

The wooden table between them suddenly seems wider. They try not to let the blood rushing to their cheeks show. Both of them are deliberately trying to focus on the work that lies ahead, but Ruff unwittingly keeps sneaking glances at Laila.

Laila clears her throat. Ruff takes the cue and buries his nose in his book. A few minutes later, Laila clears her throat again. Ruff looks up, a taunting look on his face.

Yes, sahiba? Your wish is my command.

Laila sighs. 'I don't know what I want. I'm sorry. I just have so many things running through my mind, even apart from this case. I try to focus on only the trial, but my mind does not stop.'

Ruff smiles at her. 'So tell me; it'll help you clear your mind.'

Laila hesitates for a moment. She purses her lips together before letting out a sigh and then says, 'I've always wanted to…to change the way society thinks. It thinks only in boundaries, very restrictive boundaries. Not saying that the way that I think is perfect, but I know that I think in terms of freedom and that has to be better than boundaries, right? I've always wanted to fight for the rights of those who are oppressed, help make them realize that they do have a voice. And now, it's probably going to happen. A woman is going to stand for the council elections and I should feel satisfied. But I don't; I just feel like I have so much more to offer.'

Ruff shoots Laila a confused look. She continues after a brief pause.

'The council elections. Yes, women are now allowed to be voted into the national council, but what's the use of it if no woman stands for the election? So, I asked Jasmine to convince Naya Roben. I mean, she's perfect. In fact, Jasmine is supposed to go there today, but I just don't feel –'

'Laila, wait. Do you mean Naya Roben, the founder of Wings, wife of ex-chief of police Ayen Roben?' Ruff thunders, cutting her off.

Laila nods, but is visibly confused by his reaction.

Ruff begins his story in a hushed voice. 'Five years ago, her training institute approached one of my cousins to work as a receptionist there. It wasn't that well known then, so I decided to look into it and do a background check. Everything looked fine on the surface, but when I wanted to track down a few Wings graduates to find their employment status, things started to get suspicious. I could not find them at their listed organizations of employment, so I dug deeper.'

Laila is silent. Ruff continues, 'Laila, she runs a trafficking ring under the guise of a legitimate organization. And she has many more illegal businesses. I've been onto her for years now, trying to gather evidence to file a case against her. But there's no solid proof. She leaves no trail.'

Laila, shocked at the revelation, tries to get her thoughts in order, 'Ruff, are you sure about this?'

'Yes. I found one of the women who was supposed to be employed at a printing press. She was sold to a wealthy man in Baugh. I went to their house in the guise of a cloth merchant and was able to have a conversation with the woman in private. The woman told me about Naya's trafficking trade, but refused to come out in public. A few weeks after that meeting, the woman and the man both moved out of their house and I wasn't able to track them again.'

Numbness surrounds Laila as she repeats, 'But do you believe her? Are you sure?'

'Laila, like I said, I don't have any concrete proof. But yes, I believe her.'

Laila's breath becomes shorter. She trusts Ruff's judgement. Jasmine was supposed to have a meeting with Naya this evening. She could be there right now and could be in danger. Without waiting a moment and without warning, Laila gets up and runs out the door.

Oh my god, I have to stop Jasmine.

forty-one

Jasmine

Jasmine hastily straightens the small wrinkle on her blouse before Naya makes her entrance. Jasmine has made sure to iron out every crease in her outfit. She is wearing a peach blouse with white pants borrowed from Laila. Subtle, yet elegant. Not a single strand of hair sneaks out of Jasmine's white scarf. It is difficult to match Naya's elegance and perfection; Jasmine can't help but try.

She taps her fingers on the leather couch as Naya takes longer than anticipated to arrive and then forces herself to stop fidgeting. *Would Naya do this?* She repositions herself, placing one knee on another, her hands gracefully folded on top of her legs.

As always, Naya makes a stellar entrance. Her striped silk pants and matching jacket reflect light, her presence quite literally illuminating the room. She smiles at Jasmine as she takes a seat opposite her. What really impresses Jasmine is how respectfully Naya treats her; her stature, experience, social standing notwithstanding. Naya's presence overwhelms Jasmine. It reminds her of another time, a time when she looked up to someone else kinder, wiser, more intelligent, more cultured than her, a time when she looked up to her father. Suddenly, she finds in Naya what she wasn't even aware she was looking for, what she was never able to find in her mother – a role model.

Two women bring in plates of exotic fruit and an assortment of pastries. Instead of diving right into the rich piece of chocolate cake making her mouth water, Jasmine waits for Naya's invitation.

'Jasmine, have some.'

Jasmine proceeds to indulge herself in the chocolate cake. Naya picks up a wedge of a perfectly sliced peach.

'So, I assume you liked the writing workshop.'

'Yes. I didn't even know that I could write so well.'

'But aren't you an aspiring writer?'

Swimming in Naya's charm, Jasmine has forgotten her guise once again. She covers up her lapse quickly. 'Yes, yes, but that workshop took me beyond what I thought I could do with my words.'

They chat for a few minutes, until Naya's half an hour allotted to their meeting is almost up.

'So, Jasmine, is there anything else you'd like to know?' Naya asks. Jasmine notices Naya signalling something to one of the girls waiting on her, perhaps something about making certain arrangements for the next meeting. Still there is no sense of urgency in her voice, only politeness.

Jasmine hesitates, but she knows that this is as good a chance as she will ever get. 'Well, I'm sure that you're aware of the council's decision to allow women to be a part of it. What are your thoughts on it?'

Naya smiles. 'From the first time I saw you, I knew you were a girl who asks the right questions; questions that matter.' Jasmine tries unsuccessfully to hide the red in her cheeks. Naya continues, 'I think it's one of the most progressive decisions our council has made. I am certain that it will change the course of the nation, and pave the way for a fairer, more equal society. 'Though this should have happened decades ago, I am happy that this absolutely necessary step has finally been taken.'

Now Jasmine is too eager. 'Who do you think would make a good councilwoman, if you had to suggest someone?'

'I can't think of anyone at this moment, but I'm sure that there is a wise woman out there who's cut out for it.' She smiles nonchalantly.

'I, I think you'd make a brilliant councilwoman. You're smart, elegant, someone that people can look up to, and you're already making such a huge difference to young women's lives,' Jasmine gushes.

Naya Roben's fixed smile changes to something a lot more pensive. Her brows knit to form the first crease that Jasmine has seen on her face. Her lips twitch, and for a few minutes she says nothing. There is almost a look of regret on her face, as if she's wondering why she hadn't thought of this idea herself.

She finally says, 'Jasmine, I can't thank you enough. I've been trying to find a way to reach out to more people, and you just gave me the answer.'

Jasmine has crumbs of pastry around her lips that she clumsily dusts off. Naya Roben doesn't seem to care very much about it though. She asks one of the servants to get Jasmine a napkin and signals for her to enjoy herself some more.

A young girl hands the napkin to Jasmine. As Jasmine looks up to thank the girl, she realizes that it's the same young girl she had met at the writing workshop. She tries to voice the words 'thank you', but her mind and tongue don't seem to be able to coordinate.

Suddenly, the bright living room of Naya's house appears grey, and the queasy feeling from her visit to Wings returns to her stomach. She tries to hide her uneasiness, and continues talking to Naya.

At one point, Naya even asks what Jasmine has been waiting to hear.

'I think you're a smart girl. Would you like to be a part of my organization?'

Jasmine smiles, elated.

It takes her a while to realize that the queasy feeling in her stomach is quite real. She looks at the cake and wonders if she has gotten sick from eating it. Her palms begin to sweat, and she fights her body's urge to collapse. The room around her grows dimmer. Jasmine shakes herself awake. She does not want Naya to see her in this vulnerable state.

'Can I use the washroom, please?'

Naya looks at the blonde-haired girl. 'Aneya, please show her the way to the washroom. Look after her and bring her back here.'

Aneya nods. The girl takes Jasmine by the hand. After walking for a few minutes, Aneya points towards a door. Jasmine opens it only to be hit by cold wind and a few drops of rain. She looks at Aneya accusingly – *that's not a washroom* – not realizing in her sedative state that Aneya has taken her to the back exit of Naya's house.

Jasmine is unsure of what is happening. She doesn't want to leave without giving Naya a reasonable explanation, but her senses are fading, so it would perhaps be better to get home? Jasmine feels Aneya's hands vigorously shake her shoulders. Aneya gets Jasmine to look at her and mouths a three-letter word that Jasmine understands perfectly.

'RUN!'

forty-two

Laila

The blue plastic sheet is nowhere to be found, and splatters of rain from the window fall directly on Jasmine's face. Laila directs all of her strength into dragging the mattress that Jasmine is lying on to the other side of the room and places a blanket over her.

Laila and Ruff had just reached the vicinity of Naya Roben's house, when they found Jasmine stumbling out of the smaller rear gates of the mansion. Laila had never seen anyone's face so completely pale before. Laila had put Jasmine's life at risk, and for what? Trying to put a woman in the council?

A woman that I *thought fit the bill?*

Ahmed's words echo in her ears. *Your reckless behaviour is going to cause big trouble one day, Laila. It's high time that you stop. You're not a child any more!*

She thrashes away any attempt at an explanation that doesn't involve her being guilty. As she wonders if the people she loves would be safer, happier, without her in their lives, Laila feels the rare pang of guilt intensify, and understands its lure. Perhaps guilt rids the brain of the need to step out of its patterns, offers an odd comfort. It provides an explanation for life's apparent unfairness, and makes the mind more at home, if only for a brief moment. But Laila has also noticed that guilt very quickly transforms into an incessant anxiety, an inability to think clearly, and cajoles the mind into inaction. It is not going to help her better people's lives; it is not going to help her stay strong right now, when it is most necessary. So, she allows herself to swim in it for the night, but knows that with the fresh morning air, she must let go of the guilt.

forty-three

Jasmine

Jasmine's hand fails to find the pot of water that usually lies near her bed. Her throat is dry and her body feels sore. She opens her eyes to see that Laila has moved her across the room.

Surprisingly, Laila is still asleep. It takes Jasmine a few minutes to recall the events of the previous evening, but even then she can only fill so many blanks. She waits for Laila to wake up.

Naya Roben. Her lips twitch even at the thought of her name.

Her heart stops when she realizes that she could have just *disappeared* yesterday. She had been drugged, that she is sure of. If Laila and Ruff hadn't immediately come searching for her, she would have just vanished. *Would Amer think I betrayed him?* Jasmine draws a sharp breath. That's what she, Nina and Sabaar had done to her father. They just assumed that he had betrayed them; for so many years, not one of them tried to find him. They didn't think that he could be in trouble. For the first time, Jasmine completely forgives Kaiza. She stops the tears from forming in her eyes. She *has* to find out what happened to her father, but before that she has something more important to do. She has a nation to save. From a woman.

A thought has been brewing inside Jasmine for a long time. In that atmosphere of gloom, Jasmine lets her tired muscles smile. *It is perfect.*

Jasmine sprinkles a few drops of water on Laila's face. She is surprised to see Laila still asleep. Laila is an early riser and it's late in the afternoon already. Jasmine slept a long while because of the sedative in Naya's chocolate cake.

When the water droplets touch Laila's eyelids, she stirs hesitantly. Once Laila opens her eyes and Jasmine's face comes into view, she immediately sits up, holds Jasmine lightly by her shoulders and asks, 'Jasmine, how are you feeling? Are you okay?'

Jasmine nods and then proceeds to hug Laila. They briefly discuss the previous night's events and Laila explains what she found out through Ruff. As Jasmine fully realizes what could have happened last night, her expression morphs into one of fear.

'I cannot even begin to explain how sorry I am, Jasmine,' Laila continues, 'I should have found out…'

'Laila, how could you have known?' Jasmine says, still shaken. 'It isn't your fault. This is a lot to take in for both of us, but I think you should know that Naya is planning to stand for the elections.'

'Wait, you managed to have that conversation with her? You managed to convince her?'

'What can I say, even when I'm in trouble, I'm resourceful,' Jasmine teases Laila, easing the grim atmosphere.

Laila looks heartened by Jasmine's unfazed spirit. Then she grows reflective before she says, 'I know that Gulzar Uncle is also going to stand for the elections. He doesn't really want to, but Grandfather will force him. If we help him defeat Naya, there won't be a woman on the council, but at least there will be a good man. Though Naya is a master of hiding evidence, Ruff has been observing her for years. We may find something in his files. Plus, we have your testimony. Of course, Gulzar Uncle isn't the most charming, but grandfather will put in all his resources and, with a little help, he can win. It's not –'

'Laila, stop!' Jasmine swallows the lump in her throat. She cannot keep it to herself any longer. As she watched Laila take charge of her life over the last few weeks, this thought crossed her mind many times, but she hadn't acknowledged it fully till this morning. 'Your uncle can't defeat Naya. But I know someone who can.'

Jasmine enjoys the curious glance that Laila throws at her.

'You, Laila. You should stand for the council election. I don't know of anyone more capable. Or deserving.'

forty-four

Laila

The thin white sheets of printed paper flutter with the wind. It has taken her a couple of days, along with Jasmine and Ruff's counsel, to come up with the proposal. She would have liked more time, but with the decision for the final council nominees due next week, she needs to submit the proposal as soon as possible. She's sure that most of her competitors have already handed over theirs.

The existing council decides who the candidates for the next election are going to be. Each hopeful's proposal is submitted anonymously, which is the only reason that Laila is even considering her chances. One council member cannot approve more than one proposal, and an existing council member can directly stand for the elections without presenting a proposal. This allows for a maximum of five candidates to stand for the election in any given year. If a minimum of three proposals are not approved, the council takes a collective decision on whom to nominate. Laila knows how exactly to bring her father's attention to her proposal. But his loyalties already lie with his brother; his *real* family, the kind of family that a daughter can never be.

Laila gets out of bed to look at her proposal again. It has ten signatures. *Jasmine. Amer. Mr Ruff. Ruff Junior. And a few more people from Jasmine's old workplace.* A proposal must have at least a hundred signatures from the people of the district that the candidate is standing from before it can be passed on to the council for approval.

A proposal also needs to have a manifesto, containing a list of points describing what a candidate intends to work towards if elected to the council. Her proposal is simple and clearly worded.

One. Movement for the inclusion of more girls in schools, through a ten-year period of 10 per cent reservations and through awareness programmes.

Five. Strengthening the sewage network to avoid flooding during the monsoons through active re-engineering.

Thirteen. Increasing the transparency of the accounts of council candidates and council members through full disclosure of finances and sources of income.

There's a long way ahead, but for the first time, she's sure of her path. Laila was taken aback when Jasmine suggested that she stand for the council elections. Despite being from the Jagir family, despite always wanting to work for the betterment of the nation, this thought had never crossed her mind. But the more she thought of Jasmine's suggestion, the more it seemed right. She knows she is a deserving councilwoman for Rahat because she truly wants to see its people live better lives, and she has spent a large part of her life trying to make that happen in whatever way she could. Her decision reminds her of the times she saw her father campaign, of how her heart swelled with pride every time she saw his campaign flag. This is a fresh turn her life has taken, and still she feels a certain sense of homecoming. Perhaps she had always wanted to be a change maker, a leader, a councilwoman, but had never realized it before.

She checks the proposal for any creases and errors. She has already made Ruff's typist print it twice. Once she is satisfied, she places the papers in a cream cloth folder and holds it close to her chest. The folder might be safer elsewhere but having it beside her calms her nerves. Her excitement and anxiety don't allow her to sleep for long.

She wakes up early the next morning. It is still dark outside. Jasmine is asleep; her usually soft snores are louder today. Looking at the four bare walls and the tiny window, Laila sighs; she has a feeling that these are her last few days here.

forty-five

Jasmine

The rubbery smell of the train station fills her up. Jasmine doesn't welcome the nostalgia. Once again, watching the trains rush by; once again, seeking help from strangers. It reminds her of the time she had just arrived in Rahat to look for her father. But instead of a black-and-white photograph, today she holds a copy of a document in her hand.

They have decided that Laila needs to stay out of the public eye before the council approves her proposal. Nobody is going to sign it if they find out that it's by one of the most controversial women in Rahat. Jasmine has promised Laila that she will get the hundred required signatures for her. Meanwhile, Laila can work on Jai's case. But it's turning out to be more difficult than Jasmine had thought.

It has been over an hour since Jasmine reached the station. She started by being polite but has now taken to waving the proposal in people's faces. Neither approach has worked. Exhausted, Jasmine sits down on a bench. A young woman takes a seat beside her. She looks a couple of years younger than Jasmine. Jasmine notices that the girl is fidgeting with her sleeves and is constantly shifting her reddened eyes from one side of the train station to another.

'Hey, is everything all right?' Jasmine asks her.

'Yes,' says the girl with the bloodshot eyes.

Jasmine isn't convinced. She worries that the girl is in trouble or is hiding from someone. To allow her to open up, Jasmine takes a deep breath, then softly, says, 'You know, I ran away from home a few months ago. You can tell me if something's bothering you; I won't cause any trouble. Maybe I can help.'

'Thank you,' the girl responds kindly, 'I don't need any help. I work at a tailor's shop as an apprentice and my family doesn't know it. I spotted my father here a few minutes ago. I am waiting so I don't run into him on my way out.'

Jasmine smiles, relieved, and instinctively shows the proposal to the young girl. As the girl finishes reading it, she takes the pen from Jasmine's hand and signs her name at the bottom. Eleven. Before the girl leaves, she looks at Jasmine and says, 'I hope you get the number of signatures that you need. And I hope it's for a woman.'

Jasmine retrieves the key from under the jute mat and unlocks the door. Laila is not home yet. It will give her some time to prepare to tell Laila of her failure. She wants to run out into the streets, try, try harder. Helplessness overcomes her.

She glances at the number of signatures again. *Eleven.*

For the rest of the day, Jasmine tried to get signatures at the metro station, at the promenade and at bus stands. But no one was willing to stop for, read, let alone sign a proposal being handed out by a seventeen-year-old girl.

Jasmine looks outside the window. It is becoming dark already. Then, a knock on the door. Jasmine walks to the door nervously, expecting to see Laila.

But when she opens the door, Amer stands before her, soaking wet. He always forgets to carry an umbrella. As he steps inside the room, she catches, with her lips, a drop of water sliding off his jaw then slowly moves upwards to meet his. There's nothing like Amer to brighten a disheartening day for Jasmine.

'How come you're here? Didn't you have a late meeting today?' Jasmine pulls away from him and asks.

Amer answers with a rush in his voice, as if he'd remembered some urgency at hand. 'It's about the proposal. We need to leave right away.'

Amer changes into a dry shirt before they walk into a brightly lit room in the hotel Amer is staying at. Inside, already assembled are about twenty jewellers and their families. The thick smell of the old dusty maroon carpet in the room fills Jasmine's nose. Jasmine used to be allergic to dust when she was a child. But years of living around sofas that never got dusted, and windowsills that never got wiped clean, have made her body immune to more things than just dust.

Amer proceeds to address the gathering. Jasmine looks on bemused as he holds the proposal in front of him and begins to read it aloud, word by word. He has to repeat a lot of the sentences. There are too many people in the small room and their internal chatter is drowning out his voice. It takes him more than a few minutes to reach the end of Laila's proposal. Once he finishes, he clears his throat. 'Does anyone have any questions?'

A hand shoots up in the air. 'So if each of us gets at least five people to sign this, you will sell cut diamonds to us at 10 per cent below the market price for the next two years?'

Jasmine watches intently as Amer nods. 'Yes, and I want to make it clear that you are all signing this because you have heard the entire proposal and support what it has to say.'

Jasmine pulls Amer aside and whispers urgently, 'Amer, are you sure you want to do this?'

Amer smiles at Jasmine. 'It's a small price to pay. Don't worry, it's not as bad as it sounds. Even if it was, I think it's worth it.'

Traders and their families line up to sign the ten-page document. Jasmine reckons that most of them would have signed it even if Amer hadn't read out the proposal to them. It was probably his attempt to add some legitimacy to the barter.

Jasmine knows this is not the right way to collect signatures, and she doesn't know if she should tell Laila about this. The result is fair, Jasmine is sure of that. Laila needs to run for council. But what's the point if they use money and power to get her there? *Doesn't that make us like everyone else, like the people who took away the diner?*

Jasmine tries to disperse these thoughts. *Do you sometimes need a crooked finger to properly clean a jar?*

The jewellers sign and leave, not forgetting to threaten Amer on their way out.

'If you don't hold up your side of the deal, just remember that no amount of money can fight a hundred angry hands.'

Jasmine counts the signatures.

One hundred and eleven.

One night *can* make a difference.

forty-six

Laila

The wind morphs the red and blue of the paper windmill in Laila's hand into a violet blur. As the sun starts to go down, the shopkeepers switch on their incandescent bulbs, and rows of small colourful lights shine brightly. The sky, transitioning from its tangerine hues to make way for the moonlight, continuously shifts, its surface coloured sometimes ivory, sometimes sand.

As Jasmine leads Laila towards a kulfi stall, they pass the same sign that she'd seen years ago in a newspaper. A golden setting sun with animated firecrackers around it.

The Twilight Fair. It happens once every year in Rahat. Hundreds of shopkeepers set up makeshift stalls to sell handmade leather goods, bags, woollen shawls, scarves and stone and marble carvings. There are food vendors located every few steps offering everything from ice cream to kebabs. There's even a musician, singing for tips, and another performer, juggling five blue-and-red balls. And importantly, there are women; mostly with their husbands, but there are women, shopping by themselves too.

Laila had always wanted to visit this fair but Ahmed never let her. He never liked being in crowded places, so he didn't let Laila go either.

The malai kulfi melts in Laila's mouth. Jasmine has ordered the mango-flavoured one. It was Laila's idea to take Jasmine to the fair. It's difficult to not pamper the woman who is the reason that she has a chance to be part of the national council. The *national council.* Regardless of whether her candidacy is approved, Laila wants to show her appreciation for Jasmine's hard work and constant support. Plus, they both need a bit of festivity in their lives. Laila has noticed that Jasmine has a flair for such things – the food, the dresses, the culture. As a child, Laila often wondered how people alien to her lived, but she never had an affinity towards exploring the world. Laila's world was, and is, Rahat, this nation. She suspects that it's not the same for Jasmine.

Laila picks out a fuchsia scarf for Jasmine, one with a white leaf design. Jasmine knows that there is no denying Laila something once she has her mind on it, and so she accepts the scarf and wraps it around her neck.

Laila smiles. 'It suits you.'

They walk past the shops, stopping every few minutes to examine the exquisite handicrafts on display. Laila wonders what could be done to increase the income of local craftsmen. Then she grins at how she already pictures herself as a councilwoman. But she soon takes a couple of steps back in her mind to avoid potential heartbreak.

The market's firework display starts later than expected. Jasmine tells Laila that she has never seen a rocket go up in the air and burst into colourful stars of light before. When the spectacle begins and the sparks light up the sky, some shooting straight into the air, some spiralling, Laila gawks, just as enchanted as Jasmine, at the million tiny specks of dancing light which for that one brief moment turn the dark night sky into a colourful celebration.

Sitting in Ruff's comfortable chair, Laila stares at the letter before her in a daze. It has been a week since her proposal was submitted to the council. She had given Ruff's address in the proposal. Even though the proposals are submitted anonymously to the voting council members, personal information needs to be filled out at the time of submission so the court can look into the potential candidate's records and conduct a cursory background check. Laila reads the letter again just to make sure. Goosebumps erupt over her body.

'Your candidacy has been approved.'

She doesn't know who approved her proposal. Four candidates have been chosen this year, including Naya Roben. The others are Gulzar Jagir and Ibra Nader. Ibra Nader is the son of industrialist Petra Nader. Their family is into coal mining and construction. Laila had seen both father and son at a party once. Ibra is a few years older than she is, and she remembers that she had hit it off with him quite well.

Ruff and Jasmine envelop Laila in a tight hug. Laila swears that she even saw Jasmine do a little dance when she read the letter. Jasmine vehemently denies the accusation. This is the first time that Jasmine has come to Ruff's office, and Ruff has made his special coffee to welcome her. As Jasmine tastes it, Laila can tell that she doesn't like it. Laila laughs as she continues to drink it anyway. *I like my coffee with milk*, she would tell Laila later, who would then fill in Ruff on her trusted adviser's preferences.

Laila wishes that Jai could be with her during these happy times; all the boy has seen with her is sorrow. Jai has to come home. Laila wonders what she will do if she loses to Raymond in the custody trial. Can she still take Jai and run now that she is at the centre of the public eye? She would though; she would take him and run somewhere far away without giving her candidacy a second thought.

As it starts to get dark, the three of them head back to Jasmine's one-room home to continue their discussion about the campaign. The first step is to look for sponsors. They will need money for almost any campaign-related activity. A campaign also needs a symbol, a theme that will resonate with the people; something other candidates haven't thought of that will hit the right spot. She remembers her father's campaign. 'A complete life'. His was a perfect campaign. He was up in the polls throughout and his victory was anything but surprising. Both the Jagirs standing for this year's election don't know perfection.

Laila saw an advertisement for a fizzy drink that sparked the idea. A man jumping up in the air. Freedom; or so they promise one will feel after a few sips of their lemon fizz. There wasn't really much in the advertisement, but sometimes certain images pop up at the right moment to spark what is necessary. Laila has decided to have three upward pointing arrowheads as her campaign symbol, conveying freedom, fairness and moving ahead. Free. Fair. Forward.

Laila hopes this symbol will stir people. She wants to make people first see the problem, acknowledge that it exists instead of making the problem so commonplace everyone is indifferent to it. She wants equal treatment for all citizens. Equality is a necessity for the future. She wants to build programmes to change mindsets. She wants all people to live their fullest lives, not just women. For example, someone like Gulzar. He would have contributed a lot more to the world as an artist than he does as an aspiring councilman. Or Ruff's fathers, who never got the opportunities others did. Laila wants to create social change and break the barriers that people have built in their minds, make them look beyond the rigid traditions they hold so dear and believe they must follow for a better life.

Laila thinks about her symbol again and wonders if her campaign would have stood a chance against her father's. But after a moment of quiet reflection, Laila does something that surprises herself. She peeks in her head, picks Ahmed up from the pedestal and places him on the floor, right in front of her.

forty-seven

Jasmine

He is seated at the other end of the first row, between his foster parents, and dressed in a white silk shirt and striped black trousers; far nicer than anything Jasmine can afford. His dark hair has been combed back. His brown eyes peek at her through the mesh of arms between them. When her eyes meet Jai's, she can tell that he is afraid.

As he walks into the courtroom, Jasmine gets her first look at Raymond. He is wearing a maroon cotton kurta with matching pants. Jai has definitely got his eyes from his father, but fortunately, he hasn't inherited the constant look of superiority in them.

Jasmine looks around for a Jagir in the courtroom. Amer points her to Laila's uncle who is seated a few seats away from them.

It has been two weeks since Laila and Raymond's separation was announced. The judge had given both sides time to prepare for the custody trial, but the day is finally here.

This is the first time that Jasmine has ever been in a courtroom. Laila had hesitated when Jasmine said that she wanted to attend, but now that Laila is in every newspaper and Jasmine is helping with her campaign, there is no use hiding. They can also use this gathering of wealthy people as an opportunity to seek some funds. Most importantly, Jasmine wants to be here for Laila.

They watch in anticipation as Ruff walks up to deliver his opening statement.

His hands are shaking, but his voice is loud and clear. He wastes no time in getting to the point. 'On the second Tuesday of the last month, Jai Tony was awakened by his father, Raymond Tony, in the middle of the night. What was the emergency, you ask? Raymond woke Jai up and dragged him to a room where Laila had locked herself to be safe from Raymond's harassment, *physical and sexual* harassment. He brought the boy to the door and threatened to beat him up if she failed to give in to his demands. My client, being extremely affectionate towards the child, opened the door when she heard his cries and realized that it was not a bluff. The threats were not made in vain, your honour. When she opened the door, she found Jai lying on the floor, red-faced and teary-eyed. Raymond is a man who held his kid hostage, a man who didn't think twice before hurting his child. It is unsafe for Jai to live with his father.'

When both sides are done presenting their statements, Raymond's lawyer calls Jai to the stand.

Laila

The crowd starts to leave, and soon, only Laila and Ruff are in the courtroom. She is happy that the case has at least been granted an extension. At one point, even that seemed impossible. The next session will be in five days.

She knew it even before Jai's words came out of his mouth. The widening of his brown eyes, the constant clicking of his tongue, the heavy breathing, the guilt. When he spoke, it hardly came as a shock; more like an end to hopeful anticipation. 'Father never hit me. Father would never hurt me.' And then, with more pain in his voice than any ten-year-old should have, 'He is the one who truly loves me.'

Jai ran out of the witness box as soon as he finished uttering those words. Ruff immediately complained of witness tampering. Laila knows that the judge also saw the nervousness in Jai. That's the only reason she can think of for him not giving Raymond a clear win.

One of the officers comes in and requests them to leave the courtroom. As they walk out, Laila looks at Ruff, who seems to be panicking. Surprisingly, Laila herself is not shaken. The fact that Raymond would go to the lengths of threatening and blackmailing Jai has made her furious; it has made her stronger. She is now standing with a crossbow aimed at his head.

forty-eight

Jasmine

The man's pointed black hat distracts from his flat nose. The skin on his pale face is too taut for a sixty-year-old. Jasmine wonders why he is keen on watching this trial. But the wealthy and the retired have their own ways to pass time. Maybe they're even betting on the result. She tries not to club every well-to-do man into the category of Raymond, but it's hard for her not to do so.

Jasmine doesn't have time to think about the events that unfolded. As soon as they leave the courtroom, Jasmine walks up to the man in the black hat and introduces herself. 'Hello, Mr Wolfe, I'm from Laila's campaign team. I was wondering if I could take two minutes of your time?'

Wolfe stops walking and looks straight at Jasmine, his piercing grey eyes looking straight into her dark eyes. 'So, Laila has a campaign team, huh? At least she managed to convince someone that she can win. I don't think she's going to win this case. And I don't think she's going to win the election. Women like her are born to sin and I don't support a sinner, a home-breaker, a child stealer. If you're looking for funding, please go elsewhere.'

He walks away with an air of superiority. But beggars can't be choosers and Jasmine has to make do with the few wealthy men who are in the courtroom today.

Jasmine grunts as she thinks about the other hopefuls, especially Naya Roben. She wonders how much of her trafficking money Naya will put into her campaign. She remembers the face of the green-eyed girl who saved her life. She wonders if she will ever be able to repay the favour.

As she walks up to other wealthy men, she hears variations of the same answers. 'A woman? I will not support a woman being elected to the council.' 'Laila is a home-breaker, a sinner.' 'Oh dear, I don't think she has it in her.'

There are also a few indirect and more tolerable answers. 'Sorry, I'm not interested.' 'I don't want to align myself with any candidate yet.' 'We don't have those kinds of funds right now.'

A few people even make a dash to try and save Jasmine. 'Poor girl, how did she convince you to do this? Tell me, is she hurting you? Has Laila abducted your son too?'

It is necessary for Laila to win Jai's custody, not just to save Jai, not just to bring justice for herself, but also to save a campaign that hasn't even begun yet.

Mr Ruff and Amer have contributed whatever they could. Jasmine reckons that they will have to start campaigning with the little that they have. Laila refused to ask the Jagirs for a donation. Even though the tensions between Laila and Ahmed seem to have eased slightly after Ahmed's testimony, Jasmine senses that Laila still harbours years of grievances. Jasmine wonders if she should reach out to Ahmed in private for monetary help on behalf of Laila. Jasmine cannot believe that she is thinking of reaching out to the man who took away the diner from her. But she isn't looking at Ahmed as the ruthless businessman; she is looking at him as a father. *Father.* Jasmine does not know if she will ever find hers. Also, they do really need the funding. There isn't much time left for the elections, and Laila doesn't just have an image to build; first she has an image to repair.

forty-nine

Laila

The loud knocks on the door jerk her out of her sleep. She looks over to the other side of the room. Jasmine is still fast asleep. It was a rough day at the court and they are both exhausted. Laila wonders who it could be this early in the morning.

'Who is it?' she yells, waking Jasmine up.

Ruff shouts from the other side, 'It's Ruff, Laila. Open up.'

Jasmine, who is now sitting up on her mattress, can't resist the temptation. 'Yes, it's a *rough* life, I understand. But isn't it too early in the morning to rant about it?'

Laila chuckles as she opens the door. The morning dew makes her want to grab his face and plant a kiss on his lips. But all she can give him is an unsolicited, yet welcome hug. When she pulls away, she feels a strong pull drawing her back into his arms. Their minds try and resist the attraction, but their bodies are like two magnets being forced apart.

Laila notices the expression on Ruff's face and her smile quickly fades.

'What's wrong?'

Ruff hands a newspaper to Laila. *Rahat Times*. It is the most widely read paper in the entire nation. Laila doesn't have to turn the page to find out the reason behind Ruff's glum countenance. It is right there, at the bottom-left corner of the front page.

Laila passes the newspaper to Jasmine, who looks visibly embarrassed by what she is seeing. There is a small picture of Jasmine talking to Ryan Fermago, an established realtor. Above the picture are two lines intent on ruining Laila's non-existent political career.

'Laila Jagir forces young girl to beg for money for her campaign at the trial'. Then, in smaller font, 'Is she using a ten-year-old boy to give her political campaign some much-needed momentum?'

Beg *for money*? Forces *young girl*? The tabloids are at it again. The article inside mentions how the newspaper had predicted Laila's downfall when she was only eighteen. The entire town was talking about it then. Laila still remembers the headline. 'Jagir girl passes marriageable age. Has this cinnamon-haired beauty's behaviour caused her future to head down a spiral?'

Laila grunts. Years of being in the news have taught her to ignore the press. But Jasmine and Ruff are still new to this world of media. The *free* press. Perhaps the only thing that's free in this country. Free to sell print based on assumption instead of fact. Free to add spice to make the assumption readable. Sometimes even free to get paid to put other people's assumptions in print. Anything to sell a paper. Anything to make a quick rehat.

Jasmine

As she blows on the paper to dry the black ink, she wonders if this is the right thing to do. She's sure that Laila wouldn't approve. But if this works, it could prove to be extremely fruitful.

In the few days that have passed after her courtroom debacle, they've written letters, approached people at events and even gone knocking from door to door. Jasmine is sure she saw one of the house's security guards holding her picture from the newspaper. Do not let this girl in. There is not much they can do when every potential investor runs away at the sight of Laila's name. They don't even want to give her a chance to prove herself. But Jasmine understands that if someone knows of Laila's potential, it is her father. She is sure that behind the cold relationship, there is still a warm heart waiting to melt. She often forgets that everyone is not Kaiza.

You know that Laila will make the perfect councilwoman. You know that she is cut out for this. Your daughter needs your help now, more than ever before. Giving funds to her will not affect your financial position, but it will help her immensely. I am sure that you will not disappoint your daughter. Ahmed, please.

Once the ink dries, she folds the letter, seals it in an envelope and writes down Ahmed's home address. She almost forgets that this was once a place that Laila called home. She wonders what it would have been like to know her back then. *Would she even make the effort to talk to someone like me?*

Jasmine brushes these inconsequential thoughts away and heads straight to the post office. Once again, she ignores the queasy feeling in her gut and listens to her mind. If Ahmed agrees, he could well provide all the funds they need for the campaign.

On her way back home, Jasmine makes a slight detour to her favourite kulcha stand. Laila has gone to visit Jai. Jasmine is sure that she will take time to get back. Also, the kulchawallah always seems to have up-to-date information about Raymond's life.

The stuffed kulcha is better than usual, largely due to the new yogurt chutney that the kulchawallah has been experimenting with. Jasmine doesn't mind the few drops of rain that are falling on her face. She is disappointed that he isn't sharing much gossip today. He seems to be busy rounding up orders. Fortunately, the kulchawallah hasn't seen Jasmine's picture in the newspaper; or maybe he has and still chooses to be friendly to the girl who supports his sahib's ex-wife. She wonders then if that is the reason he isn't doling out information or gushing about Raymond.

Jasmine's questions are soon answered when Raymond's long black car passes them. She can't see through the tinted windows, but the kulchawallah seems to know what's going on behind them.

'Oh, I think that Raymond sahib has a new sahiba now. No one seems to be aware of it, but I swear I saw a new sahiba coming out of his house multiple times this week,' he chuckles. 'Maybe she's in there with him.'

Jasmine doesn't wait too long. She stuffs the kulcha down her throat and makes her way through the streets, to hide behind a tree in front of Raymond's house. She arrives just in time to watch the car pull into the driveway. As the chauffeur steps out and opens the door, she can see the silhouette of a woman. The kulchawallah could be right.

While it doesn't take Jasmine long to recognize the woman, it does take her some time to come out of the initial shock. The short, permed hair, the fitted white skirt accentuating her hips, the buttoned navy blouse. Even though they are quite far away, Jasmine is sure that it is her. Her cheeks turn red with fury and also flush with embarrassment. She can't help but crinkle her nose with disgust as she sees Raymond place a hand on Naya Roben's fanny and squeeze it as they enter the house. A common enemy has the power to unite even the most unlikely people.

fifty

Laila

Jai refuses to look at Laila. Ruff has got her thirty minutes with him. There were conditions, of course. Laila and Jai must meet at his foster home, with a third person present. Ruff sits on a couch at the back of the living room as Laila tries to talk to Jai.

His foster home is a well-made single-storeyed house. The carpeted living room has olive-green and cream couches. A small glass chandelier hangs in the middle of the room. The walls are decorated with pictures of the family. Among the pictures now also hangs a picture of Jai. Laila has learned that the Milers are one of the designated short-term foster families that are part of the system, so she assumes that the pictures on the walls keep changing. But there is a small blue-eyed boy in most pictures of the couple from when they were younger.

Jai is standing in the middle of the room. Laila moves closer to him and kneels down so both their faces are in line. She lifts her hands up to cup Jai's face. A tear drips down his cheek as Laila speaks to him slowly and softly.

'Jai, what you said at the court was not your fault. I'm not mad at you at all. In fact, I think you were very brave.'

More tears roll out of Jai's eyes. Laila continues, 'Listen to me, Jai. If you want to come home to me, you have to talk to me. I promise there is no one else listening to you. Ruff is my friend. You can trust him. You've met him before.'

Finally, Jai looks up. His eyes are red and swollen. He falls into Laila's arms and talks, his voice interspersed with sniffles.

'I'm sorry. He said that they would hurt you, put a knife in your throat. And in mine too.'

Jai's tears have wet Laila's turquoise blouse. She pats his back to console him.

'Who said it, Jai? Who told you this?'

'Mikel Uncle, our security guard.'

'Did he tell you anything else, Jai?'

Laila can tell that Jai is still frightened. 'He said that he will also hurt you if I tell anyone that he spoke to me.'

Laila pulls Jai away from the hug. She holds him by his shoulders and looks into his little eyes. 'Listen to me carefully, Jai. You will be called to speak in court again tomorrow. When they ask you to speak, tell them the truth. I promise that nothing, absolutely nothing, will happen to both of us. Jai, they are hoping for you to be scared. They will win if we are scared. So we have to be strong.'

Laila smiles and holds out her palm. 'Promise me, Jai, that you will not be scared tomorrow, and that you will tell the truth.'

Jai dries his tears and places his hand on Laila's. 'I promise.'

Laila gives him a tight hug and prepares to depart. Jai doesn't let go of her hand. It breaks Laila's heart to leave him.

'Don't worry, Jai. I promise that you will come home to me very soon.'

Laila waits. Only when Jai flashes his wide smile does she tell Ruff that she's ready to leave.

fifty-one

Laila

The little boy, clad in a red silk shirt and black pants, looks at her for approval before he steps down from the witness stand. Laila smiles at Jai encouragingly. He had promised to tell the truth and he kept his word.

The day has been a repetition of the last. The same arguments from both sides. The case rests on Jai's testimony, and he has now narrated two different versions of the same incident.

Ruff said the additional information about Raymond possibly being involved with Naya cannot be used. There is no proof; and yet Jasmine saw it with her own eyes. Laila and Ruff were both dumbfounded when Jasmine told them about Raymond and Naya. They worry about what it could mean for Laila's campaign, but for now, the custody case takes precedence.

A written copy of the statements from both sides needs to be submitted to the judge by the next morning. The judge will then announce a verdict in seven days. Laila asks the judge for protection for Jai. He assigns two security guards to keep an eye on the child day and night and disallows any visitors until the verdict has been declared. Laila knows that Raymond will not physically harm either of them because the case is too prominent in the public eye for him to blow his chances for his re-election into the council, but she still doesn't want to take any risks. This time Laila is one of the first people out of the courtroom. As she walks down the hallway, she is stopped by a familiar voice. She is sure that when she turns around, she will find a man with crinkles around his nose. She doesn't know why he is here; he didn't attend the trial. She doesn't know what he wants, but a lifetime of experiences has taught her that Thakur never delivers any good news.

The door shuts loudly behind Laila, though not as loudly as she would have liked. It is raining outside, and Laila angrily brushes away the few drops that have settled on the letter. She opens it and dread fills her as she reads those words again.

'Ahmed, please.'

She had no right.

Jasmine is sitting on her mattress combing through the knots in her hair when Laila returns home in a fury, after facing the wrath of her grandfather. It created a media spectacle. Two Jagirs fighting, yelling at each other even.

'What would make you think that this family would spare one more rehat on you? We gave you a chance to make your home, and you, what did you do? You've brought disrespect and shame to two families. I came here all the way myself so that our answer is loud and clear. No one in the Jagir family wants to be associated with you any more.'

Oblivious to Jasmine's involvement, Laila had berated Thakur, telling him how she would never come asking any of them for help. It was when Thakur threw the letter at her that she fell in shock. In the letter Jasmine was *begging* the Jagirs for money for Laila's campaign.

Jasmine looks up as she hears the door slam. Laila's eyes grow wide with rage as she holds out the letter for Jasmine to see.

'My grandfather threw this in my face at the court today.' Her voice quivers. 'How can you assume that you know more about my relationship with my family than I do? You could have at least asked me about it first.'

Jasmine speaks softly, almost inaudibly. 'I'm sorry; I'm really sorry, Laila. I really wanted to help you and I thought this would work. We need funds. I knew you wouldn't allow it if you found out. I didn't think the letter would get to your grandfather.'

'The letter getting to my grandfather? That's not the problem, Jasmine. The problem is that you wrote the letter in the first place. Addressed to whom? To my father? He is *my* father, and he and I determine the relationship we have, not you. Do you understand that by tomorrow morning the whole of Rahat will know that we don't have any funds?'

'Laila, I'm sorry. But we could really use your father's help. Maybe the letter never got to him. I'm sure he still cares about you. I don't think you should give up on him. I don't even know where my father is; at least you still have yours.'

'And I have never seen my mother. But your mother is alone, withering away in a house in another district. And you're here. Right, Jasmine? You've conveniently forgotten about the one parent you know for sure is alive and suffering, because you're so hung up on the one who might as well be dead.'

Laila immediately brings her hand to her mouth. She knows she's crossed the line.

Jasmine says coldly, 'You know nothing about my life.' Then, under her breath, 'I don't know why I thought you would be any different.' She opens the door and walks out into the pouring rain.

fifty-two

Jasmine

Her beige blouse is soaking wet, but Jasmine doesn't want to go back inside. It's easy to disguise her tears in the rain. Unable to think or even see clearly because of the water in her eyes, she finally stops under a tree to catch her breath. She knows that it's not her fault that Nina is living alone in Mahlah, but all of a sudden, she can't stop feeling guilty about it. What if Laila is right? What if she has conveniently forgotten about Nina without even realizing it? What if, engaged in her new life, she has also conveniently forgotten about Kaiza?

She decides to go to get some warm food; it's the only thing that will calm her down.

She walks to a samosa stall a few streets away. As a stout man fries her some crisp, minced meat samosas, Jasmine tries to dry her tears, but instead, breaks down completely. The vendor hands her two samosas instead of just the one she'd asked for. She looks at him questioningly, but he only smiles and says, 'The second one is from me.'

Jasmine manages to smile back. She dips the piping hot samosa into the tangy tamarind chutney and takes a bite. She always feels better after she eats. Some small talk later, Jasmine decides to leave. Before she departs, she asks the vendor to pack two more samosas. She is sure that a certain hazel-eyed girl is staring out of a tiny window, lost in her thoughts, and has completely ignored her growling stomach.

About fifteen muscular men stand at the corner of the street. They are busy picking out stones and collecting them in a cloth bag.

Curious, Jasmine lingers a little longer than she ought to. She notices a second cloth bag on the ground. One of the men, presumably the leader, orders one of the other men to push the bag aside. As that man slides it away carelessly with his leg, the loose knot over the bag comes undone. Jasmine spots knives inside it and a sense of fear immediately overtakes her. She tries to keep out of their sight as she resumes her walk home, pacing behind the cars parked on the road. One of the men stops an unsuspecting kid riding his bicycle. Jasmine continues walking, but slows down enough to be able to help the kid if needed. Not that she would be a match for these men, but maybe she could run and call for help.

The boy seems scared. He looks just a few years older than Jai. The man who Jasmine thinks is the leader walks up to the boy. This man has a pointed nose and big black eyes. He talks to the kid loudly, making most of the conversation audible to Jasmine. Surprisingly though, he is stern, but polite. Jasmine can see that he doesn't want to scare the kid away. That's not the trouble he's here to cause.

'Boy, can you help me out with an address?'

The boy nods. There's not much else that he can do.

'Building number 44, Street 3. Do you know where that is?'

Jasmine doesn't wait to see if the boy pointed the men in the right direction. She doesn't know how they got her address. There are ten apartments in that building, but Jasmine is sure these men are coming for the small room on the ground floor. She sprints through the smaller by-lanes. She has to get to Laila before they do.

fifty-three

Laila

When the door finally opens, Laila expects a cold stare from Jasmine. But instead, Jasmine rushes to the makeshift cupboard and pulls out one of her larger bags. Her face is pale, and Laila can see that an explanation is not what she should ask for at the moment. When Jasmine asks Laila to help her pack their important belongings, Laila immediately jumps into action. They take only a few minutes to pack. Neither of them owns too many items.

Jasmine asks Laila to tie a scarf over her face and she does the same. Jasmine is wearing the pink scarf that Laila had bought for her at the fair. Laila wonders if she has worn it as a peace offering. Quietly, Laila follows Jasmine out of the door. By the time she exits the gate of the building, Jasmine has already stopped a cab. She holds the door open for Laila, who scoots inside without asking a single question.

Before they turn at the end of the street, Laila notices fifteen men walking towards their building. Most of them have knives in their hands. One of them is carrying a bag full of stones. As she recognizes the man with the pointed nose, the leader, her face turns white. *Mikel. One of Raymond's security guards.*

Laila gives the cab driver Ruff's office address. She's not sure if Raymond's intention was to threaten her or finish her off for good. She can't trust him to stay quiet for the sake of his political image any longer. She is grateful that Jai has additional security. Laila meets Jasmine's eyes as they both realize it at the same time. *Naya Robe*n. It's not only about the custody battle. Raymond probably sent the goons to scare Laila off the election campaign before it even begins. A display of his power; he has sent a familiar face as the leader so that Laila knows that no court battle can stop him.

As they exit the neighbourhood, Jasmine hands over the samosas to Laila.

'Thought you might be hungry.'

Laila takes them and unwraps the newspaper.

'Jasmine, I'm so –'

'Me too.'

That night, a small article goes into print on the fifth page of a local newspaper. Neither Laila nor Jasmine come across the hundred words.

'Protesters pelt stones at a servants' quarter on Street Three in Russel. It is rumoured that the council candidate from Rahat, Laila Jagir, used to live there. These protests could be a mark of people being unhappy with Ms Jagir standing for the election amidst all the controversy that surrounds her. The police are on the lookout for the offenders, who have been charged with the destruction of private property, after a case was filed by the owner of the building.'

fifty-four

Jasmine

Laila and Jasmine have been living in Ruff's office for a couple of days now, using the storeroom as a makeshift accommodation. The room is bigger than Jasmine's closet-sized, four-walled house but is quite stuffy since there's no window to let any air in. Ruff himself lives in a small studio apartment in the building next to the office. Ruff has now shifted Shadow to the office.

Jasmine has never seen Laila feel as liberated as she does around the little black terrier.

With limited funds, Laila's ongoing custody battle, and unexpected shifting of homes, they haven't been able to start campaigning yet.

Rahat University's poll results came in a couple of days ago. They had expected the result to be bad, but this was abysmal. In fact, calling it abysmal would be understating it.

Ibra Nader was leading, with 40 per cent of the likely votes. Jasmine has seen Ibra's posters on bus stands, buses and even on a few hoardings across the city. His picture with him flashing a thumbs-up sign.

'Ibra for a greater Rahat.'

Gulzar was just two points behind with 38 per cent. Naya Roben came in third, with 21 per cent. That left just 1 per cent of the votes for Laila. *One* per cent.

The controversies are doing her no good. Money or no money, they cannot delay this campaign any more.

fifty-five

Laila

The cream scarf and the matching full-sleeved kurta remind her of the Tony family dress code. Ruff and Jasmine insisted that she dress in a socially acceptable fashion at her first rally, clothes that people identify with, that make her seem more like them, less out of the box, less *threatening*.

'You don't want them to look at you and run away now, do you?' they said.

They've printed their logo, the arrowheads, with her campaign's motto on simple, thin white sheets of paper – Free. Fair. Forward. – along with the date and time for the rally. They've paid the newspaper delivery boys to put the flyers between the folds of newspapers. Jasmine requested the two waitresses who used to work with her to help by pinning posters in public places, on bus stands and the walls outside theatres.

The talk is being held at a small plot just behind the slums in Rore, a poorer part of the city. It's a small 100-square-foot lot filled with sand, being rented out until construction begins. They can't afford anything better. There is no stage, but they've managed to rent a microphone for an hour. Laila hopes it's her words that will matter the most, not the set-up. She goes through her speech in her head, at the end of which she plans to invite the audience members to ask questions.

Just before the speech though, Laila's mind begins to cloud. She sits still as Ruff and Jasmine hover around her, giving her instructions. Be polite to the audience. Talk about the issues that matter. It has been a long time since she stood in front of an audience. The last time she did, the reaction was quite phenomenal. It was one of the first few rallies that Ahmed had held. Laila was only twelve at the time. She came up onstage after Ahmed's speech and shouted into the microphone, 'Vote for my father. He takes very good care of me and he'll take good care of you too.' The audience roared with appreciation. Of course, it was all planned down to the last detail. Ahmed had rehearsed every word with her tens of times before she was allowed onto the stage. As they sit in Ruff's car and head towards Rore, for the first time in a long time, Laila's heart longs for Ahmed. He would know exactly what to do to get her campaign going.

As the sun sets and the golden sand turns brown, Laila is dragged out of the ground by Ruff and Jasmine. She's glad that not many were present to witness the debacle that was her first public rally.

All the staff from Jasmine's old workplace, the diner, showed up. Even Mr Ruff came. This is the first time Laila saw the man she'd heard so much about, a father figure to two of the most important people in her life. Amer came too. He had always looked familiar, and she now remembers that she'd met him once before, when he'd sold her some jewellery. Earrings and a matching necklace. Beautiful pieces of white pearl.

There were thirty more people present. Half of them were reporters, as Laila later realized. As soon as she stood behind the microphone, her legs started to quiver, and she lost all sense of who she was. She never thought she could be this nervous. Words refused to form in her mouth. Still, out of respect for the hard work that so many people had put in to make this event happen, and considering the large chunk of their already scarce resources that they had spent on it, she began talking hesitantly. She stuttered as she emotionlessly read out what was written on the flimsy piece of paper in her hands. It got worse when she opened the session to questions. Only personal and irrelevant topics came up.

'So, Laila. Did you have an extramarital affair? Is that why you asked for a separation?'

'You ran away from your husband's house. How can you justify standing for the election after you've committed so many sins?'

'Why have you abducted Raymond's child? You know that a court of law will not let you have him, right? Snatching a son away from his father? You should be punished.'

And then, a flash of hope.

'What are your views on small businesses? What kind of changes will you make that will benefit us?'

Laila should have described the policies that she had already thought of. The laws she hoped to change. The fast-track registration system that she planned to introduce. But she didn't say any of that. The heat of the afternoon had got to her. The last two months of her life, her marriage to Raymond and the ensuing abuse, the battles in court, the regretful decisions; all came rushing back to her, and with it, a fear, *what if she isn't meant for this, what if she isn't good enough, what if she is what Raymond and those tabloids think of her – a girl without a mother, a rebel without a cause, with no actual substance.* She knew her fears were just that: fears, nothing more, but she couldn't make herself believe it in that moment. She tried but no words came to her rescue.

'Yes, businesses will definitely be...*umm*...be...*uh*...better. By ... *umm* –'

Laila's palms become sweaty and her body grew cold in the sharp afternoon sun. It didn't rain all day. At least the weather was on their side. Laila tried to pull out sentences from her brain. But there was nothing, just empty space. As Laila's face grew pale, Ruff pulled her frozen self from the microphone and closed the session.

As Ruff and Jasmine walk Laila through the doors of Ruff's office, her body is still just as cold. She feels as though she cannot breathe; the fear returns. *What have I done? If I can't even answer simple questions about myself, I am definitely not capable of making decisions for an entire nation.*

At night Jasmine and Laila quietly prepare for bed. Ruff bids them a tired goodnight and leaves. A few minutes later he returns with a suspicious look on his face and describes a long black car that is parked outside. Laila asks if he remembers the number plate. She knows the numbers of all Raymond's cars. They're all two digits instead of four, a privilege that only council members and their immediate family members enjoy. The head of state's cars have single-digit number plates.

'14,' Ruff says.

Laila's eyes widen. Rahat. 1. Baugh. 2. Mahlah. 3. Attara. 4. Hera. 5.

'That's a Jagir car!'

Still weary, but confused and curious, Laila rushes to the door. As soon as she makes herself visible, the chauffeur steps out of the car.

'Sahiba, I was asked to deliver this to you.'

He hands her a thick white envelope bearing the Jagir family seal – royal blue with a golden leaf etched on it. When Laila asks who has sent it, the chauffeur refuses to reply and instead walks back to the car. Laila hastily opens the seal as Jasmine and Ruff look over her shoulder. She removes a hundred pieces of coloured paper from within. 500,000 rehats. There is also a note attached.

This is how much I can contribute from my campaign funds without anyone getting suspicious. I know it's nowhere close to what you need, but I hope it's enough to start. You deserve it way more than I do, Laila.

~ Gulzar

Laila smiles. Perhaps she was wrong to give up hope on all the Jagirs. But that her uncle believes in her does not take away the embarrassment of the rally. Jasmine and Ruff have both tried to console her. She knows her fears were momentary; she knows that she will make a good councilwoman. But for the first time, she is questioning her belief in herself. She isn't sure yet how she must pick herself up and move forward.

fifty-six

Laila

The grey floor blurs as she lets the teardrops in her eyes fall. Laila walks out of the courtroom without a little hand clutching hers. She had promised him.

Ruff catches up and places his hands on her shoulders. He says softly, 'You did the right thing.' A small consolation.

There were more audience members in the courtroom today. People hate incomplete stories, and Jai's custody case has become a source of national entertainment. Jai was present as well, his innocent brown eyes filled with hope, waiting to go back home with Laila.

The judge started off by summarizing the case, before he announced his final decision.

Laila remembers the look on Raymond's face. The red-faced look of shock and embarrassment hidden behind a veil of feigned tears. But instead of rejoicing, she was busy thinking about something else.

After the incident at Jasmine's house, she knows that it is not safe to go back. And after the incident at the rally, she knows that she is not in her best mental state. She doesn't know if she will be able to protect Jai from Raymond's goons if they come after him, and that is a risk she is not willing to take.

The judge's decision attracted more gasps than claps.

'Keeping in mind all the facts presented before the court of law, I announce that the child is under considerable physical and emotional threat from Raymond Tony. The court gives Laila Jagir the custody of Jai Tony.'

Since Laila's reputation hasn't gotten better since the last trial; the onlookers did not expect the decision to go her way, so the mood in the courtroom was one of general surprise. But Jai's admission of being blackmailed in the last trial seemed to have tipped the scales in Laila's favour. The judge also mentioned that for a period of one year there will be bi-monthly checks by the childcare team to ensure that Laila is keeping Jai safe and taking adequate care of him. In case the report by the childcare team indicated otherwise, Jai would be sent back to a foster home.

Laila's eyes filled with tears. She didn't know how to differentiate between the ones that had formed due to glee and the ones that had formed because of the heartbreak she was about to cause. Then, she sent in her request.

When the judge ended his announcement, Laila turned around to catch Jasmine's eye. Jai was going to be away from two women who loved him, not just one. But when Jasmine's eyes met hers, there was no accusation in them. They held a slight smile. 'I stand by you,' they seemed to tell her.

The judge's voice was loud and passionless. 'As requested by the custodial parent, the court announces that Jai Tony is to remain at the foster home for a period of five weeks, until the council elections are complete and its results are declared.'

Laila went to Jai to apologize, ask him for some more of the patience that he had displayed until now. She sat on the chair beside him, trying to explain what had just happened. When the tears in her eyes didn't allow her to speak, Jai raised his tiny hands and brushed them off her cheeks.

'It's all right, Laila. I will come home to you when it is right, and I know that you will be a councilwoman then.'

fifty-seven

Jasmine

The water falling from the white dolphin-shaped fountain is overshadowed by the drops of rain pouring from the sky. Jasmine takes shelter beneath one of the many umbrella stands set up in the garden where they had their first date. Amer has asked her to meet him at six in the evening. She's early.

The garden isn't crowded since the rain has reduced its serviceability. Jasmine can hardly see anyone. A middle-aged couple has taken shelter under an umbrella a few metres away from her. An old man holding a bright-red umbrella is walking towards the exit gate. That's it; there is nobody else in her vicinity.

As the rain starts to get heavier, Jasmine takes the precaution and shifts slightly more inwards, into the shelter of the umbrella. She is wearing a white blouse which is sure to become transparent when wet. Jasmine's hair is tied up in an intricate braid, and counterfeit pearls adorn her ears. She likes that she has dressed herself up; she doesn't often get the chance to do so these days. She is thankful to Amer for asking her to meet with him. Jasmine has been so occupied with Laila's campaign that she needs a breath of fresh air.

A few minutes later, Amer walks in. The rain has made his hair fall flat on his face. Jasmine resists the urge to run towards him and plant a kiss on his pink lips. They see each other and smile. Amer lowers his eyes and looks at the wet grass on the ground. Jasmine wonders why he is suddenly being shy. They have been dating for a while now.

As he reaches the umbrella stand, instead of opening his arms and inviting Jasmine for a hug, he comes closer and lightly brushes his fingers on her face. Then he takes a few steps away from her and asks if they could sit down on a bench and talk.

They sit in silence for five long minutes, before Amer's husky voice fills the air. 'I love you, Jasmine. And I want to spend the rest of my life loving you. I'm not sure what the right way to do this is, and this is perhaps not the best time to do this, but Jasmine Mir,' he takes two deep, long breaths, 'if you are willing, I would love to marry you.'

The tears forming in her eyes soon begin to wet her cheeks. She has never been so overwhelmed in her entire now-almost-eighteen-years of existence. Jasmine looks into Amer's blue eyes. The vastness of the ocean has condensed into those two tiny spheres.

'Amer Moran, I would love to marry you too.'

In a few minutes, the rain dies down, but the excitement does not.

Jasmine hesitates for a moment, and then finally asks, 'Amer, but what about your parents? They've rejected me once before.'

'I've already spoken to them, Jasmine, and told them that my decision is final. My parents come from a different time and mindset. But things between us are not like they were when we first met in your home; we are not strangers any more. I explained that to them – about how close we've become and how wonderful you are, and, most importantly, how happy you make me. It's true, they took a little convincing, but they trust me.'

Jasmine smiles. 'But we can't marry till the election is over.'

Amer shoots her an understanding look. I know.'

Jasmine notices Amer's face become serious. She strokes his cheek with her hand.

'What's the matter?'

Amer takes both of Jasmine's hands in his and turns to face her.

'We're going to spend the rest of our lives together. I don't want there to be any secrets between us. There's something that I need to tell you.'

Colour refuses to return to Jasmine's face. She looks at Amer, baffled and unsure. No anger, nor sadness, no emotion inhibits her. Her entire system is in shock. She now understands why she caught Amer glancing at Laila so many times. She understands his support for her campaign. But she feels no sense of betrayal.

A few minutes later, an uncalled-for sensation takes form in her as she smiles.

She doesn't hear when Amer tells her, 'I'm sorry. I should have told you earlier.'

Jasmine is lost in her thoughts. Laila is not family merely in her head. They are going to be *sisters*. Amer looks dumbfounded as an overjoyed Jasmine starts grinning.

And then it strikes her. This new information could allow Laila to seek help from another, more experienced person.

She takes Amer's face in her hands. 'Amer, you have to tell Laila.'

This time, Amer's face goes white. He barely manages to get the words out. 'Jasmine, no.'

'I know I shouldn't ask you to do this. You trusted me with this information. I'm not going to force you. I can't. This is too delicate. But hear me out and then make your decision. Laila hasn't been herself since the rally. She needs to believe in herself again, and I know talking to her father, remembering herself as she was when she was still at home, will assure her that she deserves what she has earned. Ahmed is also the only person who can get Laila's campaign on track. She won't ask him for help unless you tell her this. She will know that she wasn't someone who Ahmed had to take care of, that she isn't his burden; she is his choice. Perhaps her father also needs to be reminded of the love he felt when he took Laila into his arms for the first time.'

Amer doesn't reply as Jasmine wraps her arms around him and lays her head on his shoulder. She stretches one hand out towards his chest to feel his racing heartbeat.

fifty-eight

Laila

The fried onion pakoras, chicken curry and pieces of naan are spread out on the table. Accompanying them are disks of thinly sliced onion and some tangy mint chutney.

Laila notices the ring on Jasmine's finger as the two of them sit down to have lunch. Jasmine can't seem to stop blushing.

'Have you guys fixed a date?'

Jasmine munches on a crisp pakora. 'Not yet.'

Laila sees the expression change on Jasmine's face. They both stay quiet and continue eating. Once they've finished, to Laila's surprise, Jasmine gets up from her seat, picks up her umbrella and signals for Laila to follow her.

'Come on, there's someone you have to meet.'

Laila is perplexed at the suddenness of Jasmine's request, but once again she follows her out of the door without asking any questions. She knows that it's always better to trust this girl.

The elevator grinds to a halt on the third floor. Laila and Jasmine step into the carpeted hallway. Jasmine leads the way, and they stop in front of a small wooden door.

Room 326.

As the door opens, Laila is surprised to see Amer inside. He is dressed in a blue shirt and white pants. His eyes seem to tear up when he sees Laila. As they walk into the room, Laila looks at Jasmine in confusion.

What is happening here? Does Amer want to donate more money to the campaign? Or do they want me to look over their wedding? Did they bring me here to bestow some honour upon me?

Laila tries, but she cannot fathom what the two of them would want to talk to her about.

It's an average-sized hotel room. It has a double bed, carpeted floors, a table, a chair and a couch by the side. Laila wonders how much Amer spends on his stay. Wouldn't it be more economical for him to rent an apartment in the city?

Amer pulls up a chair as Jasmine and Laila take a seat on the beige-coloured couch. Laila notices as Jasmine looks Amer in the eye. 'It's time now,' she seems to be telling him. Jasmine then turns towards her.

'Laila, Amer has something to tell you. I think you two should talk. I'll be waiting in the lobby outside.'

Once Jasmine leaves, Laila and Amer share an uncomfortable silence. Laila doesn't have time to assess the situation. She has no idea what the conversation is going to be about. She is completely baffled when teardrops fall from Amer's eyes. For a long time, they sit like that; Laila fidgeting, trying to make sense of the situation, and Amer trying to find the right words.

Finally, Laila takes the initiative. 'So, what do you want to talk about? Or does Jasmine expect me to have the "don't hurt my friend or I'll kill you" talk with you? Because if that's the case, you should know that if you ever hurt her –'

'I love her more than anything in this world. I will never ever hurt her, I promise.' Then Amer rubs his brow with his fingers. 'But that's not why we're here.'

Then he talks and she listens.

The wind starts to violently rattle the window behind her, but Laila remains oblivious to it. She doesn't notice when Amer slides his chair back into the table and takes a seat beside her on the couch. No, her mind is blank, completely blank. Thoughts refuse to form. Seconds turn into minutes. She just sits there, completely and utterly numb, drowning in a sense of blankness she didn't know could exist.

The first thing she hears is Jasmine's voice. *Wasn't Jasmine in the lobby?* Laila doesn't know any more. She has entered a parallel world where nothing is as it seems. She doesn't know where reality ends and fiction begins. Nothing, she knows nothing. A skin-coloured blob splits into two and rests itself on both of Laila's shoulders.

'Laila, are you all right?' it asks from a distance. Laila steps out of the nothingness to find Jasmine's hands on her shoulders and water in her own eyes.

And then the tears fall. She's not sure why she's crying. She can't feel anything. She turns to look at Amer. Amer *Moran*. Laila *Moran*. No, she cannot bring herself to accept it. The shock engulfs her as Jasmine locks her in a tight embrace.

In between tears and sniffles, Amer tries to speak. 'Laila, this doesn't make you any less of a Jagir. They are your family and will always be. They chose you when your own blood sold you. If that is not family, then what is?'

The words enter Laila's ears, but they fail to reach her brain. All her systems seem to be shutting down. Air refuses to enter her body. Her vision starts to blur again. In a hushed voice, she tries to get the words out.

'Jasmine, let's leave.'

Jasmine holds Laila's hand, carries her down the elevator and calls for a cab. Laila doesn't turn back to look at Amer. *My brother.* He stands by the door till he loses sight of two of the most important women in his life.

fifty-nine

Laila

It has been a long time. It has been a difficult time. She refuses to look out of the window as they pull into the driveway.

'I'll wait outside,' Ruff says. He takes her hand and squeezes it before she gets out of his car. The guard recognizes her but hesitates to let her in. She is sure that Thakur will send her away from the door. Or rather have her sent away. She hopes he isn't at home. *Home.* He usually goes to play cards and carom with his friends for a few hours in the afternoons on weekends.

It all makes sense now – Thakur's insults, his disapproval of Laila. It doesn't justify his behaviour, but it's easier for Laila to finally piece it all together in her head.

She remembers his words as if they'd been said yesterday.

You want to let that little brat in here as well? Just having her in our house is an insult to our family. Ahmed, don't slay away our legacy, Ahmed, listen to me, Ahmed –

Laila tries to ward off thoughts of her grandfather. She has been preparing all day, practising how to focus on the task at hand, how to bring herself to talk to her father. But as soon as she walks through the large wooden door, a sudden and overwhelming sense of nostalgia fills her senses. She wants to stay longer, linger in the hall. The cream-and-red sofas, the wide pillars, the marble staircase that leads up to her room. She wants to run up there, sit on her desk by the window and let the million ideas she used to have come flooding back to her. Her bed – she's forgotten what it feels like to have a good night's sleep. The large balcony that she thought was her escape to the world. The bookcase in her room, which has more handwritten journals than printed books. She longs to touch them, read them once again, remember what she used to be like, how she used to feel and think when she was bathed in innocence, untouched by tragedy.

One of the servants asks her to sit on the sofa as he calls for Ahmed. They are trying their best to treat her as they would any other guest. They half-heartedly try to stop her from entering the kitchen. They stand back and watch as she does anyway. Laila instinctively pours out some cold milk and cocoa cereal in a bowl. She picks up a spoon, and then another. Sitting down at her usual spot on the small marble kitchen table, she decides that is where they will have the conversation.

Instead of diving straight into the bowl, she places both her hands on the table and spreads them along the cold surface. She attempts to hug the table while holding back her tears. There is nothing she can do to turn back time. Then, slowly, she realizes she doesn't actually want to live here again. She cannot imagine a life without Jai, Jasmine, without Ruff – who's outside waiting in the car for as long as it takes – without Amer. She cannot imagine a life without the Laila she is now.

When Ahmed doesn't arrive for quite some time, Laila decides to start without him. As she takes a bite of the chocolate-flavoured cereal submerged in cold milk, her mouth remembers all the sensations that it had missed for so long. She decides to enjoy the cereal instead of worrying about her father's impending arrival. But when Ahmed walks in, in his white kurta and the rarely worn spectacles on his nose, she freezes.

Father and daughter sit across from each other, to have a conversation they should have had years ago.

'I miss you,' Ahmed says. They've been seated in front of each other for a long time. The silence hasn't been as uncomfortable as Laila expected. Still, someone had to break it. Laila doesn't reply. She doesn't know how to. That her father chose her proves to her that he does love her and that he truly wanted her as his child. She knows that the last few years haven't been kind to both of them, his principles and her anger pulling them apart. But the truth, now that she can see it, is that she loves her father and misses him terribly. Perhaps she wasn't angry at how he treated her, but just angry at the loss of what they shared. But here she is, finally ready to let go of that anger, if only to have one moment stolen from the past and returned to them.

A few minutes later, she manages to softly say, 'But it hasn't seemed like it.'

Ahmed smiles. There's not much else he can do. It's true; it really hasn't seemed like it. But every passing moment he thinks of his daughter. He's a father. If nothing else, at least worrying comes to him naturally.

'I'm sorry,' Ahmed says quietly. 'I don't know if that's what you've come to hear. But I truly am.'

Laila had been waiting for years to hear her father apologize, but now that he has, she realizes that it's not the apology, it's the love, respect and affection that she so craved. Laila wants to tell him that she knows that he loves her, that he chose to bring her home when no one wanted her. But she doesn't. There is no need for it. It would break his heart if he found out that she knew.

Ahmed reaches out to hold his daughter's hand and continues, 'Laila jaan, I am very proud of you. But tell me that you have been okay.' Laila takes her father's hands in hers and nods.

'When I heard about you standing for the council elections, I was surprised, but immediately knew that it was the right step.'

'I thought so too, but I'm not sure any more,' Laila says, still holding onto her father, 'I had a rally a few days…'

'I know,' Ahmed smiles as he interjects, 'I like to keep an eye on my daughter's affairs.'

'Are you proud of me despite that then?' Laila asks, once again becoming the little kid looking for herself in her father's approval.

'I am, Laila jaan, I have been. But you, my Laila, you weren't present at the rally that day. Where was my fearless girl, who isn't afraid to challenge stigmas and norms? Who doesn't dress up in a specific way, doesn't behave in a specific manner only to please people. Where was the girl who speaks with passion because she believes she wants to do good for the people?'

Ahmed's smile disappears as he looks Laila in the eye. 'Your biggest strength has been that you speak from your heart; that you fight for what you believe in, and that you stand up with all that you have, for yours and everybody else's right to have a good life. You're already a councilwoman at heart. You don't need to mould yourself into something else for the elections. You need to show yourself.'

Laila can't believe her ears. *The same man who disparaged my behaviour all these years is now telling me that that it is my biggest strength?* As she looks into Ahmed's eyes, she notices a spark in them that she hasn't seen in almost a decade.

'I have another suggestion, if you'd be willing to take it,' Ahmed asks, worrying if he's already said too much.

'Of course,' Laila replies.

'I suggest you change your logo. It looks like something straight out of a transport company's profile. You need something that connects with the people; something that gives them…' Ahmed stops for a moment as he searches for the right word, '…hope.'

Smiling, Laila nods. Even if only for a brief while, her father and she are on the same side, once again. And he believes in her, he truly does. Perhaps she wasn't wrong to believe in herself either.

Ahmed pulls the cereal bowl towards himself, takes a bite, and continues, 'I'll write down a list of other minor changes and improvements you can make and have them sent over. Where do you live now, Laila?'

It almost seems like a guise to dig deeper into her life.

'Just have them sent over to Ruff's office.'

Ahmed continues to look at her. 'Is that where you live now?'

'Yes.'

Ahmed seems slightly shaken. He wants to ask, but doesn't. *How are you managing that? Does it have a bed? For how long have you been living there?*

But then there are some things that a parent just cannot give up on. 'What do you eat? Or have you been surviving on cereal and milk?' Ahmed says, suddenly easing the mood, bringing a little of his younger self back.

Laila lets out a chuckle, wishing her father would stop trying to be sarcastic. He's miserable at it.

'I live with Jasmine. She is nice enough to cook for both of us. You should meet her. I think you'll like her.'

'And what about the lawyer? He seems like a decent boy. He is a decent boy, isn't he? With you living in his...'

Parents. They never know when to stop once they start. Laila gets up from her seat. A leave taken too early. But the longer she stays, the more difficult it will get, and Laila knows that she has another life she wants to get back to.

Before she leaves the kitchen, Laila turns around and ties Ahmed in an embrace. She finally brings herself to say it. 'I've missed you too, Father.'

sixty

Jasmine

The clouds are rolling in the sky. Jasmine walks down the road, poll results in one hand and a vanilla milkshake in the other. She drinks the last of the milkshake and throws the container into a bin. Then she opens the sheet of printed paper and reads: 'Naya Roben. 39 per cent. Gulzar Jagir. 30 per cent. Ibra Nader. 27 per cent. Laila Jagir. 4 per cent.'

Jasmine is sure that Laila's numbers have gone up because she won Jai's custody. If the court puts its faith in someone, it inspires the same in at least a few social groups. Very few, in this case. But what Jasmine is worried about is not Laila's low numbers. It's the woman who is at the front of the race.

Naya Roben.

She has decided to visit Naya's next rally, to understand her campaign better, analyse it and see what could be done to counter it. She doesn't know to what extent Naya's criminal reach goes. As she thinks about the woman who rose so quickly as a shining example before her eyes and then fell down even faster, blood rushes to her face. She would work to expose Naya Roben even if it wasn't in the interest of Laila's campaign. Jasmine has never felt as terrorized as she did that day, for those few minutes, rushing out of Naya's house. *Naya makes so many others live in that terror every single moment of their lives.*

As she walks, lost in her thoughts, she disturbs some pigeons pecking at grains on the footpath. As the birds take flight around her, the sudden burst of wind brings a smile on her face. Jasmine looks as they soar into the sky, with their wings wide open. Then it hits her.

Jasmine rushes to Ruff's office.

On a rough sheet of paper, she outlines a bird soaring diagonally upwards, with its wings wide open. Hope. *Free. Fair. Forward.*

She holds the paper up to Laila, who is sitting on the other side of the table, trying to figure out her next move.

Jasmine's heart races, but then calms down when Laila smiles.

'Sometimes I feel that you should be running for the council,' Laila says.

'Nah,' Jasmine chuckles. 'I prefer kulchas to human beings. I don't think that's an acceptable councilwoman trait.'

They both laugh. Jasmine hands over the drawing. Perhaps it is the symbol of a new beginning.

The sun is about to set. There are thousands of plastic chairs arranged in sections. Jasmine had to pay a guy extra money to get his seat so that she could sit in one of the front rows. In the next few minutes, the ground fills up completely. As the audience waits for Naya Roben to arrive, they are served glasses of orange soda and simple vegetable sandwiches. The staff is dressed in well-ironed black pants and white shirts, and they don't refuse when asked for a second serving. It's clear that for Naya Roben free food and free drinks equal a happy public that will vote for you.

The small white flags with a golden sun printed on them shine in the twilight. Jasmine was also given one at the entrance but she makes sure not to wave it. Jasmine finishes her glass of orange soda and asks for a refill, in a petty attempt to spend some more of Naya's campaign money.

Half an hour later, Naya emerges from behind the stage amid her chaperones. The stage has a large banner with Naya's face on it; below it is her campaign slogan: 'Let's make Rahat shine again.' Jasmine grunts. *What does that even mean?* There is a podium at the centre of the stage and a few couches on the side for Naya's advisers. Jasmine recognizes Naya's husband from the pictures in her house and in magazines. Ayen Roben. And then, out of nowhere, the picture of Raymond squeezing Naya's behind flashes, uninvited, in her mind.

As soon as Naya is clearly visible onstage, the crowd rises in a deafening cheer. Naya is dressed in white pants and a white blouse. Her ears and neck are adorned with sparkling diamonds. She is not afraid to show her wealth. Wealth means power. She's not here to please the audience; she is here to make them aspire to be like her. Her speech begins and the crowd cheers louder every few minutes. Establish more skill schools to help people find work. Cheer. Fight disease together with better healthcare. Cheer. Jasmine understands why the audience is so mesmerized by Naya. She too was, once.

An hour later, the half-time break is announced. The waiters start service again. This time around it's a glass of water and a puff pastry stuffed with a spiced vegetable filling. When one of the waitresses comes around, Jasmine looks up to thank her and is taken aback when a pair of familiar green eyes stare back at her. Jasmine swallows the lump that has formed in her throat, thankful that the girl who saved her life is still alive.

'Thank you,' Jasmine says, slowly. The girl knows that it's not for the water she has just served.

Jasmine wants to ask her about the events that took place after she escaped; if Naya Roben found out she'd helped, if she was punished. But Jasmine knows it's not the right time to satisfy her curiosity. Instead, she quickly realizes the opportunity, fishes out a piece of paper from her purse and writes, *I want information to expose Naya. Are you willing to help me?*

Reading the note the waitress nods. Then she disappears into the crowd and doesn't return. The interval ends and the show resumes. Jasmine wonders if she scared the girl away. An hour later, Naya finally concludes her talk. Before finishing, she raises her fist in the air and screams into the microphone: 'Let's make Rahat shine again!' The crowd is pumped, making victorious fists in the air. Even after

Naya takes her leave and disappears behind the stage, the crowd continues chanting the slogan.

Jasmine stands up to cramps in her legs and pins and needles in her feet. She looks around but there's no sign of the waitress. Disappointed she's lost her only potential source, she turns to leave when all of a sudden a waiter positions himself too close to Jasmine. He speaks quietly. 'There's a message for you.'

Jasmine follows his eyes to his hand pressed against his leg. He slides a small sheet of folded paper from between his fingers into her palms. Once she leaves the rally, she opens the note and reads: *Meet me at the Diamond petrol station beside the club diner, two lanes away from her house. 5 p.m. Tomorrow.*

sixty-one

Laila

Laila enters the office excitedly only to find Ruff sitting in his chair with his head in a book. She coughs to catch his attention. As she unfurls the flag in her hand, Ruff gasps. It is royal blue with an ivory-coloured bird on it. She passes it to Ruff. As he holds it up, she knows that Ahmed was right. What a logo or a symbol signifies doesn't matter as much as what it makes you feel, what it stirs up within that little corner of your chest. As Ruff's eyes meet Laila's, she wishes that she could ask him to wrap his arms around her.

Ruff puts the flag down and hands Laila an envelope. The envelope doesn't have a seal and is instead held shut by a simple adhesive.

'Another chauffeur delivered it.'

Laila tears open the envelope. Inside is a message.

Bluebell Café. 4 p.m. Setha Moor will interview you for the Rahat Heritage. *If she likes you enough, she'll print a glimpse of your interview on the front page.*

Yours, Ahmed.

Laila picks up the glass of water even as the thin paper coaster clings to it and takes a sip to clear her dry throat. She moves around to adjust her spine. The white chairs in the restaurant, with their thin, wired arches for a backrest look elegant but offer no support. The white tables match the chairs. Each table is decorated with blue flowers in multicoloured pots. There aren't many people in the café. Only one other table is occupied by a man and a woman. The food on their table is untouched because they are busy nervously assessing the tension between them.

Laila, dressed in her old white blazer sent over by Ahmed, has let her hair freely fall to her waist, no headscarf covering it. She is early. It is still ten minutes to four. At least Setha can't complain of Laila being tardy in her article.

She hopes Setha goes beyond the usual questions about her personal life. Ruff has asked her to use those questions as an opportunity to explain herself. It would be much simpler if Laila used her past with Raymond to attract sympathy but that is not how Laila wants to win this election.

At a minute past four, a small, pastel-green car parks itself outside the café. A woman, dressed in an elegant green linen skirt, and a black, well fitted blouse that almost blends into her black hair, gets out of the car and enters the café. A simple red scarf is wrapped around her neck. Colourful *jhumkas* hang from her ears, complementing her beautiful dusky face; a couple of silver-coloured metal bangles softly clink on her wrists. Her lips are coated with a lightly applied pink stain and her large black eyes are lined with kohl, making them look even more striking. The woman breaks into a warm smile as soon as she spots Laila.

Taking the seat opposite Laila, Setha fishes out her journal from a cloth bag and places it on the table. Before she begins, she asks, 'Let's order something first, shall we?'

Laila orders a filter coffee while Setha quickly decides on a ginger tea.

'So, Laila. I have another meeting at six, and it's best if we don't waste any time.'

Laila nods. She tries to ignore the nervousness churning in her stomach.

'Before we begin, I want to ask you if you're okay with answering personal questions?'

For a second Laila hesitates. She fears that blankness has taken over her mind once again. She remembers Jasmine's advice. *Talk to her as if you're talking to me.* Then her father's. *You don't need to mould yourself into something else for the elections. You need to show yourself.* And then, as if by the sudden arrival of long-awaited sunshine, the fog in her head clears. Laila looks Setha in the eye and returns her smile. 'You can ask me anything that you think the people of Rahat would want to know about me. They are going to give me the authority to make decisions about their lives; they definitely have the right to know what's going on in mine.'

Setha's eyes widen. She seems surprised by Laila's frank and confident reply. Perhaps the headlines of a girl shivering with nervousness before being pulled away from the microphone had formed a different image in her mind. For the next two hours, Laila eloquently answers the journalist's questions. She talks about her failed marriage and how it was as difficult for her as it would have been for any woman in her situation. She talks about the bond that she and her father share, and how since she was a little child, her heart has been drawn towards fighting for everyone's happiness. Laila smiles as Setha mentions that she remembers reading about her in the newspapers when she herself was still a struggling journalist. She always thought that Laila was inspiring, but the negative publicity over the last few years had made her forget the respect she used to have for the young girl who was only trying to make the world a better place. Laila doesn't miss an opportunity to talk about her plans for the future. She explains the essence of her campaign, saying she wants to bring in policies that will give equal access to all in different areas of life, allowing people to live freer, more just lives. Setha listens on, impressed. When her two hours are up, she takes Laila's picture with a point-and-shoot camera for the article.

'Thank you, Laila, for your time.'

Laila smiles. She rises as Setha stands up and gives her a firm handshake.

'Thank you for listening to me. I trust you will give me fair representation in your publication.'

sixty-two

Jasmine

The ochre-coloured file stares back at her from atop the large wooden desk. It must have not been easy for that girl to procure it.

She starts to untie the jute string holding the file shut. Then she stops. She should wait for Ruff. He has gone to fetch a copy of the public records available on the Robens. He's already been through them but Jasmine wants to be thorough. The same piece of information looked at by someone else could offer a different perspective.

Earlier this evening, Jasmine went to meet the green-eyed girl who promised her information on Naya. The young girl stood hidden behind a large dustbin near the petrol station. It took Jasmine more than a few minutes to find her. When she spotted her, the girl stealthily handed the file to her. There was no time for pleasantries. She didn't even want to look Jasmine in the eye.

In an emotionless voice, she said, 'This has a list of all the companies that the Robens own, and a list of their major suppliers and customers.'

Suppliers? Customers?

Then the girl covered her face with a scarf and proceeded to leave.

'Wait,' Jasmine said urgently. 'Thank you!'

The girl didn't reply. She walked away as fast as she could.

Jasmine doesn't know if she will ever be able to repay her. Then she realizes that she can – by exposing Naya and freeing the girl.

When the door to Ruff's office opens, Laila stands on the other side trying to unsuccessfully hide a grin. Jasmine breathes a sigh of relief. The interview seems to have gone well.

The next morning, a front-page article in the *Rahat Heritage* proves it. In big bold letters, it says, 'The Real Laila Jagir', and then in a smaller font, 'All that you should know about her before you pick a side'.

A few kilometres away, unknown to the relieved two women in the office, Ahmed's face beams with pride. The smile will be plastered on his face for the rest of the day.

Twenty companies are listed in the file. Ruff says that these cannot be all of Naya's businesses. To his knowledge, Naya started and shut down more than fifty of them.

'Maybe they're the ones that are still in operation,' Jasmine tries to reason.

There aren't any details about what any company does. The sheet just lists the names of people and their addresses, divided in two columns and written below the corresponding company. Some are suppliers and some customers. Jasmine shudders as she realizes what they could be buying and selling. Or rather, whom. Jasmine proceeds to 'W' and finds Wings.

'I don't think she would be carrying out illegal activities in the name of a company she publicizes so much,' Ruff remarks.

Jasmine rereads the twenty names, sliding her index finger from top to bottom to make sure that she doesn't skip any. All the names are quite bizarre. Pole. Loop. Quiver. Jasmine's finger stops when she reaches the company named Swing. There's something familiar about it. Then it hits her; it's an anagram. Wings. As she rechecks the list, she realizes that all the companies are in sets of anagrams. If Wings carries out legal activities, perhaps Swing is the corresponding company that handles its illegal activities. There is only one address written down in the supplier column below Swing. Perhaps that is where they can begin their search.

She doesn't realize that maybe they're acting too quickly. As they carry out their plan, the public record files accessed by Ruff lie stacked in the corner of the room, gathering dust.

sixty-three

Laila

The campaign has picked up in the last week. Laila sits down to prepare for her speech to be delivered at the Rahat University tomorrow. She realizes that it's quite late and Jasmine and Ruff haven't returned yet. They'd said they were going to be at the library, digging through some files about Naya.

After Setha's glowing article was published, people are no longer afraid of letting Laila advertise in their space. Blue banners with the ivory bird, emblazoned with the words 'Vote for Laila' have been put up on bus stands, on the sides of taxis, in public parks, on some hoardings, and even in front yards.

Laila has got notepads printed instead of brochures to pass around. The first two pages of the notepad have information about Laila and her campaign. Every subsequent page has two lines about the ideas that Laila plans to implement. The words 'Vote for Laila' and the campaign symbol have been printed at the bottom of each page. The notepad has Laila's picture on the cover to establish recognition and make her a part of people's everyday lives; when they're in class taking notes, when they're at home making grocery lists, or just sitting by the window and writing. The notepads were expensive to print, but Laila believes that they will work. A brochure is usually thrown away, but people keep and use notepads on a regular basis.

Laila has personally gone to each person she knows and asked them to support her and spread the word about her campaign. When Mr Ruff got the owner of his favourite coffee shop to support her, Laila even went and met the owner to cement his vote. Her empathetic personality helped him connect with her. He even offered to put up her campaign collateral, the notepads, pens, mugs in another café of his. Along with this, she gets the votes of most of the patrons of his shop.

Laila has realized that it's the everyday people with affable personalities, and passionate students, who are going to win her the election.

Most candidates take money from corporates or rich donors for their campaigns. Laila has planned to do something different. She has decided to take little amounts of money from the people that believe in her ideas, from the voters. She has started circulating letters asking people to send small amounts of money, anything from one to 1,000 rehats to her campaign fund anonymously. She's also earning money by selling stalls and banner spaces in her rallies.

After going through her speech once more, she shuts her journal and decides to call it a night.

Ruff and Jasmine had gone to investigate one of Naya's companies and haven't returned yet, but she wards her tension away. *Ruff and Jasmine have each other for company; they'll be all right.*

sixty-four

Jasmine

The wild wind eclipses the sound of Ruff's knocks. The flimsy door appears to be made out of the asbestos left over from making the roof. Swing's supplier's address has led them to an old warehouse on the outskirts of Rahat. There is no other construction around it. They had to make their way across a thick stretch of trees to find it.

Jasmine asked Ruff not to tell Laila about the exact nature of their research. She worries a little too much and she's already got an entire campaign to worry about.

Jasmine has fitted herself with a voice recorder. Being aware of the nature of Naya's businesses, Ruff and Jasmine both know that it's a dangerous mission, but they've written a letter to Amer with the warehouse's address. *Come looking for me if I am not at your hotel by six in the morning.* They've left the letter at his hotel's lobby, and asked the receptionist to give it to him when he comes down for breakfast the next morning. If all goes according to plan, Jasmine will reach Amer's hotel and Ruff will reach his office before Laila or Amer wake up. Neither Laila nor Amer would allow this to happen if they knew about this plan.

If Ruff and Jasmine are right, the suppliers mentioned in the sheet are suppliers of trafficked women, who Naya then grooms and sells as per requirement. Their plan is for Ruff to try and make the people in charge of the supplier's company believe that he is here to trade Jasmine for an opportunity to get in touch with Naya and do regular business with her. Once they do admit to being in business with Naya, Ruff is to stir up a disagreement, take Jasmine and leave, with audio proof of Naya's involvement safely recorded.

Ruff knocks on the door once, then once again, louder to make sure that he is heard. When there is no response, Ruff starts banging on the door with both his hands. Small droplets of rain start to fall. Jasmine covers her shoulders with a scarf to protect herself from the cold. Jasmine can see that just like her, Ruff is nervous too. The drops of water trickling down his forehead are not rain.

The door slowly creaks open. A large, muscular man eyes them with a straight face. His upper body is bare and roughed-up denim pants cover his legs. He looks disinterested in the two strangers standing in front of him.

'What do you want? If you two children are lost and need shelter, go somewhere else.'

Ruff's voice is shaking. 'No. I'm here for business.'

The man starts laughing and calls three other men to the door, all well built.

'Fellas, this little man is here to do business with us.'

The room erupts with laughter. These men are right though. Ruff is about half their size. Jasmine's immediate instinct is to flee but she stays put. They haven't come so far to run. Ruff extends his hand towards Jasmine, grips her arm tightly and pushes her into the warehouse.

'How much will you pay for her?'

The man who had opened the door takes Jasmine's chin in his hand. He examines her face then takes a step back to examine the rest of her.

'So, you're serious, eh?'

Ruff nods.

'She's a beauty,' one of the men remarks. 'Where did you find her?'

'Where did you find us?' the man who had opened the door lets them in and asks firmly.

The warehouse is dimly lit, with just two light bulbs trying to illuminate an area far beyond their reach. Anything farther than two feet away is not visible.

'Found her lying at a train station. Fed her and promised to give her a job. Fulfilling my promise now,' Ruff laughs, in a futile attempt to make the men more comfortable with him. 'I tried to sell her to a big-shot lady. One of her men said that she only buys from you guys. Thought I'd sell her to you instead, and you can maybe pave a way for me to connect to her?'

'Who did you get this information from? Whose men sent you here? Give me a name.'

Ruff tries to act coy. 'I happen to be fond of my life.'

The man pulls Jasmine closer and turns her around, pressing her back against his chest and wrapping his arm around her neck.

'I'll kill the both of you right now if you don't tell me.' Then, he loosens his grip around Jasmine. 'Not her. I won't kill her. I can just pass her around. She's a pretty one; she has decent-sized breasts that ought to satisfy my men. They're always hungry.'

Jasmine tries not to react. She can't see Ruff, but she knows he must be trying all he can to remain calm.

'All right,' Ruff says. 'I'll tell you, but I don't need any trouble after this.'

Ruff takes a deep breath and says, 'Naya Roben.'

Instead of an acknowledgement, instead of being furious, the men start to laugh again. The laughter grows louder until it echoes in the empty warehouse. The man who is holding Jasmine says in a deep, mocking voice, 'I think you're talking about the same woman who sent us here to take care of a sneaky little girl,' he laughs. 'I'm sure she'll pay us more if we also take care of the sneaky man she's brought along.'

Jasmine becomes breathless as she realizes that this was a set-up. She watches helplessly as two of the men take hold of Ruff. Then the man holding her slides his free hand into Jasmine's peach kurta. She freezes as his hand reaches her breasts and stops. He squeezes her right breast, then her left breast. He traces her body with his hand, his cold palm tightly pressed against her skin as it moves up and down. It stops again, at the voice recorder pinned just below her neckline. He pulls the voice recorder out forcefully, causing her kurta to tear. Then he drops the device to the floor and crushes it with his feet.

sixty-five

Laila

She doesn't recognize the man chasing her down the stairs. The building is rickety. She's sure she did not climb up more than five storeys but as she runs down them the spiral staircase doesn't seem to end. The lift is stuck on the fifth floor. Yet, as she goes around, she keeps seeing it again and again. That's when she realizes it's a loop, a glitch in the system. Her breathing becomes shorter and heavier. She starts running faster and faster until everything becomes a blur. Slowly, the blur turns into a suffocating white blankness all around her. She tries to breathe but air refuses to move into her lungs.

Then she wakes up with a jerk.

Shadow is barking loudly. Still reeling from the effects of the nightmare, Laila looks around and finds Jasmine's mattress is empty. She springs out of bed to go into the office room and check the time. As soon as she switches the lights on, Shadow runs to her feet and quietens down. A storm brews outside, with rumbling thunder and flashes of lightning that illuminate the sky. Laila pets Shadow and then glances at the clock on the wall. It's 3 a.m.

Without a second's delay, she changes into a pair of pants and a blouse and runs to the building next door. She knocks on Ruff's door repeatedly. His neighbours wake up and ask her to shut up.

Fear overcomes Laila. Her mouth dries up. She doesn't even know where to start looking for them. It's not safe for her to be out alone at this hour of the night. But she has nowhere to go for help. Then she remembers that she does. She runs onto the street and wakes the driver sleeping in one of the taxis. She sits in the car, tells him that she'll pay twice the fare and gives him directions to Amer's hotel.

As soon as he opens the door, she storms into Amer's room without any warning. In his groggy state, he is unable to fathom why Laila could be here. Laila races up and down the room while speaking in a high-pitched voice, 'Amer, Jasmine's not at home. Ruff's not there either. I haven't seen them since I got back home at nine. We have to do something.'

That's when Amer fully wakes up. Laila subconsciously feels more comfortable around Amer, her brother, since finding out the truth.

'What do you mean? Did either of them tell you where they were going?'

Laila shakes her head. Dread fills her chest as she imagines the worst-case scenario. 'They did mention that they were going to look into one of Naya's companies, but I have no idea where they went.'

'Perhaps...perhaps to the library? Jasmine and I had found a lot of magazines mentioning Naya's life and businesses...' Amer suggests

'That's where we should start looking then.'

Amer changes into a pair of pants and fetches his jacket.

Half-heartedly he says, 'Laila, I think you should wait here. It'll be safer.'

Laila glares at him.

'No? Yup, didn't think so.' Amer follows up quickly.

For a fleeting moment, they look at each other and share a soft smile. Then they get back to being their tense selves.

They don't wait for the lift to arrive and run down the stairs instead. As they rush past the lobby, the receptionist calls out Amer's name in an attempt to stop them, 'Sir, someone has left a letter for you. Someone by the name of Jasmine.'

Amer and Laila stop in their tracks. As they open the letter and read its contents, their faces go pale. The letter has an address and says that Amer must act if he doesn't see Jasmine by six in the morning. They're a little more than two hours away from that time, but neither of them is ready to wait.

sixty-six

Jasmine

They're playing a game.

Jasmine and Ruff's hands and legs have been bound tightly with a rope. The game is simple. Whichever one of them hurts Ruff enough for him to tell them to pass his punishment onto Jasmine gets to fuck her first, and whichever one hurts Jasmine badly enough to get her to pass her punishment onto Ruff gets to kill him. They have to wait for their turns to try. One minute for each person.

The first man walks up to Jasmine. He holds a loop of thick rope. As the rope slashes her stomach, a pulse of pain shoots through her. When her tongue decides to let out a shriek, she lets it. There's no use in trying to act strong. The more unbreakable they seem, the harder these men will try to break them. When the rope hits her body for the fifth time, darkness surrounds her and her mind jumps back to being home in Mahlah.

She's in an empty room, dimly lit by a small lamp. Sabaar is standing in front of her, with the whip in his hand. 'No,' Jasmine screams, less for the impending pain, more for the loss of his soul. But Sabaar is under the control of the beast. He won't stop. He hits her a few more times with the whip. Jasmine wails, 'No, Sabaar, please don't do this. We're siblings; we're family. I love you, Sabaar. Please don't make me hate you.'

Suddenly, the pain stops. She is back in the living room, playing a game of cards with her brother. They're enjoying some rose sherbet that Nina has made for them. Jasmine laughs as she wins another game. Nina brings them some piping hot samosas. They are waiting for Kaiza to come home from work so they can pounce on the biryani that Nina has prepared for dinner. The sky turns black and Kaiza still doesn't return. Nina and Sabaar look at Jasmine, furious, like it is all her fault. She must be punished. And so, the whip strikes once more.

Then Jasmine wakes up in Amer's arms, covered in a pool of her own blood.

sixty-seven

Laila

Laila forces the window shut and hopes that its glass won't shatter. The wind refuses to calm down. It rattles and almost breaks the pot lying on the bedside table. Ruff lives in an average-sized apartment, with one room and a kitchen.

It's past six in the morning and the sun is still nowhere to be seen. Ruff is laid down on his bed, and Laila sits beside him and strokes his cheek. His system is still in shock. Laila herself is shaken. She has a nightmare to thank for the safety of her friends.

Laila doesn't know what would have happened if they got there any later than they had. Amer knew a few men who he usually called upon to get rid of anyone causing trouble at any of his workshops. They had been in the army once and now live off petty jobs. Five large, well-built men were needed to stop the bloodbath. Unfortunately, the culprits managed to flee. Amer has taken Jasmine to a hospital. Laila came back with Ruff.

As Laila gets up to fetch him a glass of water, Ruff wraps his hand around her wrist to stop her.

'I'm sorry!' His voice is quivering.

Instinctively, Laila bends down and kisses his forehead.

'Shhh. Everything's okay.'

Tears fall from Ruff's eyes. She's never seen him this vulnerable. She moves her lips down from his forehead to the bridge of his nose, then the tip of his nose, until they reach his lips. She lingers for a few seconds and then presses onto his lips. He lifts his hands and cups her chin. A much-needed, sweet buzz of electricity fills them as they kiss for a long time, only to stop when breathlessness takes over.

Ruff pulls away from Laila and parts his lips. 'You...your campaign?' He feels like it's his duty to remind her.

Laila closes the gap between their lips and continues to kiss him. His lips curve into a smile. She then holds him as he buries his head in her arms. Just before Ruff falls asleep, he says resolutely, 'I'm not going to stop. I have to do something; I have to expose Naya.'

Laila looks at him and smiles. 'We'll do it together.'

Ruff pulls Laila closer. Laila strokes his hair as he rests his head on her chest and falls asleep to the sound of her heartbeat.

sixty-eight

Laila

Blue flags flutter in the air as she steps onto the stage. She is nervous, but at the same time she can't wait to speak to the students. She holds in her hand a list of key points. Ruff is standing backstage. His eyes follow Laila as she walks to the podium.

Laila surveys the view in front of her. There are hundreds of Rahat University students seated in the auditorium, waiting to hear what she has to say. A few hired hands and volunteers stand along the edges of the room and wave three-foot-wide flags. Laila reaches the podium and takes a deep breath. Just like Ahmed had taught her; in through the nose, out through pursed lips. The spotlight blinds her for a second. Once her eyes start to adjust, she looks at the faint faces of the audience and smiles. Her nervousness from a few seconds ago disappears. She moves closer to the microphone and talks in a loud, clear voice. 'I am Laila Jagir and I am here to be your councilwoman. But I'm not here to be your councilwoman because I am Laila *Jagir*, but because I know that I can truly bridge the gap between what you want and what the government provides. I am here to move a nation forward and help not just our systems, but our minds progress. I am not here just to command; I am also here to listen.'

Half an hour later, when Laila concludes her speech, she watches the silhouettes rise as almost half the audience stands up in applause. She remembers that she has more to ask of the students. 'I trust you to make the right choice and cast your votes in my favour. But I have a greater task for you. Something that not one of you here is obliged to do, but should, because you will be helping the nation make the right choice.' Laila pauses and looks at the audience that has gone back to keenly listening to her. 'I need you to volunteer for my campaign. I believe the youth has the power to herald a change. I am as old as some of you. But I never got the chance to go to university solely because I was born a woman. Yet, I see so many women sitting in the audience today. I am proud that such a diverse university exists right here in Rahat. I am proud of every single one of you for making the right decision and choosing, even fighting, for your education. I know that you believe I am right for the nation, and I believe that each one of you has an important part to play in moving our nation in the right direction.'

Laila then gives them the information on how they can register to be volunteers in her campaign. After a quick break, she starts the interactive session. It was her idea to let the students come onstage and ask her questions. To make the selection process fair and interesting, she had asked for a poll to be conducted at the university. Students submitted their questions, and the ten questions with the highest votes were chosen.

Once the session is over, more than a thousand students register to volunteer for Laila's campaign. Rahat University has decided its vote.

Laila is up by 14 points now. At 18 per cent, she still trails behind all the candidates, but she is only two points away from Ibra, who seems to have slowed down after his blazing start. Naya is still leading, but is only two points ahead of Gulzar, who is at 30 per cent.

Laila has an interview with *Live!*, a lifestyle magazine, in the evening. Ruff had said that it was a good opportunity to show people who Laila was as a person. It will help humanize Laila, he added. Also, as Jasmine pointed out, these kinds of lifestyle magazines have maximum readership.

People have also started sending money for Laila's campaign. They've received almost 400,000 rehats from anonymous donations.

A determining point of her campaign will be the candidate debate next week. It is the only time where all four candidates go head-to-head. Jon Wilins, an accomplished writer of politics and history, will be hosting the debate, asking questions put forward by the public. The debate comes just two weeks before the elections. Laila knows that it is the biggest opportunity she has to get ahead of her competitors.

sixty-nine

Jasmine

The bruise on her stomach stings as she bends down to pick up the heavy stack of files. Jasmine blows the dust off them as she places the pile of public records on Ruff's table. She unties the rope that has been holding them together. Sitting in front of her is all the public information available on the Robens. She has a choice to make: safety or justice – and she's chosen the safety of the hundreds of people affected by Naya's wrongdoings.

After the scare at the warehouse, Jasmine is even more determined to expose Naya. She can't even begin to imagine what state she would have been in if Laila and Amer hadn't arrived when they did. Luckily, she survived with only a few bruises.

Naya must have instructed the green-eyed girl to give that file to Jasmine. She's sure it was the girl's only chance to save herself from Naya's organization. Perhaps she got caught when she helped Jasmine escape the first time.

The ochre and brown of the files remind her of home, of when it was so windy that they had to shut all the windows to protect the household items from getting covered with a light coat of sand. Yellow here is just a colour on a fruit, or the brightening of the sun; in Mahlah, it was a way of life. Suddenly her heart longs to be in those familiar lanes, inside those familiar walls, with the sound of Nina and Kaiza lovingly bickering, with the *choo-choo* of the toy train that Kaiza had got them when Jasmine was five. The train didn't survive for too long though. The sand got into it.

Jasmine slowly opens the first document in front of her. She reaches the fourth page before realizing that her mind hasn't taken note of any word after the third line on the first page. She turns the pages back again and rereads the words carefully.

seventy

Laila

The foster home doesn't look as uninviting any more since Jai will definitely be coming back to stay with Laila in a few weeks. As they walk inside, the house help requests Laila and Jasmine to take a seat. Jasmine still looks quite beaten down. She still looks pale and drawn, her usual glow yet to make an appearance again. She says she's fine but her shrieks in the middle of the night tell Laila otherwise. Only after Laila embraces her does Jasmine go back to sleep. She wishes that Jasmine and Ruff would step away from trying to expose Naya. But didn't Laila herself do the same thing; fight her hardest when Raymond came at her the strongest?

Soft footsteps enter the living room. Laila and Jasmine run over to him and pull Jai into a tight hug. Jai laughs as Jasmine tickles him. His little giggles put a smile on Laila's face. She looks over at Jasmine and sees her laugh for the first time in days.

'You've grown taller,' Jasmine tells Jai. An inch, or perhaps more.

'They make me drink milk every day. I hate its taste but they say drinking it will make me taller,' Jai explains, between his chuckles.

Laila realizes how ignored Jai's nutrition was when he lived with her and Jasmine. How many times a week did they give him milk? Once, maybe twice, and always mixed with chocolate. Laila knows she will take better care of Jai now; now that at least legally his father is off their backs and they don't have to hide in a four-walled closet-sized box any more. She suddenly shakes her head. She almost apologizes to the room under her breath. That one room gave them a fresh lease on life. It protected them when nothing else would. Jasmine protected them when no one else would.

'Jai, do you like it here? Are they treating you well?' Laila asks.

'Yes, Laila. They are really nice. They take me to parks to play, and even to the movies.'

Jai notices the smile on Laila's face fade and steps forward to give her a hug.

'But I miss you so much. I wouldn't want any of the outings if I got to see you and Jasmine every day.'

Laila's eyes moisten but the tears don't fall. She tightly wraps her arms around Jai.

'Just a few more days, Jai.'

'Well, I suppose we'll have to take you out for chocolate cake once you get back…' Jasmine goes back to tickling Jai.

He jumps up and down with excitement. Jasmine walks out of the living room and brings in the sweet basket they've got for him. It has chocolate cookies, pastries and a few different kinds of candy bars. As soon as Jasmine hands it over to him, he begins unwrapping it.

'Don't finish it all –' before Laila can finish the sentence, he gobbles down an entire cookie, '– in one day.'

seventy-one

Jasmine

She has read through tens of files. Only five documents remain. Jasmine is starting to believe that Ruff was right. There is nothing in these public records to help form a case against Naya. But her gut tells her that Naya has left a loose thread somewhere.

Having learned their lesson on being sly, Jasmine and Ruff decide to take action in a much more open and public way from now on. Once they find some evidence, they plan to file a complaint against Naya and simultaneously put some reporters on the case. Once it is in the public eye, Naya will not be able to threaten or buy her way out of it, at least not with ease. Jasmine wonders how the families of the girls that Naya employs or, she shudders, trades, have never tried to look for their daughters. Perhaps they have. Perhaps Naya stopped them, like she almost stopped Jasmine and Ruff. She probably had them taken care of.

The only businesses that are mentioned in her public records are the legal ones. Some are still functional; some were open-and-shut shops. But there is nothing in these files that sheds light on her criminal activities. Still, Jasmine picks up the first of the five remaining documents and gets to work, trying to be as thorough as she can. By the time she reaches the tenth page, she is already yawning widely. She decides to shut the file and call it a night. Laila has gone to meet a few sponsors. She should be home soon as well.

A few minutes later, Jasmine's stomach starts growling. The early dinner she had has already been digested. Jasmine heats a leftover piece of naan and breaks an egg over it. As she sits down to eat, she decides to read through a few more pages. When she turns the page, she freezes. She glances at it once, twice, three times, just to be sure. Naya started this company six years ago and shut it within two years. Jasmine's mind goes numb as she reads the company's name once more, a name too familiar for she had spent weeks looking for it when she first came to Rahat.

Fern Tree!

Ruff says it's nothing. Fern Tree was a consultancy company, one of many started by the Robens around that same period, mostly because accountancy laws were getting stricter and Naya Roben had the money to hire experts to advise other corporations. Ruff thinks they probably shut down the company either because once businesses understood the process the consultancy became obsolete or because the Robens lost interest in it. There have been many companies that Naya has started and quickly shut because an idea first caught her fancy and then fizzled out. But Fern Tree was completely, 100 per cent legal.

'That's the company my father came to Rahat to work for,' Jasmine finally manages to tell Ruff. 'And you know what happened after that. You know I haven't seen him since.'

Ruff pauses, unsure how to react, then says, 'All right, I'll check all the records available for Fern Tree.'

'I checked everywhere when I first came to Rahat. There is no trace of it anywhere. I don't understand how it appears in Naya's records but there's no mention of it anywhere otherwise.'

'You couldn't find it because it's not currently operational. And what did I tell you when you asked to go through Naya Roben's public records?' Ruff asks.

Jasmine doesn't know what Ruff is getting at, so she doesn't answer.

'I said that I've already gone through them and there's no use in going through them again.' Ruff looks at Jasmine with a kind smile. 'But you were right; everyone does offer a different perspective.'

Jasmine returns his smile. Finding out about Naya Roben's wrongdoings will not only help the people she has affected, but it also seems to offer a key to both, helping Laila and finding her father. Jasmine hasn't ever felt this determined before.

'But I'll look with you,' she says. 'This has come as an unexpected chance. There's no way I'm giving up on my father again.'

Once they finish the lamb kebabs, Jasmine helps Laila put on the black, collarless jacket over her snug black dress. The dress is plain and ends slightly below her knees. This is the first one that Laila has got stitched for her campaign.

Jasmine combs Laila's hair carefully, which now falls only to her shoulders, after she cut it the previous night. She watches as Laila lightly lines her eyes with kohl and dabs her lips with an almost unnoticeable red stain.

Laila radiates confidence. She goes through her notes again and again. Ruff and Jasmine helped her to prepare for this debate, and by the end of their rehearsals, she could answer every question with aplomb. Rahat has finally accepted that Laila is a worthy candidate, but this is her chance to prove that she is a more deserving candidate than the others.

Jasmine wishes Laila luck as she and Ruff get into the hired campaign car. They want to be there early, well before the debate starts. It will help calm Laila's nerves. Amer will pick Jasmine up in half an hour.

Jasmine knows that the election is only two weeks away and Laila needs all the support she can get. But instead, ever since she read that name in the file, all she can think about is Kaiza. It has now been almost six years since she last saw him. He will be forty-three years old now and she is almost eighteen. Kaiza left her a child; will he recognize her as a woman?

A sudden thought sends her heart fluttering. She and Amer are going to get married after the elections. There will be no greater joy than to see her father by her side on her wedding day. She knows that her marriage was never on his mind, but she's sure that he will be extremely proud of her choice, of Amer. Jasmine is sure that Kaiza will like Amer. Maybe they will get together at family lunches and joke about Jasmine's love for ice cream and laugh innocently at Kaiza's idiosyncrasies. Perhaps Nina will forgive Kaiza; perhaps they will be a family again.

Jasmine forcefully shifts her attention back to Laila's debate. This is not the time to indulge in flights of fancy.

seventy-two

Laila

The three-tiered auditorium can seat almost 3,000 people. Laila is sure that not a single seat will be empty. There have been six council debates in the years prior and, barring the one that happened on the day of a storm, not one has seen less than a full house. Right now, though, there is not a single person in the audience. The doors open in twenty minutes but the candidates are allowed entry backstage half an hour before the start of the debate.

None of the other candidates are here yet. Laila has brushed up on all their campaigns. Gulzar is taking it slow, playing it safe, using the family name and support whenever he can. Naya Roben is quite the opposite. Her campaign is all about showing the nation how powerful and resourceful she is. She has even distributed free meals in certain poorer sections of Rahat, to solidify their votes. Ibra Nader's campaign took off really well. His pockets are deep, but his campaign doesn't have a solid ideological direction, and he has been doing pretty much the same things from the beginning – putting up posters and bombarding people with pictures of his face. People have started to lose interest in him.

Ruff stands alongside Laila onstage. Four podiums have been set up in a curve, all facing the audience. Laila's name is etched onto a metal plate that is stuck on the third podium from the left. She stands behind the podium and looks at the empty seats in front of her. She takes a deep breath to calm her nerves and then practises her opening statement. She is happy that she was able to take Ahmed's counsel on it.

'There is a difference between choosing any candidate that could possibly run the council and choosing the right candidate. I am not standing here to tell you that my fellow colleagues won't do a decent job at running the nation, but I am standing here to tell you why I will do the best one. I have dedicated my entire life to helping people gain their rights, their freedom, and to helping this nation move forward. I wouldn't be standing here today if getting elected as a councilwoman wasn't the best way to further that cause.'

The packed auditorium breaks into a loud round of applause as Laila ends her opening statement. Occupying the podium to Laila's left is Ibra; Naya is standing on her right. Gulzar has occupied the podium on the extreme left. Hanging behind the candidates are banners with their respective logos and slogans. The upward soaring bird with 'Free. Fair. Forward' for Laila, the golden sun with 'Let's make Rahat shine again' for Naya. Gulzar's logo is the picture of mountains, with a sun rising from between them and a river beneath them, all confined in a circle, with the words 'Towards a better life'. Ibra Nader's is an animated version of his fist with a thumbs-up sign, emblazoned with the words 'Ibra for a greater Rahat'.

Jasmine, Amer, Thakur, Ahmed; they're all seated in the audience. Ahmed's face beams with pride as he applauds his daughter's opening statement. Laila twitches as she spots Raymond seated in the front row. She suspects that Naya Roben has managed to gather a great deal of information from Raymond about Laila. Perhaps that is the reason she went to Raymond. Laila is sure that Raymond would have helped her even if Naya wouldn't have offered anything. But maybe their relationship, Laila is unsure of what nature, exists because Naya doesn't want Raymond's help to loom over her as a favour she has to repay in the future.

As Laila turns and looks at Naya, she tries not to grunt in disgust. Rage builds inside her as she remembers a bleeding Jasmine and a horrified Ruff tied up inside the warehouse. Naya moulds her lips into a smile that quickly transforms into a smirk. Laila wonders if Naya knows what Laila is thinking about; if she intends to use those emotions against her. Laila tries to think clearly. She is not here to pin Naya down; she is here to win the audience over.

The debate is a three-hour-long engagement, where five questions posed by the existing council members and ten questions chosen by a public poll are answered by the candidates. Each candidate responds and then the floor is thrown open for them to counter each other on their responses, after which members of the audience can ask questions directed at individual candidates.

The first few answers by the candidates go uncontested. Everybody seems to wait for momentum to build before taking on their opponents.

'What steps do you plan on taking to get more girls to go to school, and to reduce their drop-out rates?' All the questions are anonymous. Jon Wilins randomly picks the order that the council members are to speak in. The audience goes silent at this question, but it's a relatively more forward-thinking lot present in the auditorium, so Laila knows that they expect the council members to stand for the education of women.

Gulzar gives a safe, generic answer. Ibra says that he will hold a public forum on it once he becomes a councilman and then implement the best suggestions. Jon Wilins then moves on to Naya. Naya has more to say on the topic than the two men who've already spoken. 'I think we need to give monetary incentives. Very few parents will refuse to send girls to school if they are paid to do it, right?' The audience cheers. Even if Naya had spoken gibberish, they would have cheered. They are mesmerized by her.

When the floor opens for rebuttals, Laila takes Naya head-on. 'I don't think monetary incentives are the answer. I agree that it has a great potential to improve enrolment, but there will be no incentive for parents to keep their child in school or to make sure that the child is going to her classes regularly. Plus, it leaves room for parents to cross ethical boundaries to get the money. What about wealthy families? Do they also get paid to send their daughters to school? Is the state going to waste its financial resources by giving more money to those who don't need it?'

Naya grins. 'Miss Laila, a girl's education may not be important enough for you to *waste* money on it. But to me and to this nation, it is a priority.'

Laila grunts as the audience applauds. 'Female education is one of the top priorities of this nation right now. It's alarming, how many girls are out of school –'

Naya cuts her off, albeit with a smile. 'Laila Jagir is trying to fill words in the air to divert attention from the fact that she, in spite of being a woman, thinks that saving the state's money is a greater cause than educating its girls. How will she, a woman who couldn't keep her own home together, who even pulled her boy, perhaps only because he wasn't her own, out of school, understand the importance of education, understand which policies are better?'

The moderator warns Naya about interjecting when another candidate is speaking.

Laila turns towards the audience and raises her voice. 'Miss Roben, I'm just saying that your way is not the best way. There is a better way than to *bribe* people into sending their girls to school.' Laila pauses and regains her composure. There is no benefit in responding to personal attacks. 'Naya Roben here believes that everything can be bought with money, but I believe that it shouldn't. Some things need to be imbibed in our systems. When you elect me as your councilwoman, I will implement progressive schemes that aim to change the mindset towards education in the long run. I will make it compulsory for schools to reserve 10 per cent of their seats for girls, for ten years. I will start a drive to educate the parents on the importance of sending their girls to school. I will provide aid to schools to set up facilities, such as hygienic washrooms for girls, vehicles to ensure their safe travel, and extra educational support for older students, so that they don't have to start from a lower grade. I will subsidize education for girls; even make it free for a few years. But I will not pay parents to send girls to school because I believe in long-term sustenance, not a short-term easy solution.'

Laila pretty much takes it home from there. By the end of the debate, more than half of the audience is chanting her name. That ought to change the poll numbers. Due to a shortage of time, only two audience questions per candidate are allowed. When it's Laila's turn, the first question is asked by a short-haired, tall woman, who is a reporter from a leading women's magazine.

Apparently, Ruff was right; it's difficult to keep an affair a secret for too long. The question is direct. 'Are you and your adviser, Ruff, romantically involved?'

Laila is fazed for a few seconds. Then she replies, 'Yes. We started our relationship very recently. I think it is difficult to not give in when you're in love, don't you agree?'

The reporter blushes and quietly takes her seat.

Laila turns around to see an equally flushed Ruff backstage. The way he looks at her forms tiny goosebumps on her body. When the session ends Laila runs backstage, straight into Ruff's arms. They steal a short kiss after which Ruff moves his lips over to Laila's ears and whispers, 'You were absolutely brilliant out there. I think I may now, *officially*, be dating the next council member from Rahat.'

seventy-three

Jasmine

The smell of sewage assaults their senses as they make their way into the slums. This area of Rahat is made up of small, one-room, unpainted cement houses, closely stuck together. They do have house numbers though, painted in white, on their thin metal doors. As Ruff and Jasmine reach their destination, they stop and knock on the door. House number 49. They are here looking for a certain Rustom Seljee. Requesting a favour from a friend at the registrar's office, Ruff pulled out from the archives, files of all of Naya Roben's now defunct companies. And there it was, the elusive Fern Tree. Jasmine and Ruff found that the office building of Fern Tree had burned down, forcing Naya to shut the company. The incident took place at night so hardly anyone was injured. A large amount of compensation was offered to the families of the few workers who lost their lives. The Robens hushed up the incident and kept it out of the media but they did pay their dues in court. When Jasmine found the report, her mind could only conjure up the worst possibilities. The feather-light pages felt like a hundred kilos in her hand. She read through the names of all the deceased men. Twice to make sure. And then she finally breathed again; there was no mention of a Kaiza Mir.

It seemed like another dead end until Ruff spotted a complaint filed by a fireman stationed in the area. Rustom Seljee. The second page of the complaint was missing. Ruff is sure that in an attempt to erase all evidence in a hurry, someone had left this one page behind.

An elderly woman opens the door. All strands of her fine hair are grey. Her pale skin is blotched and dry. A maroon cotton nightgown covers her body. Her brown eyes are barely visible under the large wrinkles that have formed on her face. That nothing about this little woman is striking is what makes her appearance striking.

'Mrs Seljee?' Jasmine asks politely.

The woman's voice is so hoarse that it's difficult to believe it is coming out of her body.

'Yes. I'm Kazine Seljee,' she says, sounding irritated. Jasmine will later realize this is how she sounds when she says just about anything. 'What do you want?'

'We're here to talk to your son, Rustom Seljee,' Jasmine explains, trying to keep her voice as calm and as gentle as possible.

'He's dead and gone a long time,' the woman hisses. 'Shoo away now. I don't want any more trouble.'

'No, no, we're here to help.'

The woman shuts the door on them without any warning. They knock again and continue knocking until the woman caves and lets them in.

The small room has just a mattress, a stove and a partitioned area to attend to nature's call. Its walls are bare and grey. A tiny window lets just enough light into the house to make everything barely visible. The woman spreads out the mattress and signals for Ruff and Jasmine to sit. She sits facing them on the cold floor.

'What do you want to know?' she asks.

'Your son, he filed a report against a company called Fern Tree. This happened about five years ago. Do you remember anything regarding this?' Jasmine asks. Ruff shows Mrs Seljee a copy of a one-page complaint from the archives.

Whatever little bit of colour the woman's face had left in it drains out. She waves her hand in the air, signalling to Ruff to move the sheet of paper away from her eyes. She vigorously shakes her head, muttering under her breath. 'How could I forget?'

Her voice grows softer. 'My son was a fireman. He was deployed in the area of Hyden, just on the outskirts of Rahat. That's where this company, Fern Tree, was located.'

'Oh.' Jasmine feels obliged to fill in the silence between the woman's pauses.

'But my boy heard of the fire only the next day. One of his friend's brothers worked in that company, so news reached him that it had burned down. He was very surprised because the fire station had not received any call the previous night.'

Jasmine and Ruff both widen their eyes.

'Even fires of a much smaller size don't go unreported. This had to have been seen by someone. My boy was a curious lad and so he went to the site of the burned building.' Amidst her sniffles, Mrs Seljee continues, 'He came back home and said to me, "Ma, there's something fishy about that building. It's down in the grounds, but it definitely did not burn down!"'

Jasmine gasps. But why would the Robens fake a fire?

'And so, the next day, he filed a report accusing the company of falsely claiming that the building was burned down, when it had, in all probability, just collapsed on its own.' Tears have started rolling out of Mrs Seljee's eyes. 'He was a fireman, you know. He thought that they ought to believe him, or at least launch an investigation.'

She covers her face with her hands. Jasmine moves to sit beside her. She places her hand on Mrs Seljee's shoulder to comfort her.

'*Did* they start the investigation?'

'No,' her tears are already starting to dry and her voice has become louder. Jasmine fears that she has done this many times before, replayed the incident in her mind, imagined running her hands over her son's head and begun crying, only to stop after realizing that nothing can be done any more, that for her own sake, she must stay strong. 'No. They came looking for my son the next day. Five men. I tried, but I could do nothing to stop them. They beat him up in my own house and then dragged him into a van. I haven't seen him since.'

'We'll get justice for your son,' Jasmine says softly.

A cold stare replaces the fear in Mrs Seljee's eyes. 'Please, don't. I don't want justice. I only want peace.'

As Jasmine and Ruff exit the house, the woman says something touching. Jasmine suspects she wishes she had said it to her son before he embarked on the same quest.

'Be careful out there. These people are dangerous. You never know, but they're always watching.'

seventy-four

Laila

Laila looks at the sheet of paper in front of her for a long time.

Naya Roben. 28 per cent. Ibra Nader. 25 per cent. Laila Jagir. 25 per cent. Gulzar Jagir. 22 per cent.

The playing field has levelled out. Naya Roben is surprisingly still leading, despite her performance at the debate. But Laila knows that Naya has other resources at hand to keep her numbers up. In fact, that's what Laila is most worried about, that she will not be able to garner as many votes as Naya will be able to buy.

Jasmine and Ruff say they are close to finding proof about Naya's illegal activities, but they haven't revealed any details to her. Laila needs to concentrate on the election, they say. The election is in ten days, and if Ruff and Jasmine can prove anything against Naya, Laila has a strong chance of winning. She can't believe how close she is to being a councilwoman and how far she has come, how hard she has fought for her place. She mentally gives herself a pat on the back. She knows that her father would have done the same.

One big advantage to her campaign has been the involvement of the student volunteers. They've gone door to door and convinced people that Laila is indeed the right choice. They have helped her in reducing the taboo that surrounds a working woman, though Laila admits that Naya did part of that job for her. When Naya used her power to convince or even bully people into supporting her, she did Laila a favour by reducing the gender-related bias from the election.

'Let's celebrate,' says Jasmine, suddenly looking up from the notes she's been making.

Laila laughs. 'Don't you think it's too soon? I'm not even in the lead.'

'Oh, come on. We deserve a little break,' Jasmine responds. 'Nothing much, we'll just go have some ice cream.' She nudges Laila's arm playfully.

Laila gives in.

The tamarind chutney spills onto the man's shirt. He doesn't notice the small stain that forms just below his pocket. He is busy enjoying the roadside snacks. Laila grins as Jasmine presses her face against the tinted window of the campaign car. It still fascinates Jasmine that they can see the outside world, but the people on the outside can't look in.

As they reach the ice cream parlour, the owner blushes as he recognizes them. They ask to be given a table at the back corner of his quaint little shop even though it isn't very crowded. Honestly, Laila wouldn't have minded even if it was. When someone interacts with a candidate in a non-political setting, it increases the likeability of the candidate. It's one of the many lessons Ahmed had taught her. He would always take small surprise trips to restaurants or libraries and take walks along the promenade.

'How's the investigation coming along?' Laila asks Jasmine as they take their seat.

'I think we're onto something –'

Jasmine is interrupted by the server. The owner hasn't waited for them to place an order. The server places on the table two portions of their popular salted butter caramel ice cream amped up with some chocolate-coated hazelnut chunks and toffee sauce, accompanied by crispy puff pastry biscuits. On the house. They dig into the dessert. A few delicious bites later, Laila looks up from her bowl. 'Just be careful, Jasmine.'

Jasmine flashes Laila a reassuring smile. Then her expression turns serious.

'I might have found a clue that could lead to my father.'

Laila listens intently as Jasmine narrates the unexpected links in their investigation. Laila realizes she might be able to add her own two rehats of help.

'Jasmine, what you said about that building, that it might have just collapsed? Two office buildings of the Jagirs also collapsed about five years ago. Fortunately, we hadn't started operations yet, so no one was injured. We called in experts and they said there was a problem with the land in both cases. Now that you mention this, I really think that there was more to it than just the land being the problem. I mean, the buildings were on different sides of the city. It has to be a huge coincidence and real hard luck that we chose those two wrecked pieces of land.'

Laila and Jasmine blurt it out together. 'We need to find out which construction companies were hired to make these buildings.'

Before they leave, the owner comes up to them and requests Laila to sign a mug. He hopes to keep it at the counter as a souvenir once she wins the election.

seventy-five

Jasmine

It is as disturbing as it is delightful. Riverland Constructions. They were right to have their doubts. All three buildings were constructed by the same company. Jasmine looks up at Ruff eagerly when he enters the office. He had gone to the company registrar to find out more about Riverland.

'Did they ask you to enquire in the archives department?'

'No,' Ruff says nonchalantly. 'They gave me the information themselves.'

'The company still exists?' Jasmine asks incredulously.

'Yes,' Ruff replies. 'And running like a well-oiled machine.'

'Who owns the company?'

'Take a guess.'

'No!' The extent of Naya's reach never ceases to amaze Jasmine.

'The husband and wife are joint owners. They started it eight years ago. Their latest project was, in fact, completed three days ago. A building right here, three lanes away.'

He continues, 'I went back to my friend in the archive department and he gave me access to the records of all collapsed commercial buildings in the last decade. A total of fifteen buildings collapsed in the last seven years, causing 300 deaths in total. Twelve of those buildings were built by Riverland. All of them collapsed five to six years ago. The land that Fern Tree was built on... it was supposed to be used by the government for the construction of a research centre. But they shifted the research centre elsewhere and sold the land to the Robens. I suppose because the government had extensively examined the land, Riverland could not blame the land for this building's collapse.'

'Hence, the fire,' Jasmine adds. 'But I still don't understand why they would build something that would collapse so easily.'

'I suspect that they substituted the building materials for much cheaper, adulterated alternatives that would drastically increase their profits. But that they stopped doing so when so many of the buildings collapsed in such a short span of time.'

Jasmine knows that this is their point of entry into bringing Naya down. Once any of Naya's illegal practices are exposed, all her secrets will spill out. Once again, Kaiza did not fail her.

seventy-six

Jasmine

The sun casts a mellow orange hue in the sky as it descends from its pedestal. The stadium lights come on and slowly all the seats start to fill up. Jasmine looks on from behind the stage. From having thirty people in the audience to having to rent the inter-district cricket stadium to accommodate all those who want to catch a glimpse of Laila, they've come a long way.

It will be Laila's race to win from tomorrow. Ruff and Jasmine met with the journalist Setha in the morning to hand over a copy of all the evidence they have collected against Naya Roben. She has promised that the news will make it to the front page tomorrow. If only Jasmine knew what fate has in store for the rest of the front page. They've also filed a case against Riverland. The timing had to be just right. By the time Naya figures out that there's a case against her, the details of her filth will be scattered all over the newspapers. She won't be able to bury the case or the evidence. If Naya doesn't do it voluntarily, Jasmine is sure that the court will ask her to withdraw her candidacy. Still, Jasmine doesn't feel a sense of victory. Yet. Perhaps it is necessary to find the scrawny, dark-eyed, long-awaited man.

This is Laila's final rally before the elections, which are just four days away. It is estimated that 15,000 people will attend the rally. When the stadium fills up and thousands of blue flags wave in the air, Jasmine, Amer and Ruff watch from behind as Laila walks onto the stage. Jasmine looks on proudly as Laila addresses a full stadium with no hesitation in her voice. She never thought she would even start to like this hazel-eyed girl, who has a knack of entering people's lives and turning them upside down, let alone feel proud of her; prouder than she has ever been of anyone in her entire life.

As Laila pauses for a break and returns backstage, Jasmine gives her a tight hug.

'Thank you,' Jasmine says.

'For what?'

'For making me, just like everyone else in this audience, believe.'

There are fifty men in total. Wearing white kurtas, they line up to collect the weapons. As the orange flame rises, Raymond stares into the fire. He lowers his hand to light the first torch. He has decided to enable his warriors with his own two hands. Naya thinks that he is doing this for her. He is glad that she fails to see the satisfaction it provides him; otherwise, she wouldn't agree to lie in his bed at his command. She has to often sneak away from her husband and the press, in the middle of the night, to satisfy Raymond's carnal needs.

Once the fifty torches are lit, the abandoned parking lot behind the stadium looks like the sun itself has set foot on earth. But there is no sun, there is no light; there is only rage, waiting to burn.

This had always been Raymond's ace trick – rumours are readily believed and sentiments are always ready to be hurt. After the attack on that little room that Laila had sought refuge in, Raymond asked his birds to fly around and spread the news that Laila's house had been attacked by men whose women had run out on them because they wanted to follow in her footsteps. The rumours grew thicker and the voices grew louder. These fifty men are volunteers. Raymond has not paid them a single rehat, but they all want to hurt Laila as badly as Raymond does. Well, almost.

The plan is not to kill her. How will she suffer if she dies? No, no; the plan is to make her grieve, to make her miserable. Before he sends his army out to the battlefield, he gives them a mandatory energy boost. 'Who is spreading sin into our society?'

The response is unanimous. And loud. Almost like a roar.

'Laila Jagir.'

'Who will teach her a lesson?'

'We will.'

'What is our mission?'

'To clean our world and make it pure.'

And the last of all, 'Will we fail?'

'Never!'

Raymond watches as the fifty men march towards the stadium. When the first torch hits a patch of dry grass, Raymond turns and walks towards his car. He sits behind his tinted windows and watches as the world in front of him lights up.

First the shock hits and then the realization. As the hot orange flames enter the stadium, ironically, Laila freezes. The men follow the flames, all clad in white kurtas. They're shouting her name. The words should have been difficult to decipher amidst all the chaos, but Laila hears their voices clearly.

'Laila Jagir, take back your candidacy.'

'Laila Jagir is a sinner.'

The fire spreads fast and like everyone else in the stadium, it is holding onto anything it can find, just so it can stay alive a little bit longer. Jasmine and Ruff rush onto the stage and cover Laila with a shawl before beginning to escort her backstage. She pulls the shawl tighter around her and descends the stairs towards the audience, ignoring the protests from her friends. There are 15,000 people down there. She cannot run away. She swore to protect these people.

She has to make her way to the other side of the stadium. The two side exits have drowned in fire and the protesters are waiting to torch anyone who tries to cross over to the stage, behind which lies the main entrance. Courtesy the safety briefing earlier in the day, she knows there is another way out through the back; a narrow gate, with a metal lock on it. The way to it is through the locker rooms. Its key is kept in a glass box right next to the door, along with other emergency supplies.

The men take control of the stage and use the microphone to send their message out loud and clear. 'Laila Jagir is a sinner. She will burn in hell, and whoever supports her will burn along with her.'

Laila is lost in a sea of panic, where no one is ready to stop. It doesn't matter if she is Laila Jagir, a hopeful for the council chair, born in one of the most respected families of Rahat; everyone is on their own when it becomes a matter of life and death. As she makes her way towards the locker room, she tries to steer the crowd away from the fire and tell them to remain calm. But the lack of oxygen is making her dizzy.

It was easy to spot the entry to the locker rooms from the stage. But now, surrounded by people on all four sides, it's difficult to even breathe, let alone know which way to go. As the men on the stage torch Laila's flag and throw it towards the audience, the panic turns into frenzied fear. A man knocks her down in an attempt to run faster. Laila tries to get back up but she can't. Footsteps trample her. She can't gather enough air to feed her body. Her vision starts to blur. A little while later, she doesn't know if it has been just seconds or minutes, a skin-coloured blob in a white shirt bends down a few feet away from her. It is a student volunteer.

'Let me help you up.'

If the volunteer tries to help Laila up, the volunteer might suffer the same fate as Laila. Laila's own safety doesn't even cross her mind. She needs to ensure that the people in the stadium are safe. Instead of taking the volunteer's extended hand, using all her energy, she yells as loudly as she can.

'Open the back exit. Go through the lockers. The key to the back exit is in the glass box beside the door.'

The last thing she sees is the volunteer's frantic nodding. Then everything turns black.

seventy-seven

Jasmine

Ruff bends down and kisses Laila's forehead. They've stretched her out on his bed, which is much nicer than the mattresses they've got back at the office. Laila woke up once at the hospital but has been asleep since. The doctor says that she needs to get as much rest as possible. Most of her body is covered in bruises. Red, blue, purple; all in different stages of their life cycle. Her dress had holes in it when they found her, making parts of her bleeding flesh visible. The injuries are not as bad as they could have been. Her body is sore, but all its parts have retained their ability to function. Almost everyone at the stadium has borne minor injuries, including Ruff and Jasmine. More than a hundred people have been heavily injured. But there were no fatalities.

Naya Roben has withdrawn her candidacy. A full investigation has been launched into her businesses. The news came out just a few hours ago. None of them feel any sense of satisfaction. The newspaper still lies wide open on the side table, with the headline 'Two candidates, two controversies: Was allowing women to stand for the council a disastrous idea?'

They are equating Laila to Naya. In fact, they're pointing fingers at all the women of the nation. The article goes on to state that women cannot handle political pressures and that there should be a recall of the decision to allow them to stand for the elections. They expect Laila to withdraw her name too. An all-male election once again; politics back to its pristine sanctuary within conservative boundaries. Jasmine does not know if Laila will withdraw her candidacy. The election is only two days away; perhaps she will wait it out. But she might give in to the pressure to ensure the safety of her supporters. *Who knows how many more men Raymond will send? How many more lives he will burn to add as logs to the fire of his ego?* She knows it had to be Raymond, perhaps influenced by Naya.

Now that Jasmine knows that the election is a lost cause, she decides once Laila is all right, she will go look for Kaiza. Though it is a bitter pill to swallow, perhaps it is better for Laila to withdraw her candidacy after all, for the sake of her own life.

seventy-eight

Laila

The colour of the drink is yellow. No one should have to drink yellow-coloured milk, but Jasmine fails to understand that. She has mixed some turmeric powder in warm milk and claims that it will help Laila heal faster. Ruff laughs as Laila holds her nose shut with the thumb and index finger and downs the concoction in a single gulp. The pain hasn't hit her yet. Perhaps the painkillers that the doctor has given her are working their magic on her emotions as well. She has decided to apologize publicly and withdraw her name from the election. The people of Rahat are due to cast their votes tomorrow and they deserve a leader who can keep them safe.

Laila has to go to court to sign her withdrawal. It's going to be difficult, considering she can't even walk two steps without stumbling. The only consolation she has is that they will pick Jai up on their way back home. He will perhaps be disappointed in her. He had hoped to come back home to a councilwoman.

'Let's go,' Ruff tells Laila. But he doesn't hurry her.

As Laila shifts her body off the bed, she can feel every single part of it burn. It hurts even when she as much as lifts her hand to adjust her sleeve. She looks over at Jasmine, who is trying her best to be strong. Jasmine even postponed her wedding for Laila's election. She wishes she could give something back to the girl, if not a victory.

As they walk towards the door, the intensity of what she is about to do hits Laila. All the effort, all the hard work, all for nothing. The nation will not have a woman in the council. Laila realizes that she has let not only herself and her principles, but all the students, an entire generation down.

Before Jasmine can reach the door and open it for Laila, someone knocks.

Two young girls are dressed in white blouses with Laila's campaign symbol, the wide-winged bird printed on the front and, 'Vote for Laila' written at the back. Laila recognizes them as two of the leaders of the volunteer group from Rahat University. She doesn't know if they are here to blame her for what happened at the stadium. Since they're wearing her campaign T-shirts Laila doubts it. They wait for Ruff to help Laila sit on the bed. Once she is comfortably seated, they extend a bouquet of flowers, purple lilies, towards her. 'These are for you.'

Laila smiles but doesn't say much. She wants to apologize, but she can't get any words out. It seems shallow somehow. Finally, she breaks the silence. 'Thank you for these lovely flowers. I know that me apologizing won't make anything –'

'No, no please,' the shorter girl with golden curls cuts her short. 'We're here to stand by you.'

Laila's eyes widen. If not anger, she expected sympathy. But support? That she hadn't even dreamed of.

The girl continues, 'I was the one you told about the back door. You fought for us without thinking about your own life. We're here to fight for you now.'

The other girl chips in. 'Please, mam. Don't withdraw your candidacy. Your speech at the Rahat University helped me stand up to my parents. You are the reason I am still in college. We genuinely believe in your ideas for the nation; we believe that we, specially us as women, deserve and can have a better future, and you made us believe that.'

Laila's eyes can't contain the teardrops any longer. As they fall, she understands what she has done; she has not only made these two women believe that they have the right to demand better and equal lives, but has empowered them to take action. That's all that she wants, for people to live more empowered, more just lives. That is why she decided to stand for the elections in the first place.

'I won't withdraw my candidacy.' Laila's voice is muffled because of her tears. So, she speaks again. This time, louder. 'I will not withdraw my candidacy. Even if I have the support of only the four people present in this room, I will fight. If you can have the courage to believe in me even after everything that has happened, I cannot give up.'

The girls look at each other and smile, 'Oh, no. When we meant we're here to fight for you, we weren't talking about *just* the two of us.' On the girls' instructions, Ruff helps Laila make her way downstairs. As she steps out of the building, she is welcomed by a deafening cheer.

When she was five and would ride her play horse in the hallway outside her room, Ahmed would always run after her. He would ask her to race him down the passage. He never won, not once. Back then Laila feared that his losing had more to do with his intentions than her riding skills. Sitting in this golf cart seems similar. But instead of Ahmed running behind her, there are thousands of Rahat citizens walking by her side, many of them students, many of them women, believing that this is a race that they will all win.

Laila turns back to glance at the noisy trail behind her. There's only one phrase that can be heard, over and over again.

'Vote for Laila!'

'Vote for Laila!'

'Vote for Laila!'

A feeling of exhilaration consumes her. A volunteer comes up to her and offers her some water. They have arranged for everything. Water, some snacks, and even loudspeakers. They want to make sure that the world hears them. They are fighting against the media, the big guns of society, the opinion makers, because they believe that the masses have the power to create change. They believe that *they* have the power to create change. Laila smiles as she sees the results of her hard work right in front of her eyes. She is not fighting for their votes any more; they are fighting for her, for a chance at a better life. Ruff, Jasmine and now Amer walk alongside the cart, waving blue flags in the air and chanting with the crowd, at the top of their voices. They all cheer enthusiastically as the rally continues late into the night.

Tomorrow is the day Rahat votes.

seventy-nine

Jasmine

It's a clear morning. The clouds have taken refuge elsewhere and left the streets of Rahat shining. People have already started lining up outside polling booths. Everyone wants to get this over with before the crowd thickens. The largest-ever voter turnout is expected this year, and women are estimated to make up almost 30 per cent. As the clock strikes seven, the first sheet is stamped against a candidate's name and dropped into the ballot box. Jasmine, though, is not heading towards the nearest voting booth. Since she is a citizen of Mahlah, she cannot vote in the Rahat elections. She has other plans for the day. She should be back before the sun sets, before the results start to come in.

The cab drops her off at Hyden. When she walks to the location she was so desperate to see, there is nothing. The ground is bare, with barbed wires surrounding it. There is a sign facing the road: 'Property of Hinterland Management. Trespassers will be prosecuted.'

With time, her suspicions have only grown that her father was indeed in the building the night it supposedly burned down. The building collapsed just a month after he left Mahlah. He was new to the place and naive. Plus, her father had always been a sincere worker. If anyone was working late in the building that night, she'd bet it was Kaiza. The only hope she has is that his name was not on the list of victims. He was not one of the dead bodies.

This locality is not very well developed. There is only one hospital within a five-kilometre radius of the site. The injured ought to have been taken there.

As Jasmine surveys the barren land, she does something that she doesn't do very often. She folds her hands and prays. She doesn't know to whom. Kaiza had taught her to fold her hands and just thank the universe – the winds, the sun, the trees, life itself.

'It will hold you together in times when nothing else does,' he'd said. She had resisted the urge whenever she previously found the need; perhaps her grievances towards her father for not returning had compelled her not to follow his advice. But today, she gives in. Then she opens her eyes and hails another cab. To Terese Hospital.

The hospital is small and has less than twenty rooms. The walls and the floor are grey, perhaps too grey. Jasmine wonders how hospitals can afford to look so glum when they're in the business of giving people hope. Perhaps she is wrong; perhaps that's what they sell, the feeling of sorrow, helplessness, that makes people feel worse so they run towards any treatment being offered in the guise of hope. Jasmine herself feels like she might be sick. She walks up to the front desk, a semicircular table positioned right opposite the front door. As the receptionist asks her what she's looking for, she realizes she doesn't know what to ask.

'I'm looking for hospital records,' she says finally.

The man at the desk is quite young. He looks up at Jasmine, confused.

'Excuse me?'

Jasmine gives the first excuse that pops into her mind.

'My father was admitted here about six years ago but we lost his records. His doctor says his recent stroke can only be treated if we understand what happened back then. So, I really need a copy of those records. His name is Kaiza Mir.'

'I'm sorry, mam, but we do not hand out patient information. Unless you have a signed letter from the doctor and the patient's ID card, I cannot help you.'

'Sir, please help me. My father is very ill, and I've travelled a long way to get here.'

'Sorry, mam, I really cannot help you.'

'This is about my father's life! Please do something. I'm sure you ca–'

Just then, an old nurse passes through the lobby. The receptionist, who has had enough of Jasmine, calls out to the nurse and asks her to show Jasmine out. The nurse is a short, stout woman. She has the same grey in her eyes that she does in her hair. Her face is slightly wrinkled, and her head is a little too big for her body and looks like it may just fall out with a single tilt of the neck.

As the nurse walks towards her, Jasmine throws herself onto the desk in a desperate attempt.

'Please, please! This is a hospital, aren't you supposed to help save lives –'

The nurse lightly grips Jasmine's arm.

'Please, it's just one file. His name is Kaiza Mir. It's a unique name; I'm sure you won't even take long to find it.'

The nurse suddenly tightens her grip on Jasmine's arm and starts pulling her away. When Jasmine refuses to budge from her position, the nurse looks her in the eye, and says sternly, 'Come with me.'

There's something about the knowing look the nurse gives her. Jasmine reluctantly starts walking towards the exit with the nurse's hand still tightly locked onto her arm. Surprisingly, the nurse doesn't stop at the door. She walks with Jasmine onto the road. As a taxi stops in front of them, Jasmine turns to the old lady.

'I'll go now. You can leave my arm. I won't cause any more trouble.'

The lady leans into the window of the cab, and to Jasmine's amazement, gives instructions to the driver. 'Drop her at house number 15-C on Gildermen Road in Houson. Do you know where Gildermen Road is?'

The driver nods. Houson is on the other side of the district. Jasmine has to get back before the results are out, and it's late already. 'What are you trying to do?' she asks confused. She then turns her attention the cab driver and says, 'No, I do not –'

The woman gives Jasmine's arm a sharp pull. She has too much strength for how little she looks. 'Go to this address. You'll meet Dr Richard. He knew your father,' she says.

Jasmine nods slowly and asks the driver to take her to Houson.

eighty

Laila

The first digit on the counting board flips. Those numbers, printed on yellow plastic, are all that Laila can think about right now. The three candidates are running neck and neck, their numbers somewhere in the 4,000s, with Gulzar leading by two votes. Every fifteen minutes the numbers change. The counting is estimated to go on till 8 p.m. Three hours of pacing, a racing heart and sweaty palms.

The counter is placed right outside the room where the counting of votes is taking place. They've placed about fifty wooden chairs near the counter for the candidates, their family members and advisers.

Laila looks around. Gulzar is seated beside Thakur and Ahmed. Ahmed comes up to Laila and wishes her luck. He is proud of Laila. She can see it in his eyes. He gives her a comforting smile every time she looks at him.

Gulzar had come over and given her a friendly handshake when he entered. She thanked him for his generosity. If she doesn't win, her heart wants Gulzar to take the seat, even though she knows that Ibra is probably a better choice. Ibra is here with his father and his campaign advisers. There is no spite in the atmosphere but the competitive spirit refuses to die down.

Laila needs Jasmine beside her. When Amer arrives and she doesn't see Jasmine with him, Laila panics.

'Where is Jasmine?'

'She said that she was coming on her own.'

'Do you know where she is?'

Ruff places his hands on Laila's shoulders.

'She's gone to finish something important. Don't worry; she'll be all right.'

On its way down, the sun has turned the sky golden. It is difficult to believe that the day is finally here.

eighty-one

Jasmine

The taxi stops in front of a small yellow cottage. Jasmine pays the driver and steps out. She hesitates a moment, wondering if this is another one of Naya's traps. But this is a populated residential area, and for Naya to know that Jasmine would find cause to end up here is a little too far-fetched, even for a lady with such an abundance of resources.

The counting must have begun. Jasmine knows that Laila is waiting for her. But she has already travelled so far; she has to at least meet with Dr Richard, on the chance that he is in.

Jasmine knocks on the door and holds her breath as the wooden door is opened by an old man. With a bald head, his already circular face looks rounder. He stands bent on his spine with his shoulders drooping forward. His eyes are grey, and his gold-rimmed round spectacles hang loosely on his flat nose. When he talks, he stretches his words, making it sound as though he is singing. 'Hello. Who are you?' He closely examines Jasmine.

'I'm Jasmine Mir –'

He doesn't wait for her to complete the sentence. His face lights up as if he had just had his Eureka moment. He speaks as though he knows her.

'Oh, Jasmine! Please come inside and have a seat.'

His house is sparsely furnished. There is only a simple couch in the living room, upholstered with plain brown cloth. Jasmine takes a seat, while Dr Richard brings her a glass of water. Jasmine gladly gulps down the entire glass. The long journey has dried her throat. The doctor seems like a nice man, a lonely man. She wishes she had time for pleasantries, but she doesn't.

'I've come here looking for my father. Kaiza Mir. Do you know him?'

The doctor's eyes gaze into the distance as he relives an old memory. 'Oh, yes. I knew him. He was admitted to my care after he sustained injuries during a building's collapse.'

Jasmine straightens up. So Dr Richard *knows* the Fern Tree building did not burn down. She does not raise this question, however, she only listens, though she fears that after all this time she might find only answers, and not a person.

His eyes open slowly to see a faint figure bent over him.

'Kaiza?'

Jasmine?

Kaiza imagines his daughter running to embrace him as he returns from work. She drags him to the dinner table, where Sabaar and Nina are already seated, waiting to devour the freshly cooked dinner. Kaiza pats Sabaar's head and gives Nina's cheek a slight peck before he sits down. There is light chatter in the air, and the whiff of delicious spices lingers in his nose.

'Kaiza, do you want another serving?'

'Kaiza…?'

'Kaiza…?'

'Kaiza, are you awake?' Dr Richard's voice finally breaks through the fog in Kaiza's mind and he fully awakens. It takes him a minute to realize where he is. He was brought to the hospital two days ago. Someone dragged him out from beneath the rubble and admitted him here. Though he never fully lost consciousness, his memories of the last two days are fuzzy. Today though, his head is clear. In fact, he feels an upsurge of energy, a certain degree of happiness and peace. His mind rushes to place the sense of déjà vu, and when he remembers, Kaiza only smiles. He had read in a novel by the acclaimed Dr Silverman of how some patients suddenly feel alert and get better a day or two before their demise. Kaiza doesn't feel any sense of dread as he calmly accepts his fate. But he knows that there is one last thing that he needs to do.

'I need a pen and paper,' the frail man tells the doctor.

Though surprised at this unusual request, the doctor obliges. Kaiza spends a few minutes bent over the sheet, filling it with words, and then with moist eyes, looks up and asks, 'Do you have my address on your file?'

'Yes, we do.'

'I am going to ask a huge favour of you. Please, if something happens to me, will you deliver this letter to my house in Mahlah, to my daughter Jasmine? Jasmine Mir.'

Dr Richard smiles as he takes the letter from Kaiza's hand. 'I will. But don't lose hope for yourself, Kaiza.'

Kaiza nods as the doctor takes his leave. Soon, he closes his eyes for one last time and slips back into his dreams, back to the dinner table in Mahlah, where he knows he will remain forever.

In her head Jasmine is screaming, wailing, but her face is devoid of all emotion.

'I am sorry, Jasmine, there's not much that we could do. He looked like he was getting better, but he had sustained too many injuries and...'

'But... but... I checked all the names in Fern Tree's case file. His name was not there,' Jasmine chants under her breath. 'His name was not there...'

'Jasmine! Jasmine, listen to me! The only death certificates made were of the bodies that were claimed. The hospital was paid and, might I say, even threatened to fake reports, to put in burn injuries where there weren't any. That is why I resigned, because I refused to be a part of it.' Then he adds softly, 'Only the people who could not be erased were named in the file.'

Thoughts refuse to form in her mind. Feelings refuse to consume her heart. Only an overwhelming sense of helplessness takes residence in her. She will *never* be able to see Kaiza again. His arms will only be a memory, his wise words only a sweet hymn in her mind. She wishes she hadn't knocked on the door. She wishes she hadn't come looking for him at all. Then there would be hope; at least there would be hope.

Jasmine doesn't notice as Dr Richard signals with his hand, *I'll be back in a minute*, and leaves the room. All Jasmine can see is Kaiza, sitting right in front of her, reading out from one of his books. He is telling her about animals, about cows. She has seen a few cows by now. She's even had their milk. He extends his hand for Jasmine to place hers in it. She holds out her hand to touch his. But it doesn't. It can't. Instead, her hand only finds emptiness. There is a vacuum inside her that she has felt only once before. The time when he first left, leaving behind only his warmth, which would slowly fade with time. Now he has left for a second time. The pain is much, much worse.

eighty-two

Laila

The night carries with it an unusual chill in the air. Unless something momentous happens, the numbers suggest that Gulzar is almost certainly out of the race, whereas Laila and Ibra are nearly at par. As Laila turns to look at Gulzar, he greets her with a smile. He doesn't seem to mind the loss at all. Laila thinks that he might have even voted for her.

Jasmine is still missing. Amer has gone to look for her. But the impending decision about the council's future does not allow much room for any other worry to creep into her mind just yet.

As the clock strikes eight, a man steps out with a sheet of paper and starts rolling the yellow counter one last time. Laila takes Ruff's hand and squeezes it tight. This is it. This is the moment. She shuts her eyes tight, opening them only when the rolling stops.

Gulzar Jagir. 690,234

Ibra Nader. 1,124,435

Laila Jagir. 1,124,389

Laila's heart sinks as she stares at the numbers in disbelief. She flops down on the wooden chair. She cannot believe that it is over. She cannot believe that she has lost. In the last few moments, with the people of Rahat standing up for her, Laila was really beginning to believe that she would win. The realization will hit her later, and after it hits, the pain will follow. But right now, her mind is only in shock, in disbelief. Still, before she takes time to understand the situation, form her next steps, she knows that she must first go up to Ibra and congratulate him. As she gets up from her chair, she can hear Ruff, who has gone closer to the counter call out to her.

'Laila!'

'Laila!'

As Ruff comes back, he holds her by the shoulders. 'Laila, listen! Laila, the difference is less than 200 votes. We are going to call for a recount.'

Jasmine

Jasmine unfolds the yellowing paper to find her father's handwriting on it. The doctor said he had written it in his final moments and had left it for her. 'I am sorry I could not deliver it to you. I found out later that the only address we had in our files was his office address here,' he said.

When she starts reading the letter, her mind silences Dr Richard's chatter. She doesn't hear when he says that he never opened the letter once, when he goes on about how sorry he is about Kaiza. Jasmine's eyes and her mind, in their entirety, stay focused on her father's words.

Jasmine, laado,

I want to start by admitting that you were right. You were right when you said that if you love someone, you should never leave them and go. You were right when you said that I should stay back in Mahlah. I hardly ever tell you this, but you're almost always right. I left to work so that we could have a better life, but we already had a beautiful one, with all of us together.

I'm writing this letter to remind you that you hold the potential to do anything that your heart desires. You are special, Jasmine. You are special because you have a mind of your own and I trust you to use it to your best ability. But I am mostly writing this letter to tell you that I love you. And that I love Sabaar. And even though it might not have always looked like it, I have always loved your mother and I love her till this very moment.

I hope you can forgive me for leaving my family behind. I hope you have learned to never leave yours.

Please, Jasmine, take care of Nina. She will not be able to hold herself together for very long. Please offer support to Sabaar. He looks strong, but he hides his grief behind a thick guise of stubbornness. But, most importantly, and above everything, take care of and be there for yourself.

Remember, Jasmine, that I am always there by your side. Look within you and here I will be, forever, waiting. I have and will always be proud to call you my daughter. You're the best gift that life could have ever given me, and for that I will always be grateful.

I love you.

Forever,

Your Father,

Kaiza

Jasmine closes the letter and then her eyes. She quickly wipes her tears. She knows it's getting late and that the council results must have already been declared. Even though she would have wanted to stay and talk to Dr Richard about her father, she thanks him and proceeds to leave. When she walks out of the door, she is surprised as her helplessness is replaced by a sudden sense of calm. She then rushes to catch a cab.

Her family is waiting for her.

eighty-three

Laila

As the silhouette of a girl appears through the wooden gates, Ruff taps Laila's shoulder and points in her direction. Jasmine and Amer enter the premises. Laila runs towards Jasmine as soon as she spots her, the pain in her legs notwithstanding. It is almost midnight. At least one of her worries has been pacified. When she reaches Jasmine, Laila cannot contain herself. She tries to narrate the entire evening's proceedings in a single breath.

Jasmine looks at Laila with moist eyes and wraps her in a warm embrace. Laila wants to know where Jasmine has been all day, but all that her mind can focus on right now is the counting board.

At half past twelve, the man walks out of the room with another sheet of paper. He starts by changing the numbers next to Laila's name. She tightly clasps Ruff's hand with her right and Jasmine's with her left. The counter stops moving.

1,124,354.

That's even fewer votes than the last count. As the counter moves onto Ibra's name, she is certain that she has lost.

And then, all of a sudden, Jasmine and Ruff both pull Laila into a hug.

Laila opens her eyes and peeks at the board.

Gulzar Jagir. 690,601.

Ibra Nader. 1,124,103.

Laila Jagir. 1,124,354.

Laila's knees buckle and she falls to the floor. Her face is in her hands. The tears refuse to stop flowing while the smile refuses to fade from her face.

Ahmed walks up to Laila, and gives his daughter a hug, his face beaming with pride. Gulzar and Ibra both congratulate her.

Laila looks up to see Amer, Jasmine and Ruff dancing around her. Outside, her supporters, led by the students, have gathered for a victory rally. Laila walks out and joins them, knowing that there is a long way ahead. Her story has only begun.

eighty-four

Jasmine

The hand-painted banner they've hung at the entrance is spelled wrong. In Jasmine's defence, she has never had to write Jai's name before, and so she has unintentionally swapped the 'I' for a 'Y'.

They couldn't get multicoloured balloons so they had to make do with just red. The balloons are scattered all over the floor, since Ruff forbade them from sticking them onto the walls. A decadent chocolate cake is laid out on the table, alongside some samosas, fried potato crisps, vegetable fritters and some jalebis. Laila got Amjad Uncle from the Jagir household to bake the cake.

An air of festivity surrounds Ruff's office. Laila and Jasmine have been chirping with excitement all morning.

'Welcome Home, Jay,' the banner announces.

It's not much of a home really; it's just Ruff's office. But it has served them well over the last few weeks. They won't be here for much longer and, as Jasmine looks at the wide wooden desk, she realizes that she will miss it.

Laila has already rented a small apartment in one of the newer buildings near the council house. Her father would be more than willing to welcome her back home, but she wants to start her own life, independently. Jasmine kept her gaze to the floor when Laila incessantly went on about how Jasmine and Amer should also rent a house in the same building.

'The building even has a garden. It is beautiful, Jasmine. And the best part is that we will be neighbours. I will still get to see you every day. How will I survive if I don't get to see you every day?'

Jasmine simply chuckled, trying to hide the guilt behind her laugh. Jasmine has already made her decision, and she is sure that Laila is not going to like it.

eighty-five

Laila

As soon she hears the sound of a car's engine, Laila runs outside. It is difficult to believe that Jai is soon going to be in her arms and that henceforth she is going to be with him every single day.

The Milers requested they drop him off. They have, unsurprisingly, grown extremely fond of Jai. It's difficult not to. The boy is a bundle of joy.

As the car door opens, Jai, dressed in a red shirt and striped black pants, with the blue backpack that Jasmine had gifted him hung on his back, runs out. He jumps into Laila's arms.

'Lailaaaaa, I am back!'

As he proceeds, with equal enthusiasm, to hug Jasmine, Laila thanks the Milers and bids them farewell. When they leave, Jai faces the car and waves goodbye. Jai is going to miss his foster parents.

'Don't worry, we'll visit them.'

Jai flashes Laila an open-toothed smile. Then he opens the front zip of his backpack and fishes out two cards for the two women he loves. The one he hands to Laila has a few balloons painted on it, with a three-word message.

'Congratulations, Councilwoman Laila!'

Laila hugs Jai again. As unbelievable as it may sound, she is indeed, now a councilwoman. It gives her a thrill to know that it is her father who will be passing the office to her.

As the white car fades into the distance, the two girls and the little boy turn and walk into the office to enjoy the long-awaited homecoming.

eighty-six

Jasmine

She can already feel the sand particles settling in her hair. As she steps out of Amer's car, a warm breeze hits her face. *I've missed this.*

Before knocking on the door, she turns back and says to Amer, 'I'll see you in the evening.' As he waves goodbye and drives away, Jasmine turns to face the door. She takes a deep breath and knocks.

It took them almost six hours to get to Mahlah. Jasmine stated her intention to Amer a few days ago. They were having dinner at a small diner in Russel, discussing their wedding plans. In fact, Jasmine had been thinking about it even before she found out about Kaiza but once she read his letter, she was sure about moving back. True, Mahlah hasn't done much good for her, but it is home. Rahat made her believe in herself, exposed her to a world she didn't even imagine existed. But she wants to use her new-found empowerment to help people of Mahlah move forward, in the only way she knows how.

The idea has been brewing in her head for a while. It will be difficult to convince Nina, but hopefully it will not be impossible. As the sun climbs over her head, Jasmine knocks again. Jasmine is already sweating, but she knows that it has more to do with the impending encounter than the heat in the air. As the doorknob turns, both women, for a few moments, look at each other in disbelief. Nina is the first to speak.

'Jasmine?'

She perhaps fears that she is seeing a mirage.

'Mother, I'm so sorry.'

'Oh, so you heard.'

Jasmine does not know what her mother means, but as she enters the house, it becomes clear. A photo of Sabaar hangs on the living room wall with a garland around it. He was killed during cross-border firing. Hearing the news, Jasmine is unsure of what she feels. She lost her brother many years ago, and yet, a grief takes residence in her. But for the most part, she supposes she is relieved. Perhaps her brother is in a better place now, a place where the beast hasn't accompanied him.

As both women take a seat in the living room, Jasmine feels a sense of dread overcome her. The house has become dusty, dilapidated, worn. Despite retaining the tattered couches, the torn wallpaper, a few old stools, the living room looks empty. Jasmine cannot find Kaiza in this house any more; she cannot find herself in this house any more; she cannot find home in this house any more. She cannot picture the lively dinners, listen to the chatter happening over a game of cards, or smell the whiff of spices. Her senses only catch dust and loneliness. The house feels alien, lost. Mirroring its inhabitant.

'Have you come back to sympathize with me? To take me away from my city? You must know that I will not come. I will not be another traitor to this house.'

For the first time, Jasmine sees the pain behind the spite in her mother's voice. Nina is surprised when instead of shooting her a sharp response, Jasmine sits beside her and takes her hand.

'No, Mother. I am not going to ask you to leave.'

She then holds out Kaiza's letter and tells Nina the entire story. It is difficult to gauge if her mother would have cried if Jasmine had left at that moment. But, at least in front of Jasmine, at least for a long time, she doesn't. Then they talk; not about Kaiza, not about their family, but about the pistachio ice cream that Jasmine had on her way to Mahlah, about how Rahat is heaven for a sweet tooth. Nina tells Jasmine how she bought another cooking pot after Sabaar left. She cooks biryani in it often and eats the entire dish all by herself. She has started singing in the kitchen again. Jasmine tells Nina about Laila, about how she is the strongest person Jasmine has ever met, to which Nina surprisingly replies, 'I think you're the strongest person that I have ever come across, Jasmine. And yes, I know about the campaign. I asked the neighbours. You know I can't read, but I have been buying newspapers every day ever since I found your picture in one.'

When Jasmine tells Nina about Amer, Nina almost cries. She cannot believe that her daughter is going to get married.

Then, Jasmine narrates her idea to her mother. Surprisingly, in an instant Nina gives her nod of approval. 'I will find investors. You'll have to come and stay with me in Rahat till we can get this place renovated,' Jasmine says, her fingers crossed behind her back.

'All right. But after you get married, I am not going to stay with you and your husband. I will stay right here, in my house. You'd better get one of the bedrooms done up for me.'

Jasmine smiles. 'Of course, Mother.'

The sudden brake of the car wakes her up. When her eyes open, she finds herself outside the garden with the dolphin fountain. She glances at the back seat, to catch her mother gazing at the city in wonder. Amer switches off the engine and gets down from the car so nonchalantly that it almost makes Jasmine believe that this is where they had intended to arrive. When Jasmine asks Amer why they're not going home, he doesn't answer. Instead, he walks straight into the garden. Jasmine helps Nina out of the car and then, clueless as they are, they follow Amer inside.

As Jasmine reaches the dolphin fountain, she gasps. It doesn't need much of an explanation any more. There are three tables covered with embroidered white tablecloths. Each of them has a bouquet of flowers placed in the centre. On the first table, Ruff Junior and Jai sit alongside three empty chairs. The second table has been occupied by Mr Ruff, Janie and Lara.

On the third table, a couple she recognizes – Mr and Mrs Moran.

The dolphin fountain forms the backdrop of the small stage, which has been decorated with beautiful white, fuchsia and purple lilies. Nina takes a seat beside Mr Ruff. Amer has already taken his place on the stage. The hand-painted signboard displayed beside the stage erases any doubts that Jasmine has about her guess.

'Jasmine weds Amer'.

A pulse of anxiety rushes through her body. *Do I want this right now? Am I ready for this?*

Amer senses her hesitation and runs off the stage towards her. He leans into Jasmine's ear and whispers, 'We don't have to do this right now if you don't want to. I'm sorry. I shouldn't have –'

Jasmine wraps Amer in a hug and whispers back, 'I want this. I won't have it any other way.'

Then she asks, 'But where's Laila?'

As if on cue, Laila runs inside carrying a beautiful gown for Jasmine. Her breath comes out in short gasps from all the running.

eighty-seven

Laila

The ivory gown makes Jasmine look like a queen. It gathers at her waist, where it is encrusted with jewels, and then delicately falls to the floor. Laila is dressed in a snug red gown that shapes her body well. As the ceremony commences, Laila sneaks a glance at the adjacent table. Jasmine's mother is a frail lady, with a triangular nose. The entire time she has been here, she has had tears in her eyes. But that's not the petite lady she is interested in. When the Morans congratulated Laila on her win, she began shivering. As Mr Moran held his hand out to give Laila a handshake, she acted distracted by Ruff's supposed holler, to avoid giving Mr Moran her trembling hand. They will never know that they are sitting only a few metres away from the daughter they threw away, and she doesn't intend to tell them. But she cannot bring herself to hate them because she is thankful that they didn't keep her. She couldn't have asked for a better father than Ahmed.

As the curtain drops and Amer pulls Jasmine in for a kiss, Laila holds Ruff's hand and squeezes it. Ruff leans over and plants a kiss on Laila's forehead. A few seconds later, the audience collectively gasps as Jasmine pulls away the curtain and continues kissing Amer. Laila can see that the priest is extremely embarrassed. But Laila is proud. Love should not have to hide behind barriers. When the ceremony ends, Laila hugs Jasmine and Amer tight. 'Congratulations!'

Jasmine pulls Laila aside and whispers, 'Laila, I have something to tell you.' Jasmine looks tense, almost afraid of what Laila's reaction might be. But Laila already knows what's coming. 'I have decided to move back to Mahlah. Amer and I are looking for houses. I'm sorry, Laila, I should have told you earlier.'

Laila smiles. 'Of course you're going back, Jasmine. I knew it the day you told me about your father.'

The girls hug again. Laila tries to stop her eyes from watering, but the tears continue to flow.

'I'll keep visiting, I promise.'

'Me too.'

Jasmine tries to lighten the mood by cracking a joke. But Laila's tears are contagious. For the end of a journey, for the beginning of a new one, for all the pain, for all the happiness, for all the joy, for all that they have been through and survived, Laila and Jasmine hold each other and cry.

eighty-eight

Laila

Laila pours some cold milk over the cocoa-flavoured cereal. As she relishes her breakfast, Jai glares at her from across the marble table. He is stuck with a glass of hot chocolate milk.

'Jai, you asked for the chocolate milk today. Now you have to finish it. You can have the cereal tomorrow.'

Jai doesn't touch his milk.

'If you had the bowl of cereal and I had the chocolate milk, you would have wanted the chocolate milk. That's not the right way, Jai. You'll always think that other people have it better. So, it's best to be happy with what you have.'

Laila is surprised by her own wisdom. She has realized that raising a child is as difficult as running the nation, and she has to do both. But she's not complaining one bit.

With Ruff's help, Laila has managed to find a good school for Jai. Ruff also got a restraining order issued against Raymond. Laila has no proof that it was indeed Raymond who set her rally on fire so she cannot get him arrested. Hopefully, he will not get elected in the council for another term. But even if he does, Laila knows that she now has the strength to face him.

Once they finish their breakfast, Laila helps Jai pack his bag. He refuses to stop using the blue backpack that Jasmine had given him even though it is worn out. Laila picks up her briefcase. Before she leaves, she takes a last look at herself in the mirror. Her black skirt is perfectly complemented by a matching jacket. A pearl necklace sits on her neck. Pearl earrings adorn her ears. Her cinnamon-coloured hair falls just below her shoulders. She combs through it with her hand and heads out the door, but not before giving Shadow a pat on his head.

Today is her first council meeting. Her first chance to effect a decision that matters.

She takes her seat on the podium. It gives her a thrill as she looks at the twenty-odd people who have come to watch the session today. It feels different to be on the other side, but even when she was in the audience, she wanted the same result as she does today – a free, fair, better life for the people of this nation.

The bill to be voted on today was introduced by Hooser. It looks like the councilman is trying to do all the good he can before he leaves. The agenda is quite simple. They are voting to impose a mandatory clean-up drive on the most polluted lakes in the nation. Laila is the third council*person* to cast her vote. When the Speaker takes her name, it sends a shiver down her spine.

'Councilwoman Laila, you have one minute to decide your vote.' She uses the entire minute, not to rethink her decision, but to look around and breathe in every sight, smell and the sound of the moment. The silent eyes that stare at her from the audience, the smell of the wood of the podium, the Speaker's grating voice, the loud beating of her heart. Finally, she casts her vote.

'Yes.'

She feels a sense of pride course through her body. Because of the one word she has uttered in the room today, she has potentially saved many lives. Law has power. Words have power.

Laila enters her cabin, which is furnished with a wooden desk and a very comfortable chair. Her desk is covered with photos, of Jasmine, of Ruff, of Jai, of Ahmed, of Shadow.

Laila closes her eyes for two minutes to let the magnitude of the moment sink in. Then she fishes a file out and gets to work. She looks at the first bill she is in the process of drafting. A motion for the acknowledgement and legalization of all genders and sexual identities. Laila doesn't know if this bill will pass, but she will try, again and again, for as long as it takes. She has a nation to better, and she will never give up on its people.

eighty-nine

Jasmine

The freshly painted blue door makes her house stand out in the lane. The colour on the windows and the roof matches the door. The rest of the house has been given a coat of gleaming white paint. The slow deposit of sand on the white will eventually give the walls a beautiful texture. Laila's father, Ahmed, and Amer have both invested in her vision. When Ahmed found out, he apologized to Jasmine about the diner on behalf of his manager, and fired the manager immediately. He even helped Mr Karen set up another diner close by.

The plain white tiles have been changed to a nice cream. The faded green on the wall doesn't need to be covered up by Nina's drawings any more. Jasmine asked for new wallpaper to be put up; one that is covered with pictures of intricately painted and colourful flowers and birds. Sabaar's room has been broken down and merged with the hall. Jasmine's room has been broken down and merged with Nina's room, which has been attached with a second door that opens directly onto the street. Jasmine has also decided to find her mother a pet dog. Nina has learned to live alone, but a companion never hurts. Everybody needs love.

The star of the house is the kitchen. It has been fitted with the latest grills and ovens, and even the stove is new. The counter has been broken and remodelled with steel fittings. But what excites the mother and daughter the most is what is placed beside the counter. It is beautiful. It is a two-foot-tall clay pot, placed on its own personal burner, for all the biryani that Nina will ever want to cook.

Jasmine walks back into the hall and can already envision the place in its completely transformed state. She imagines the seven round dark-wooden tables, bunches of fuchsia-coloured flowers placed in the centre of each. A blackboard painted on the bare strip of wall above the kitchen door, displaying the menu in white chalk. There will be small lamps hanging from the ceiling. She plans to fix a bookshelf on one of the walls and fill it with as many books as she can, as many stories that she can discover, so that people can read to their heart's content. Even though the head chef at Karen's was brilliant, Jasmine knows that food has never tasted better than when cooked by Nina. Mahlah will be lining up for her mother's biryani once again. But Jasmine has also imported a few dishes from Rahat. She knows that the salted caramel ice cream will be a hit here and so will the generously stuffed kulchas. Nina never shies away from learning new recipes so she is only too eager to try out the dishes. It's one of the few things that Nina and Jasmine are realizing they have in common – the love for learning.

All of a sudden, Jasmine wishes Laila and Jai were here. She even misses Ruff's company. When Jasmine and Laila work together, they're an unstoppable force. But what Jasmine misses the most is the hustle and bustle of the city. Rahat has made her world start to spin a little too fast. She doesn't want to slow it down for Mahlah, so she has decided to bring Mahlah up to speed.

Jasmine steps out of the house to see vehicles and camels passing by. She remembers the day she packed her bags and left. Courage takes one a long way. She is grateful for the bravery that sparked within her that day, which led her to discover parts of herself. As she looks at the bend down the street, her eyes strain into the distance and she imagines a scrawny man, with dark eyes, dyed hair and a thick moustache, returning home on a camel.

She shifts her moist gaze and looks up at the large turquoise sign, shining brightly, at the top of her house:

'Kaiza's Diner'.

Acknowledgements

First, a few clarifications for the readers. The setting employed by the book is fictional, inspired by the reality of multiple cultures. The title of this book is taken from the wonderfully vivid poem 'Udaipur (early morning)' by Akhil Katyal, who was kind enough to grant us permission to use it.

I must begin by giving thanks to my friends and family, who enriched both the journey of this novel and my own personal journey. First, Urja Jain. This book would not have taken shape without Urja's constant critique, without her being passionately involved in the lives of the characters. She loved Laila, Jasmine, Kaiza, Amer, Ahmed and Ruff so deeply that she made them real; Priya Tolasaroya, who read this book cover to cover every time an edit was made, who celebrated alongside me every time a milestone was achieved and who held me through the many troughs; Abhishruti Srivastava, who helped me realize that there isn't just light at the end of the tunnel but that the tunnel itself is illuminated, full of laughter, kindness and love; Ramya Pillutla, who helped me step out of my mind and appreciate it at the same time; Harsh Shah, Mayank Biyani, Tushar Kanade, Rutwik Deshpande, Shravan Rathi, Swati Shrimali, Vivian Castelino, everyone at Annapurna and all my friends and family in Mumbai, Hyderabad and Bengaluru for being by my side as I went through multiple iterations of all aspects of the book; Anuradha Sharma Aunty, who pointed me to a mirror at the right time; my sisters Aastha Lodha and Kashish Lodha who constantly teach me to enjoy all moments in life; Raunaq Surana, without whom I wouldn't have had the courage to follow my heart;

my mother, Rupali Jangda, who, though she doesn't know it, inspires me immensely by how strong and adaptable she is; my father, Vinay Jangda, who has never been hesitant to break down his own walls to understand his daughter better; my brother, Nihar Jangda, for his love, for his sensitivity, his strength and for always being proud of his sister; and finally, my grandmother Vimala Jangda, for being the most resilient woman I know.

I am indebted to my early readers and friends, Laveena Tiwari, Manoj Gopalkrishnan, Nyamat Chada, Pankaj Sancheti, Rishikesh Bhanushali and Rakshit Khilnani for not only lending their perspectives but also for constantly extending their support. I have immense gratitude for Nidhi Dugar Kundalia and Mohit Uppal who guided me and helped me understand a world about which I had no prior knowledge; Viswanath Pillutla Uncle, Mridul Aggarwal, Pavan Surana and Showick Thorpe for trying to help my work reach a bigger platform.

Many lovely individuals have been involved in taking this book from a first draft manuscript on my desk to the version that you hold today. I want to thank Aanchal Malhotra, who not only expertly looked at it with both the lens of an editor and a reader but also enriched it with her passion for literature, art and aesthetics; who constantly inspires me through her own work. Also, Anuj Bahri, Sharvani Pandit, Sarah Zia and the entire team at Red Ink Literary Agency for believing in my work and for guiding me.

Poulomi Chatterjee, for her insightful edits that helped me look at the book from a new viewpoint; Ansila Thomas, for her patience and for taking this journey alongside me; Meena Rajasekaran for the beautiful cover design that encapsulates the essence of the novel; Sini Nair, Dipti Anand and the entire team at Hachette India for their efforts in bringing this book to the reader.

And finally, I would like to thank you, dear reader, for evolving this work each time you read it, by lending it the perspective of your own experiences.